Cassie Connor loves capsule  weekending in Nice and tal wherever she goes. She's als never finished *War and Peace* motto is CBA - Can't Be Arsed - and has resorted to writing and inventing her own men because fictional heroes are always so much better. Hudson in her debut novel, *Love Under Contract*, proves the point perfectly.

instagram.com/CassieConnor

# LOVE UNDER CONTRACT

## CASSIE CONNOR

One More Chapter
a division of HarperCollins*Publishers* Ltd
1 London Bridge Street
London SE1 9GF
www.harpercollins.co.uk

HarperCollins*Publishers*
Macken House, 39/40 Mayor Street Upper,
Dublin 1, D01 C9W8
This paperback edition 2022
1
First published in Great Britain in ebook format
by HarperCollins*Publishers* 2022

A catalogue record of this book is available from the British Library
ISBN: 978-0-00-856826-9

Printed and bound in the UK using 100% Renewable Electricity
by CPI Group (UK) Ltd

*This book is for the amazing Charlotte Ledger, her passion and enthusiasm for her authors is unmatched.*

# Chapter One

'For fuck's sake.' The words slip out before I can stop them and I slam my phone down on the bar top. Seriously? I don't freaking believe it.

Unbelievably, and by a cosmic quirk of coincidence, those same words, at the self-same moment, emerge from the mouth of the guy next to me. 'For fuck's sake.' This is the guy whose eyes I've been studiously avoiding even though our bar stools are practically wedged up against each other in the crowded hotel bar.

We look at each other, bemused.

'Date stood you up?'

I want to scowl at him because I hate the way that he immediately assumes my issue is that minor but he's got a sympathetic smile on his face.

'No.' I sigh. 'My sister's just texted me to tell me she's engaged.'

He frowns. 'And that's not a good thing.'

'Not when it's to my ex, no.'

'Ouch, that's pretty bad…' He pauses. 'I'll raise you ten.' Amusement wreathes his wide mouth and I find myself drawn to his lips. It takes me a second to wrench my gaze away to look down at the phone he's nursing in one hand.

'We're playing my bad is worse than your bad?' I ask.

'Yup.'

'I doubt it very much –' I arch a haughty brow. He's the sort of guy you need to keep on his toes '– but go on then.'

'My business partner has just pulled the plug.'

I look at him in faded jeans hugging brawny thighs and a soft white Henley T-shirt clinging to a very broad chest and unbuttoned to show a smattering of dark hair. What sort of business could he be in? He exudes masculinity with a capital M and has those flirty, I-know-I'm-hot-shag-me-now eyes. They're bright blue with an irresistible twinkle.

And he's not my type at all. Even as I'm telling myself this, there's a small part of me that wonders what he looks like naked because you'd have to be visually impaired not to see that he's got muscles in all the right places and he knows how to use them. I pull myself up sharply, narrowing my eyes at him. I do not have thoughts like this.

He grins at me as if he knows exactly what I'm thinking.

I swallow. Am I that easy to read? My type of man wears a sharp, tailored suit, he's clean shaven with short hair and he does a fine line in crisp white shirts, tasteful silk ties and unassuming cufflinks. Never trust a man in novelty cufflinks. I regard it as a barometer of arseholery. Like Andrew.

Again I try to imagine what sort of business he could be in. Dressed like that, he's no one's idea of a businessman.

2

Not with that thick, too long hair that skirts the top of his shoulders, several days' growth on his chin, and strong, large hands that are oddly elegant but also look as if they might have done a fair bit of labouring in their time.

'That's tough,' I say, trying to be totally business-like and ignore the ridiculous flutterings in my belly. If they're butterflies they can sod off back home, this is not me. I lift my chin. 'Presumably in your contract there are termination and dissolution clauses. I'd expect there to be some contractual notice period.'

He raises one eyebrow and his crooked smile comes complete with dimple. Aaargh, it's cute. 'You need to speak to your solicitor,' I add quickly and very primly. I don't do cute young men or cute older men for that matter.

The dimple deepens as if I've said something really amusing.

'It was a ... business person's agreement.'

I eye him and the what-can-you-do-about-it-after-the-event expression on his face.

'One of those shake-of-the-hands-after-you-spat-on-the-palms agreements?' I ask, tilting my head in question.

He nods and shrugs. 'Something like that. We agreed we could help each other, she offered to finance things.'

When will people learn? They want to save money on legal fees but when it all goes tits up, it costs so much more. A decent contract is watertight, bombproof, cast-iron and every other rock solid cliché you can come up with. I should know; as senior legal partner at one of the biggest city law firms in London, I draw up and check contracts. I've got a reputation for being the best, and I'm not too modest to own it. Discovering a loophole in a recent client's contract saved them a potential loss of seventy million pounds. I'm expensive but I'm worth every penny.

'Meaning she put up the money.'

'Yeah, that's about the size of it. I thought we were friends. She decided otherwise.'

Something about the barest flicker in his eyes gives him away and like a shark scenting blood I'm on it. 'Ahh, so you slept with her?'

He stares at me and then gives a shrug. 'Once or twice. Nothing serious. And not recently.'

'But she wanted to,' I prompt because I know how this goes. The adage 'don't mix business with pleasure' is there for a damn good reason. Nothing good ever comes of it. They should have had a contract drawn up between them before they stepped anywhere near a bedroom.

'She knew it wasn't serious. I was honest about that. This last year I've been trying to focus on building my business. The business has to come first, while I get it off the ground.' His chin juts out in a slightly bullish way which reinforces what he says and it intrigues me. Seems like he is passionate about *his* business.

Rather than confront the 'she-knew-it-wasn't-serious' bullshit, because, you know what, CBA, I can't be arsed – I've come across this type of guy a million times – I ask, 'So what is your business?'

The slouch which has curved his body into a C shape vanishes as he straightens, those blue eyes light up with a fervour that glows like a 100-watt bulb and I'm obviously too close because I feel some sort of weird adrenaline rush –

it must be the energy he's exuding. 'I design and make furniture.'

I wasn't expecting that. I don't know what I was expecting but now I can see it, those hands, the broad chest, muscular arms under the white T. So, he's a carpenter. 'Are you any good? Would I have heard of you?' I take a sip of my wine.

'Not yet but you will. My name's Hudson Strong.'

I snort and not in a cute piglet way – my wine comes out of my nose. What sort of a name is that?

'You made that up,' I accuse him, coughing.

He grins at me. 'Take it up with my parents. My mum and gran are huge Doris Day and Rock Hudson fans. My eldest sister is called Doris.'

'Seriously?' He shrugs again and when he does, the hair on his shoulders bounces. It shouldn't be attractive but it's soft and silky looking and it catches my attention.

'And do you have a name, Ms Contract Lawyer?' The corner of his mouth lifts with a pleased-with-himself smirk.

'Good guess.'

'Not really, it's written all over you.' He casts an eye over my black suit. Sensible it is not but smart it is. Hugo Boss for Women. I am the best dressed woman in my office which is important when you swim with sharks. My black Louboutins do great things for my calves, while my blonde hair is secured in a classy chignon which shows off the subtle, carefully maintained highlights.

'And,' he adds, 'you did use the words "termination and dissolution clauses" with the fluency of a second language.'

'Rebecca Madison. I work for Carter-Wright.'

He whistles. 'The big boys. Sorry,' he amends immediately, 'the big girls.' Which earns him a brownie point. Just the one, mind, because his lip curled slightly when he was eyeing up my suit.

'Something wrong?'

'I guess not. That's your uniform.'

'What's wrong with it?'

'You look a little buttoned-up.'

'Well I'm not,' I say primly, which makes me sound very buttoned-up. There's something about this guy that pushes my buttons.

'So, your sister.' He nods to the phone. 'What's the story with the ex?'

My natural inclination is not to say anything but there's something in the way his voice softens slightly when he asks the question, the husky timbre of a good listener. Besides, what the hell, he's a complete stranger. Why not share? But I need another drink before I go there. With a wave of my finger, the bartender glides over.

'Double Hendricks with tonic.' I order it because gin always hits the spot with me and I need some numbing. I turn to him. 'And you?'

'Glass of Merlot. Thank you.'

I can't decide if his cool acceptance is because he's used to women buying him drinks or because he really doesn't care. Most men I know still stick with the caveman 'me man, I buy drinks' routine which, given I earn just as much as them, if not more, doesn't seem equitable, although for some of them buying a drink is a green light to sex. It isn't.

'So you got a text from your sister?' He sounds

6

disbelieving.

'Yeah, we're not close.' That's the understatement of the century.

'Lucky you. I've got three sisters. If only text was their preferred form of communication.' He gives a dramatic shudder, which makes me smile even though I'm so not in a smiling mood. 'Letting Doris, that's my eldest sister, follow my Instagram was the biggest mistake of my life. She likes to comment and phone … a lot.' Despite his words he looks fondly down at his phone.

I wonder what that must be like. I have no idea what goes on in my sister's life. Her Instagram is probably full of posts of her designer handbag collection, her latest sports car (she swaps them every six months) and tons of pouty 'love you babes' type posts.

'So,' he prompts. 'The ex, how ex is he?'

'Very ex, and he's a complete dick. I have no feelings for him. He dumped me way back. Three years ago.' I can't bring myself to tell him that as soon as Andrew dumped me, he turned his attentions to Laura.

'And you're still carrying a torch for him?'

'God, no,' I say scornfully because Andrew is a fully paid-up novelty-cufflink-wearing member of the arsehole club. 'I'm pissed off because I've been summoned to go play nice at Thanksgiving next month for their engagement party.' Now it's my turn to shudder – it's heartfelt.

'Thanksgiving?'

*That's* the bit he focuses on?

'My step-dad is American, my mother is English. They spend a lot of time in New York.'

7

'So you're going to New York for Thanksgiving. That's cool.'

I glare at him. He and I have very different ideas of what's cool.

'I'll be under the microscope with everyone watching to see how I'm *handling it* when I couldn't give a toss. They deserve each other but whatever I say or do, it'll be sour grapes or I'm jealous because *of course* I'm competition with my sister. Why do people always assume that?'

He pulls a face. 'That sucks.'

I sigh. 'It is what it is.' I knock back my gin and wave the bartender over and order a second double. 'You want another?' I ask.

'My tab this time. I can still afford to buy a round of drinks.'

'It's fine, I'm staying here. My drinks will be expensed.' I've been at a conference for the last two days and then HR set up this meeting, so it was agreed I'd keep my hotel room another night even though I only live in Chelsea.

He laughs. 'Of course they will. In which case I'm happy to freeload if the company's paying. Money is going to be tight for a while.'

'What are you going to do?'

'It's no big deal. I've got a big exhibition coming up in January. I only need to sell a few pieces and I'll be up and running.'

'That doesn't sound so bad.'

'It's not, it's more what she said.' He grins. 'I'm a no-good, commitment-phobe dickhead who led her on and took advantage.'

8

'And did you?'

He shrugs. 'I never made any promises.'

I know the type. He has 'love 'em and leave 'em' written all over him. But some women believe that they'll be the one to change that mould of guy. Poor fools.

'But basically, you did. You led her on and took advantage.'

His eyes narrow, giving me a sharp assessing look, and now it's my turn to shrug.

We both sip our drinks in sudden awkward silence as if we've just remembered we're complete strangers and our conversation has come to an end.

Thankfully my phone buzzes and I snatch it up.

'Now I have been stood up,' I say as Hudson Strong turns to me. 'The guy I was supposed to meet has just bailed.' Which is really fucking annoying because I could have gone straight home tonight instead of keeping my hotel room for another night.

The only reason I'm here in this cattle market on a Friday night is because my friend in HR asked me (insisted, and I owe her – I always seem to owe Mitzie) to talk to an ex-colleague about the company's wellbeing strategy and you never know when a contact might come in useful. I'm entirely the wrong person to be talking to about wellbeing. Because every company needs a daily yoga session between eight a.m. and nine – I mentally roll my eyes. Do you know how much work you can get done before the phones start ringing when the switchboard fires up at nine a.m.? And don't get me started on how much time is wasted when people finally come back to their desks, so relaxed they're almost sliding out of their chairs, and that's after they've stopped by the pretty boy barista, Tony. He's only recently been installed in reception with a shiny Gaggia coffee machine for their mocha latte, oat milk cappuccinos and double espresso. Apparently free quality coffee is essential for mental health – I'll admit it keeps me wired, although it doesn't do much for my sleep patterns.

'That's a bummer.'

I look around the crowded bar. 'Are you supposed to be meeting someone?'

'Yeah, my *ex* business partner. This is not my kind of place.' He winces. 'Full of corporate stiffs.'

'Like me?'

There's a pause as he studies my face and then a slow smile lights up his face as he says in a low voice that I have to strain to hear. 'Yes. But I bet you could be unbuttoned.'

He glances at my tailored shirt. At the buttons.

A little thrill like an electrically charged hiccough runs through me. I stare at him. He meets it head on, one eyebrow raised ever so slightly. He's just laid down a challenge.

No one has ever unbuttoned me. Not properly. I'm not even sure I can be unbuttoned.

I swallow and lift my chin. I can't look away from him. The moment is charged, hyper charged, and then it hits like a defibrillator shock. I want to be unbuttoned by this man. By this stranger. I want to see if I can be unbuttoned.

I knock back my gin and, watching his mouth, that plump lower lip, I whisper, 'Unbutton me, then.'

## Chapter Two

I've shocked him. His pupils widen. I've called his bluff and I feel a rush of power. He stares at me for what feels like a full minute. Neither of us says a word and my heart is pounding with the enormity of what I've just said. Any minute now, he's going to get up and walk away. Of course he is. But then he looks at my lips, an amused twist to his as he considers me.

He leans over, his eyes never leaving mine and the breath is caught in my chest. I can't move. At first his lips are soft, skimming mine, a teaser of a kiss, and I'm expecting him to pull back with a mocking smile at how easy it is to mess with me. But then almost before the first pass of his mouth across mine is complete, his hand slides across my jaw with a gentleness that is belied by the unexpected hunger of his lips. His mouth swoops down on mine like a hawk dropping on prey. The touchpaper going up in flames. And I'm with him, it's like an eruption and I'm meeting with equal hunger that fierce possessive kiss as his fingers tangle in my hair, hard against my skull, desperate as if now he's here he's not letting go.

The sound of the bar around us, the chatter and laughter, recedes into the distance and it's just me and him. I'm kissing him back because I want to. He's cute, flirty and totally not my type. It's been a while since I did anything this reckless. What am I talking about? I've never done anything reckless and suddenly I want to. Fuck being the sensible, good sister. I want to walk on the wild side for once, break free – especially on the day that I find out my sister is getting married to the guy who broke my heart.

I've slipped off my stool and I'm pressed up against him between his thighs and I'm gripping them while his hands are massaging my ass. His tongue licks the edge of my lips and I open my mouth, the first touch of his tongue shooting fireworks southwards in an instant fizz of lust that I haven't felt since I was a teenager. I'm hot and crazy horny and instead of pulling back, which is what my head is telling me – hell, it's shrieking at me – but any common sense has been slashed and burned to the ground. I lean in to him as he swallows my low groan.

'We need to get out of here,' he mutters against my mouth.

Glassy-eyed I stare at him. I'm not drunk but I'm not sober. I'm just beyond tipsy and I like the buzz. I like the lack of inhibition it gives me.

I nod and take his hand and lead him out of the bar into the lobby. Without saying anything or looking back at him, I walk over to the lift practically towing him behind me, not that he seems to be complaining.

Even before the lift doors close, we're kissing again, his hands have pulled the fabric of my blouse loose from my skirt and they're now sliding up to my breasts. I moan in anticipation. It's been a while, that's all this is. Pent-up need.

He pulls back slightly but I kiss him again. I don't want him to stop or change his mind. I'm a little crazy right now, I think. My sister's text has pushed me over the edge. I'm through with always doing the right thing. At least I am for this evening. Tomorrow, I'll be back on the straight and narrow and every other cliché that sums up my dull little life. Tonight I'm going to be exciting. This man seems to think so.

We reach the third floor and the doors open. Neither of us makes a move and the doors are closing again when I make a mad grab at the door button.

We stumble out of the lift and knock off a vase on a console table. Both of us stare at each other in horrified amusement but it doesn't break the spell and he pushes me up against the wall to kiss me again. I can feel the full length of his erection grinding up against me, hard against the denim of his jeans. His hands are stroking my skin, swirling strokes that light up my nerve endings. My brain shuts down, all I can do is feel his mouth with that plump lower lip roving and capturing mine, sucking at my neck. An unbearable ache is building between my thighs and I'm antsy and agitated, almost as if I could rip my skin off. There's a need driving me. I want his hands on me, every bit of me. I want his clothes off. I can feel biceps under the soft cotton jersey of his T-shirt.

'Fuck, I want to fuck you,' he mutters against my lips and instead of the profanity shocking my normally prim sensibilities, it thrills me. He wants *me*. I'm doing this to him as much as he is to me. We pull apart, our breathing ragged. 'Fuck,' he says again and smiles, brushing my hair from my face in a touchingly gentle move. I stare at him. Am I crazy? But I've never been so consumed by desire. I've never ever done anything like this, let alone what is going to happen next. And it will happen because if it doesn't, I might just die of frustration.

I fumble for the room card in my bag which is thankfully messenger style, otherwise it would have been dropped, forgotten, abandoned by now. I find it. 'Room 306,' I say, dropping my eyes because suddenly I'm shy. I want this so badly but what are we doing? I don't even know him. Sense and lust battle in my head but lust is winning by a wide mile.

There's not a soul about which is probably just as well because it's fairly obvious what we're about to do. In cartoon land we'd have a flashing neon sign over our heads declaring a hook-up in progress. We stop outside room 306 and as I lift the key card to the electronic lock, his puts his hand over mine stopping me from opening the door. Oh God, he's changed his mind. Of course he has.

'Are you sure about this?' he asks. I look up at him in surprise.

The question hangs between us and my mouth opens but I don't say anything for a moment because I realise he's serious.

'We've had a lot to drink.'

I frown. 'Not that much.' Yes, the drink has lowered my inhibitions, I'll give it that much credit, but it's more than that. My libido has taken charge, I want to feel the planes and shape of him beneath my hands. I want to feel the weight of his brawny body naked against mine.

I lift a hand and touch the vee of skin exposed by his T-shirt and then slide my hand down his hard chest, my fingers pressing into the firm muscle, my thumb stroking the edge of one of his ribs. It's delicious, the human body, living, breathing, all those cells, blood pumping. I haul in a juddering breath. Through the fabric I can feel the warmth of his skin.

I look up at him meeting his gaze. He's looking at me, his jaw clenched as if every bit of his body is tense awaiting my answer.

'I'm sure,' I whisper and click open the door.

He swoops again and we're in my room, my back against the door, his mouth storming mine with a groan of pleasure. It's as if now we're in a safe place, we can slow the pace because the end is agreed, there's no rushing to finish. The pace turns leisurely and I wonder if I might melt under the onslaught of his slow, tantalising kisses, his mouth roving over mine with thorough intent, like he wants to explore every last inch and then some. My hands have crept up around his neck, into the soft silkiness of the hair at his nape, my breasts are pressed against his solid chest. I think at this moment in time it's quite possible I could die a happy woman. The man knows how to kiss and if I'm honest, I always thought it was an overrated pleasure, but this, this is something else. It's like being on a boat carried along on a fast moving river, flowing seamlessly over one rapid after another. There's a rise and fall of pleasure as his lips slant this way and then that, his tongue teasing mine, drawing me in.

His hands cup my face, his fingers sliding along my cheekbones before one hand slips down to the top button of my shirt. He lifts his head, his blue eyes glittering as they hold mine. The palm of his hand caresses my breast as his finger circles the button.

*Unbutton me.* The whisper of the words echoes in my head. He slips a finger beneath the button, sliding it through the fabric, and kisses his way down my throat, his palm deliberately grazing my nipple. I throw back my head, eyes closed, and a tiny whimper escapes as I push my hips against his in tiny pulsing thrusts. The heat and the pressure are building and another sigh slips out as he undoes another button, his mouth nuzzling at my cleavage as I'm pressed against the wood of the door. I'm hemmed in, caught between his body and the door, and it feels good – his thighs against mine, holding me in place.

His tongue flicks across the curve of my breast and I want to rip my shirt off but he's taking his time now. The barrier between shirt and bra and his hand is unbearable, my breasts ache with longing, a fierce tingle in my nipples. He opens another button, his fingers trailing down my sternum to the next and then the next. He opens up the shirt, parting it with his hands which skim across my skin. I swallow as he looks down and then lifts his head to give me a slow, wicked smile. The shirt slides off my shoulders, and he takes my bra straps with it, peeling them down my arms so that the cups are drawn down. This time he gives me a smile that shoots straight to my core as he lowers his head and takes one nipple into his mouth. The hot wet swirl of his tongue weakens my knees and I let out a breathy, almost panicked moan. It's almost too much for me to take. My breath is ragged and I moan again, definitely panicked now. It is too much.

'Fuck.' I have to grip his waist to stay upright. My body is flooded; a cocktail of pleasure, excitement and fear is doing an eclectic dance through every last nerve ending.

'Yes,' he says, moving to the other breast, sending another cascade of sensation bursting through my synapses. His tongue sucks, laving leisurely, as if there's so much to explore. My entire being is focused, like the bullseye on a dartboard, radiating out and down. I rub against him, desperate for some relief, my hips restless and needy. He unclasps my bra, and then both hands are on my breasts, cupping and tweaking. I want to tell him to stop. I want to regain some control but he's doing such wonderful things I can't bear it. His mouth is on mine and I'm surely going to die of pleasure.

Now his hands are at my waistband, giving my breasts a merciful rest as he undoes the zip at the back, and they slide into my panties to caress my bottom, pulling me closer against that long, hard, insistent erection. He lets out a small groan and it galvanises me. I've never been passive and I'm shocked by how I've just let him take over, I've let him play my body, which to be fair he's done like a pro. Andrew had never made me feel like this. Feel like I was going to burst out of my skin. An orgasm is gathering – it's building and rolling up like a wave about to crest. I tense at the inevitable frustration, my own inability to climax. How many times have I waited in vain for the wave to curl over the top and crash down when instead it flattens out, running into shore, sputtering into nothing. Maybe, just maybe, this time will be different.

Tentatively I insert my hand between our bodies, pushing his T-shirt upwards, my hands touching his tan skin, skimming the sides. He's broad, his ribcage wide, and he hisses in a breath as I run a finger along the waist band of his jeans. It gives me the confidence to bring my hand down across the flat plane of his belly, my index finger toying with the soft silky arrow of hair just above the button of his jeans. I can feel him straining and through the denim I cup him, sliding my hand down his length in a move that brings me a burst of pleasure right between my legs.

'God,' he groans, a real heartfelt masculine plea that fills me with feminine smugness. I can do that to him. I do it again and again. Delighting in the noises he's making deep in his throat. He grabs my hand, looks me in the eye again, and shoves my skirt down, his hand slipping into my pants. I'm so wet and he can feel it. He plunges a finger into me.

'Ahh,' I squeak, the shock of pleasure driving my voice up several octaves. He slips a second finger inside and starts to caress me, his mouth against mine as I'm panting and writhing. Unbuttoned. I'm coming undone.

His fingers start to move faster. 'That's it,' he murmurs against my lips. 'That's it.'

My hips are moving against those wicked, determined fingers as they work their clever way in and out and over my clit. I can feel the swell building and building. My sounds are incoherent now. The wave is climbing higher and higher with every stroke and he's whispering in my ear. 'Come for me. Come for me.'

I can hear my breathing loud as I'm sucking in air. Then I do come for him. The wave breaks, unleashing a flood of intense pleasure. My knees go weak as I lose control. 'Aaaah.' I cry out as sensation crashes over me, through me, around me. I'm lost, mindless for a while.

I'm limp as a noodle and Hudson is holding me up and I can feel his eyes on me. I look right back at him, a smile on my face. It must be the alcohol. I've never let go like that before. Aftershocks are rippling like tiny explosions of bright pleasure between my legs. I want to squeeze them together and hold onto them forever.

'I'm sorry,' I say looking away.

One hand is holding me up, wrapped around my waist, and with the other he lifts my chin and gently kisses me on the mouth.

'What are you sorry for?' he asks, genuine confusion on his face.

'You know, for…' I can't bring myself to say 'coming', so I shrug and instead say, 'Not doing anything for you.'

He quirks that eyebrow and gives me a crooked smile. 'Not doing anything for me?' He laughs. 'I think you've just fuelled my ego for several thousand months. It's quite something, knowing I could do that to you.' Along with the cocky, there's something like awe in his expression which makes me feel just a bit taller. It gives me the courage to pop the top button of his jeans but as I go to slide down his zip, he shakes his head, 'Uh-uh.'

I catch my lip between my teeth again.

'If you do that, it'll all be over before it starts.'

I shoot him a look of pure devilment. 'You'll just have to think of brick walls.' He laughs softly and nuzzles my neck, tugging me forward towards the bed. I step out of the skirt that has pooled around my ankles, still in my heels.

'Mmm, sexy,' he says looking at me unashamedly. I'm in my pants and heels, nothing else, but he seems to like the view and he's rubbing himself as he looks at me. It's unexpectedly erotic and a fresh pulse of desire throbs through me.

There it is again, that slow, sexy, full of wickedness smile that makes me feel like a goddess. My nipples peak, my breasts ache to be touched again.

'That was just the warm up.' He shrugs out of his jeans, taking a small square packet out of his wallet and stands beside the bed holding my hand wearing nothing but tight boxers which leave very little to the imagination. He gently pushes me down to sit on the bed and then bends down in front of me, his hand cupping the back of my knee as he slides it down my calf to remove my shoe before doing the same to my other leg. He looks up at me. I'm desperate to clamp my knees together. I feel exposed and vulnerable and it's not like me at all but for once I really don't care. I'm normally the one in charge, the ball breaker, but the sensations he creates make me happy to leave him in charge. He pushes my knees apart and leans forward to pepper my thighs with kisses, each kiss higher than the last.

He pays particular attention to the large mole on my inner thigh which looks like the outline of Australia. I freeze. I can't do this. I've never had oral sex. I'm not that kind of girl. Men don't do that to me. I'm too buttoned up and I don't think, despite the earth-shattering orgasm, that I can do it now or rather let him do it to me. I try to close my legs because I really can't and he looks up at me again. Oh God, is he going to make me? But he lifts a hand to my face and stands up, pulling me to my feet. He slides his boxers off and his dick springs against my belly as his other hand takes off my panties.

'We don't have to do anything you don't want,' he says against my mouth as he kisses me lightly. I'm completely not myself. I'm limp, molten and submissive, which isn't like me at all. I can't believe that I actually like letting him take charge. It would never happen normally, not in a million years, but he's a stranger. I'll never see him again after tonight and it's a shame this is my hotel room. I wonder how he'll feel if I ask him to leave. He'll probably fall asleep and then I'll be lying here for hours wondering how to face him in the morning. Although I guess I could sneak away and check out. I could shower tonight.

'Hey, are you still there?'

I start realising my brain has taken over and is doing its usual mile-a-minute planning-ahead thing.

In a panic I grab his erect length with clumsy fingers.

'Whoa,' he says.

'Sorry.'

'No, your hands are cold.'

'Oh,' But now I'm touching him, I'm fascinated by the

smooth skin coating the hard length of him, and the contrast of my slightly darker skin on the lightness of his. He sucks in a breath. I look up and there's a strange, contorted look on his face. I stroke him again and he closes his eyes, his face slackening.

'Yes,' he murmurs, breathing out a groan. I'm tuned to every sound he makes, adjusting my movements like I'm tuning up an instrument. It's exhilarating to know that I can do this to him and I feel some of my confidence returning. I start to explore, changing the pace, sliding my hand up and down with a slow, sure grip, listening to the accompanying lengthy groan. It's turning me on too.

Suddenly he slaps his hand over mine. 'If you keep doing that, it's all going to be over.'

'I don't mind,' I say, swallowing. How can I come twice, when I've never properly come – not with someone else – before.

He reaches for the square packet and tears it open, slipping the condom on. I brace myself because, let's face it, sex isn't that great. I'm sure some people have great sex but I'm also equally sure it's not the norm. I expect him to lunge for me and slide on top.

Hudson laughs softly. 'I'm obviously losing my touch. You've gone again.'

'Sorry,' I said wondering what he'd say if I told him I were thinking of my ex. Probably not much.

'You apologise too much.'

'Ha, not normally,' I say, a bit of my usual spirit asserting itself. Outside the bedroom I always know every move I'm going to make, I'm the one telling everyone else what to do, when to do it and how to do it – I've been called a control freak, which I don't think is necessarily a bad thing. Not when you're dealing with multi-million-pound contracts. Attention to detail is important. I'd say Hudson's attention to detail at this very moment is pretty damn good. His fingers are toying with me and the ache is back. 'Fuck me,' I whisper and then I say it again, louder this time. 'Fuck me, right now.'

I tug at his wrists pulling him on top of me. He laughs and then captures my mouth in a slow, open-mouthed kiss and the desire for him comes roaring back. And then the kissing is frantic and he moves, parting my thighs and he slides in so slowly, his face relaxing in pleasure above me.

'You're tight. Fuck,' he groans. 'So tight.' He pushes in and I close my eyes as we have the best sex I've ever experienced in my entire life.

## Chapter Three

My brain is sluggish when I wake. Daylight is filtering around the curtains of my hotel room. Daylight! What the hell is the time? Then last night floods back. Shit. I'm still here. I've slept the whole night. I can't remember the last time I did that.

Hudson Strong is lying beside me, on his back, one arm above his head, the sheet pushed down to his waist, his skin tanned against the crisp cotton sheets. I take a moment to study him, remembering with vivid clarity the weight and shape of him. I swallow. I hadn't planned to be around this morning for post-coital awkwardness.

My phone begins to ring somewhere across the room. Shit. I glance at the man next to me. I don't want to wake him. What would I say to him? I scramble out of bed to my abandoned skirt, bra and handbag, virtually diving to retrieve my phone. Shit again. It's my mother. What the hell is she doing calling me at this time of day? It must be three a.m. in New York. Has someone died? I have to answer.

'Mum,' I whisper into the phone and, watching the sleeping man, I scuttle into the bathroom.

'Rebecca, why are you whispering?' I tense at her crisp tone.

'Just woken up,' I say, which is true. 'Is everything okay?'

'Why wouldn't it be?'

'You're calling me at three in the morning your time.'

'I'm well aware of that.' This is the sort of conversation I have with my mother most of the time. We operate on different frequencies. I like to think that mine is low and measured while my mother's is high, lots of waves, lots of contained bitchy drama. 'I'm calling about your sister's engagement party.'

Great, exactly the thing I don't want to talk about.

'You are coming, aren't you?'

'I'm not sure,' I say.

'Rebecca, you said you'd come for Thanksgiving.'

That was before my sister got engaged.

'You have to come. How will it look if you don't?'

It will look as if I don't want to be there. 'I'm really busy with work.'

'Well of course you are but it's Thanksgiving. I'm sure Jonathon must know someone that knows someone on the board, I could get him to have a word.'

Because that would really go down well. I close my eyes. He would as well. I shudder at the prospect of my bullish step-father phoning Marcus Carter-Wheeler, Managing Director, or Geoffrey Wright-Davies, Finance Director, or any of the other partners. Imagine what that would do to my hard-nosed, ballsy reputation.

'I'll be there.'

'Excellent. Let me know your flight details and I'll have a car pick you up.'

With that my mother hangs up. God, I'm a thirty-three-year-old woman and my mother still has the ability to screw up my day. I have no choice now, I'll be the sad singleton sister at the party, with all eyes looking at me thinking that he ditched me for Laura. He didn't. The reason he dumped me was because I got the job he'd applied for, but funnily enough he keeps very quiet about that. It still irks me that he insisted I shouldn't apply for the position. At the time, we were living together and he expected me to let him have the promotion – even though we both knew I was by far the better candidate. When he was told he was unsuccessful, he wanted me to refuse the position. When I said no, he packed his bags and left, moving back to the States. That's when I should have realised that men and careers don't mix.

What a great start to Saturday morning. I wonder if I can lock myself in here until Hudson Strong leaves. There's no way I'm getting back into bed with him, in case he thinks I want a repeat performance. Which I do – but no. No, I don't. In the cold light of day, I just want to get back to normal. Last night, while not a mistake – the sex was off the scale – scared the shit out of me. Losing control like that, being so vulnerable in front of another human being. But there's another part of me that wants to pump the air and

27

say, 'Go me.' He was really into me. A good time was had by all. And God, he's hot.

Imagine if I could take him home to my family. Ha! That would put Andrew's and Laura's noses out of joint. I give in to the rather wonderful fantasy of me gliding into my parent's living room on Hudson Strong's arm. I have to keep calling him that ridiculous name because despite what we did in bed together last night, calling him plain Hudson feels too intimate. A forename and a surname keep it business-like and at a distance, like I'd treat a client or a colleague. Not that I'd be having wild sex with clients or colleagues.

I imagine my sister's face, her jaw dropping incredulously. A nice fantasy but that's all it is.

I huff out a sigh and turn on the shower, anything to delay going back into the bedroom. I consider using the enormous corner jacuzzi bath and have a quick rather delicious mental image of him joining me in there. Instead I get into the walk-in shower which is almost the size of my kitchen and, using the expensive Jo Malone hotel body wash, which smells of orange blossom, I take my time and even wash my hair, although I don't have my straighteners with me. I can do my hair properly once I get back to the flat before I go into work, although no one is going to see me, I don't expect anyone else to be at work today. I tell myself it's because no one else is as dedicated, not because they have better stuff to be doing.

With nothing else I can do, I emerge from the steamed-up bathroom into the coolness of the huge bedroom. It's a junior suite, complete with super king-size bed, deep teal velvet sofas, interesting art on the wall and the most sumptuous, bury-your-toes-in-the-pile carpet. Full on shag pile. The thought makes me smile.

Someone, well, there's only one person it can be, has opened the window to the big glass-fronted balcony and the voile curtain is blowing in the light breeze, lifting up to reveal the Thames flowing past the window and the iconic Tower Bridge just along the riverfront. It's definitely a room with a view and more than one view too – because Hudson Strong is standing in front of the window, naked. Although my heart sinks slightly that he's still here, I can't help admiring the rather fine bum on display. Despite my semi-American upbringing I can't quite bring myself to use the word 'ass'. It's a thing of beauty, sculpted atop well-muscled thighs. My neurones start firing up with a little – and, quite frankly, a bit too joyous – *wahey*. Even my nipples decide they want in on the action, firming in the morning breeze beneath the towel that is firmly wrapped around me.

He turns. 'Morning.' His voice has that low gravelly quality that immediately stirs a flutter of butterflies in my stomach.

'Hi,' I say crisply, wanting to make it clear our little interlude is over, but he is so damn gorgeous my mouth dries at the sight of him, which prompts me to say. 'You want the bathroom?' I deliberately keep my eyes up, on his face. Don't look down, don't look down. I look down and he gives me that sexy slow smile as if he can see right through me.

'Did you sleep well?' he asks with a cheeky grin as he

29

knows full well I'm doing everything I can to keep my eyes up top.

'Yes, thank you.' I feel stiff and awkward. Why can't he just go and use the bathroom?

Thankfully he moves past me, shutting the door behind him and I heave a quick internal sigh of relief, grabbing my abandoned knickers from the floor by the bed and hurriedly yanking them up over my still wet legs. Where the hell is my bra?

It's tossed over the chair on his side of the room.

I've just managed to get both arms into the sleeve of my silk blouse, which is sticking to my wet flesh, when his phone rings. I wriggle into my skirt, my heart pounding a little. Maybe he won't hear it? Maybe he'll ignore it? Although I never could. Ringing phones have to be answered, although I don't suppose he'd be bothered by a client on a weekend.

The strident ring silences and I breathe a small sigh. I pick up my handbag and look around for my shoes.

The bathroom door opens just as I spot them, where they'd been kicked aside last night under the dressing table.

'Was that my phone?'

He's wrapped in a towel which should make me feel better, except it doesn't. Tucked low around his hips, the white fabric contrasts with his golden skin and the sight of his dark silky hair heading down from his belly button affects me. God, he's so hot. A flush of heat races up my body.

Of course he notices. He would. He gives me another one of those knowing smiles before he turns to focus on his phone. His face wrinkles. 'Sorry, I really need to speak to this guy.'

I shrug.

'Hey, Dave.'

As he turns his back on me, I snag my shoes and slide my feet into them.

As if I'm playing musical statues I take a silent step towards the hotel door and freeze, watching him carefully. Please don't turn round, please don't turn round.

'Yes, she's no longer involved but you don't need to worry... What? You can't do that.' There's a long pause as whoever is on the other phone is talking. I take another step towards the exit.

'As soon as the exhibition is over I can pay all the rent.'

His voice raises, agitated now. 'Mate, you can't do that.' He pushes a hand through his hair, still hunched over with his back to me. 'I need my tools, my stock. I can't work if you keep me locked out. Just give me until January.'

He sounds genuinely anguished and there's no sign of the happy-go-lucky man I spent the night with. I take another couple of steps and then look back just before I move out of sight. His whole body stiffens. 'Seven grand! You're fucking kidding me. I can't lay my hands on that sort of cash.'

I feel a tug of sympathy at the mix of desperation and pleading in his voice but I'm so close to the door now, my hand is on the handle.

'You have to give me a couple of months.'

The door clicks open.

'Dave? Dave!'

Dave has obviously hung up.

The last thing I hear is the clunk of the phone being dropped and Hudson saying, 'Fuck, fuck, fuck.'

I bolt down the corridor. It was a one-night stand. Whatever his problem is, it's nothing to do with me.

## Chapter Four

I don't expect my assistants to make me coffee, go buy my lunch or wrap up birthday presents on my behalf, but I do expect them to be on time, be accurate and own up to their mistakes and not burst into tears every five minutes. We're all human, mistakes happen, but this is the second time my latest assistant (they never last long, not many can take the pace) has double booked me for a meeting and she hasn't arrived at her desk before nine a.m. once this week – admittedly it's only Tuesday but really – so yes, I ball her out and yes, I get called into HR. Again.

Mitzie Wilson, Carter-Wright human relations assistant director, tries to look sorrowful and serious. 'Rebecca, you can't keep doing this.'

'Doing what?' I ask, pursing my lips at her.

'Yelling at people.'

'How hard can it be keeping a diary straight? Or getting here on time. Seriously, it's embarrassing.'

'There are processes. You need to set up a meeting to

give appropriate feedback and feedback should include constructive criticism, focusing on strengths and weaknesses.'

I fold my arms and glare at her. We've had this conversation before.

'She's a walking catastrophe at the moment.'

'Rebecca,' she says in a warning tone. 'You do know she's just split up with a long-term boyfriend. Caught him in bed with her best friend.'

'Ooh, that's not nice. I had no idea. Poor girl, that must be shit.' I wince.

Mitzie stares suspiciously at me. 'Good lord, was that actually empathy I heard there?'

I shrug and ignore the question. 'Why didn't I know that?'

'Probably because she knew she wouldn't get any sympathy from you.'

'I'm not that bad. I just have high standards.'

She lets out a heavy sigh. 'I know you think this generation are all spoon-fed.' She pauses and pulls her rabid squirrel face. 'I do too but in this case if you could be a bit 'there, there', and show a caring side, you know, show a smidge of sisterhood…' She pins me with the sort of pointed look that says we're being serious now and we are professional senior managers.

'I'll go out and buy her some chocolate,' I say.

She blinks at me. 'I'm sorry.'

'What?'

'You said you'd go and buy her some chocolate.'

'I'm not a complete monster.'

She eyes me suspiciously, staring hard at me. 'Oh my God.'

'What?'

She studies my face before she stands and walks around me. 'Something's different.'

'I've no idea what you're talking about.' I fold my arms across my chest, which I immediately know is a mistake. That's my tell and Mitzie knows it.

'Did you get laid? Oh my God, you did.' She grins. 'Little Becca got some action. C'mon, dish the dirt? Who is he?'

'No one, it was a one-night thing. I had an itch, I scratched it.'

'Where did you meet him? Bumble? Online?'

'In a bar and don't get excited, I'm not ... seeing him again.' Although I'd had a hard time not thinking about that night. Two orgasms. The man knew what he was doing.

'But you want to?'

Mitzie has an uncanny mind-reading ability.

'I'm not anything,' I say. 'I really don't want to discuss any of this. Can I go now? Some of us have work to do and, it would appear, chocolate to buy.'

'That would be very nice of you and perhaps you can cut her a little slack. Just while she gets her head together.'

I roll my eyes. 'Seriously, Mitzie, I get she's having a tough time, but managing your boss's diary is pretty fundamental. Can you imagine if either of us had fucked our bosses' diaries up like that in our junior days?'

Mitzie gets off her HR high horse for a moment and

gives a conspiratorial shudder. 'No, we'd have been toast.' She smiles at me and rolls her eyes too and then she gets right back in the PC/HR fundamentals saddle. 'I get it, I do, but … you can't treat assistants like we were treated when we were in their shoes. We're not in the dark ages any more. We treat people with mutual respect. As we would like to be treated ourselves.' I pull a face at her corporate manual speak.

'It was only ten years ago,' I mutter. 'And these guys have no idea how lucky they are.' I went through hell and back as a trainee working for Wright Junior. I had a first class law degree from Cambridge and I spent more time picking the guy's dry cleaning up and arranging pet sitters for his dog for the first six months than I did touching legal briefs. That's how I ended up specialising in contract law. The minute I passed my probationary period, I applied for a job in the contracts department, as far away from Wright Junior as humanly possible. I learned more in my new job in three weeks than I did in three months working for him.

'You've got that face on,' Mitzie says, pointing at me. 'As if you're chewing wasps with added vinegar.'

'I'm just reflecting on how far we've come, since we started. In spite of everything. And that I made senior partner.'

'Andrew did you a favour, showing his true colours.'

I pull a face. 'Did I tell you he's got engaged?'

'No. I had no idea the two of you kept in touch.' Mitzie frowns in confusion.

'We don't,' I say with a harsh laugh, 'but he's just got

engaged to my sister.' I drop the bomb and wait for the explosion.

'Fuck! No way! What a tosspot. And your sister? I know you're not close but … what a cow.'

I grin at her, amused at her outrage. 'Fuck! Yes and … they're having an engagement party at Thanksgiving.'

'You've already got your plane ticket.' That's what I love about Mitzie, she's sharp. 'Tell me you're not going.'

I shrug. 'I bloody have to. My mother is instigating a three-line whip. The whole family has been summoned, even my Great Aunt Maude, who hasn't left Boston for five years.'

'Shit, I'm sorry.'

'Don't be, I don't care. What really pisses me off is the constant asking how I feel – as if I should give a toss – and telling me not to worry, I'll find someone soon. Half of them will be convinced I'm heartbroken, even though he's an arse and he and my sister deserve each other. Although my sister will be excessively smug feeling like she's won or something, she's welcome to him.' I huff out an angry sigh. 'That's not the worst of it. I'm not sure I can stand being asked every five fucking minutes why I'm still single. Seriously, it's like the family playlist on permanent loop with only three tracks: how is your love life, why can't you find a man and are you a lesbian?'

'You need a fake date to put them off the scent,' says Mitzie.

'Aside from romcoms – I'm pretty sure that's not a real thing – unless there's an app I've missed'

'See, there's a gap in the market,' she replies.

I laugh. 'God, can you imagine the contracts you'd have to come up with. It would be a nightmare – tying the details down. No chewing, spitting. Turn up on time.' My mind blanches at all the things that could possibly go wrong.

'Or turn up, have a great time! Seriously, Rebecca, only you would think of having a contract. Have you never seen *The Wedding Date?*'

'Going back to my earlier comment – it's a romcom.'

She gives me a sarcastic grimace. 'A good one – you should watch it. You never know, you might decide you need your own Dermot Mulroney.'

I waltz off and as soon as I get back to my office, I google the film and for the rest of the day I can't stop thinking about what Mitzie has suggested.

At three-thirty I google Hudson Strong Furniture.

## Chapter Five

The bar – it's a pub actually – he's agreed to meet in is one of those proper old London pubs with wooden floorboards, leaded coloured glass windows, iron pillars, fading red wallpaper and a big cast-iron fireplace. The customers are mainly old men in heavy overcoats hunched over their pints at the round, scarred wooden tables. It's unnecessary to point out it is not my kind of place – my heels denting the floorboards scream intruder. It's the sort of strategy I would employ. Putting people in situations outside their comfort zone is a classic ploy to gain the upper hand. Well if he wants mind games, two can play at that...

Thankfully Hudson Strong is already here because it's not the sort of establishment I'd want to sit in and wait by myself. I'm surprised the soles of my shoes haven't stuck to the floor.

He gets a brownie point for standing up as I approach his table. I shimmy out of my red cashmere coat. Early November and it's freezing out this evening, although at least it's dry, which has saved my hair. This time of year, it's a constant battle against the damp. I really ought to invest in a hat.

'Nice suit,' he says and I eye him suspiciously. And I'm right to. His gaze glides up button by button to my face. I sit down, slowly crossing my legs. I'm wearing my favourite office outfit, and the pencil skirt rises to mid-thigh as I sit down and I give him a cool, self-possessed smile as I follow his gaze, which tracks the progress of the fabric. I like that he clearly likes what he sees. It gives me a quick kick of power. I watch as his eyes move upwards, studying the tailored jacket which gives me a well-defined waist and hints at the swell of my boobs. You can do a lot with clothes, especially expensive ones that hide the bits you want hidden and enhance the bits you want enhanced. Not that I should be the least bit worried because after all, unlike most people who see me in this suit, only Hudson Strong has seen me naked, although that's not going to happen again, as I've made clear in the contract.

I lay the brown envelope down on the table and push it towards him.

His mouth quirks. 'You want to get down to business straightaway? No foreplay?' There's a scrape of wood on wood as the old man at the table by the window moves his stool to get a better look at the pair of us until I shoot him the Madison ice queen look, which makes him turn away.

I glower at the feeble joke, wishing this place wasn't quite so empty and echoey.

'Would you like a drink?' He puts his beer glass down. He's drinking real ale in a traditional glass which says Sam

Smiths on it. I nod. 'Gin and tonic, please, but only if they've got Hendricks and Fever Tree slimline tonic and I'd rather have it with cucumber but lemon will do if they don't have any.'

'Is that everything?' he asks in a dry voice and I give him a sharp look. Is he taking the piss?

I watch him, now taking the time to study him. He's in faded jeans, no surprise there –I've already put a dress code clause into the contract – he's wearing another Henley – navy blue this time – clearly his T-shirt of choice. I wonder if he owns a whole rainbow of them.

'Here you go.' He hands over the drink and I taste it. Surprise, surprise, it's not slimline tonic but it doesn't taste too bad as the barman has been heavy-handed with the gin, which almost blows my head off.

'Thank you.'

'Meets with your approval?' he asks.

'Yes.'

'Good.'

I tap the envelope because suddenly I have no idea what to say to him. What seemed like a brilliant idea two days ago suddenly doesn't feel quite so genius.

I take a deep breath. 'Like I explained on the phone, I have a proposition for you.'

He just looks at me – he's not about to make this easier.

I suck in another breath and dive in. 'You need money. I need…' Oh God, I have to say it. Focus on the business side of the deal. I have something he wants, he has something he can give me. 'I've drawn up a contract for a … a part.' A part, where did that come from? I get a grip and blurt the rest out.

'I need a fake-date for Thanksgiving. You need seven thousand pounds. I'm offering to pay you that sum if you'll act as my boyfriend while I visit my family for four days plus travel.' I'm on a roll now as his eyes go wide. 'All your expenses will be covered and I'll pay you a deposit on signature and the full balance at the end of the period.'

He stares at me, his eyes widening as I draw to a close, not that I blame him. It does sound a little crazy.

'Have you watched *The Wedding Date* too many times?'

It seems everyone but me knows this damn film.

'You know the film where she hires an escort…'

'I understand the premise,' I say shortly.

'So you want me to be your escort?'

'In principle, yes,' I say stiffly. Now he's used the word 'escort', the idea suddenly sounds very cold-blooded rather than a solution to a problem, which is the ledge it had previously been residing on in my brain.

'Won't people be surprised if you rock up with someone they've never heard of?'

'All the more fulfilling on my part. Besides my folks don't expect to know the details of my life. They're not that interested.'

He shrugs. 'Can I think about it?'

'No. I need to book flights.'

'Flights?'

'Remember, my parents live in New York.'

He goggles at me, there's no other word for it, and it's

kind of cute. It makes him look dorky instead of naked sex god, which quite frankly is intimidating as hell.

'You're offering to pay me seven thousand pounds to go to New York with you.' He grins. 'Hell yeah! You've got yourself a deal.'

'It's a job not a holiday,' I say severely. 'And we won't be there that long.'

He grins. 'You mean you're not going to show your English boyfriend – that's what I am – the sights?' Then he pouts and gives me heart-melting puppy-dog eyes which are so over the top I almost smile.

'There might be time for sightseeing,' I accede because, hey, it would get us out of the house and away from scrutiny. I don't want my family guessing what's going on – now that would be truly humiliating.

'I'll do it if you add a clause that guarantees a trip to the Empire State Building.'

I roll my eyes because it's about as clichéd as it gets when it comes to New York. 'There are a million better places to visit that are less touristy. My favourite is Grand Central Station.'

He ignores me. 'Oh and Central Park and the *Friends* apartment.'

'It's a business proposition, not a holiday,' I point out, a touch haughtily. 'Like I said, I've drawn up a contract.' I've been very thorough. I push the envelope towards him.

'Whoa! Whoa! Whoa! Back up a minute.' He holds up a hand, his forehead crinkling in disbelief and asks, 'Why?'

'Why?' I repeat. 'I've just told you need I need a pretend boyfriend.'

'But you're…' He indicates my form with a wave of his hands. 'I can't believe you can't get a date.'

I roll my eyes. 'Of course I can get a date. I don't want one.'

He shakes his head. 'Why not?'

Do I really have to explain this? Why don't men get that my career comes first?

'I don't date because I don't have time and I'm not interested.'

'Okay,' he says slowly as if he's talking to a child.

Clearly, I do have to explain.

'Look, I love my career. I've learned the hard way that men I date have expectations. They expect me to put them ahead of my work. Andrew, my sister's fiancé, was a case in point. He walked out when I made partner instead of him.'

My career is the most important thing in my life, especially since my dad died. He was so proud of my achievements. My sister is the mummy's girl and I was always the daddy's girl. He said when I got into Cambridge to do law that it was his proudest day. He was ill by my finals and never saw me graduate but he was my biggest supporter. I want always to know that he would have been proud of me.

'Let me get this straight. Andrew, the bloke that is marrying your sister, left you because you got promoted and he didn't?'

'Yes,' I say, not wanting to dwell on it.

'What a dick.'

'You see, we're agreed on something already.'

'So you want a fake boyfriend to show him what he's missing.'

'No! Not at all. I couldn't care less about him. I just need to get my family off my back with the constant worrying and nagging. All the questions. Why haven't you got a man? Are you a lesbian?'

He laughs. 'Okay,' he says. 'I get that that's irritating but seriously, a fake boyfriend? Isn't that taking things a bit far?'

I fold my arms. 'It might seem it to you but you wouldn't understand. Men don't have this pressure. No one seems to worry that the human race will die out without you doing your bit. Bachelors are celebrated, feted even. Spinsters never. Not that I call myself a spinster but it is a constant preoccupation of my mother's. As she frequently tells me, having a spinster daughter is giving her stress lines. I don't want to be responsible for a worldwide shortage of Botox.'

'Complicated,' agrees Hudson. 'Worried mothers are not good news. I get that.' He shoots me a reassuring, empathetic smile.

'I would pay you seven thousand pounds.'

He frowns. 'That's a lot of money.'

I nod. 'But you need it?' It comes out as a question because for all I know he might have solved his problem. For a second, I wonder why he agreed to meet me. He had no idea I was about to play fairy godmother.

'How do you know about that?'

'Dave? The phone call?'

'You heard that much before you ran, then.'

'I didn't run. I had somewhere to be.' My lofty tone doesn't wipe the knowing smile from his face. 'So you owe money to someone?'

'No,' he rears back a little as if stung. 'You make it sound like a gambling or drug debt. I told you that night that my business partner had pulled the plug but what she didn't tell me was she'd stopped paying the rent on the workshop I use. Dave, the owner, has locked me out, until the back rent is paid. All my tools, my samples and my materials are in there. It's Catch 22, I can't make any money if I can't get into the studio. All my stock for the exhibition is in there. If I don't get that back I'm sunk.' As he sinks his forehead onto his hand, he's reminiscent of Rodin's thinker.

He leans forward and picks up his beer, taking a long slug. My eyes are drawn to his throat and I watch the smooth column of skin and immediately I have a flashback of his chest, the light dusting of hair across it and the way he groans when he comes. Yes, that's right, comes plural. The memory of those orgasms has me doubting that I'm doing the right thing. Maybe I should have found someone I wasn't in any way attracted to.

'So, this contract.' Hudson pulls the envelope towards him. My breath catches in my throat. Is he seriously considering it? 'What's in it?'

'Why don't you look?'

'In a minute,' He flashes me a sudden grin. 'You're the contracts expert. It's a bit like sending the poacher in to do the gamekeeper's job. It's unlikely you're going to point out any dodgy things in there.'

'There aren't any dodgy things in there,' I snap and then

try to soften my face. I am supposed to be persuading him to do this, after all. 'They're all practical, common-sense suggestions.'

He pulls the contract out of the envelope and glances down, skimming the first page and then the second.

'I'm your contractor?'

He reads. '"This service agreement is dated blank day of blank between client Rebecca Madison and the contractor – Hudson Strong."'

'It's a technical term. You are being contracted to undertake the agreement. Ergo you're a contractor.

'Okay.' His eyes go back to the sheet of paper and a small smirk plays around his mouth.

'What?' I ask.

'"The client is of the opinion that the contractor has the necessary qualifications, experience and abilities to provide services to the client."' He quirks an eyebrow.

'You're male,' I say with a touch of exasperation. 'That's the essential prerequisite. You'll see in the clauses section what the contract entails or,' my voice is suddenly prim, 'doesn't entail.'

'Ah,' he reads on, 'no sexual relations.'

'I think it should be clear going in what my expectations are,' I say, conscious that my face is turning a little pink.

'Clearly – no going in at all.' His eyes meet mine and my heart almost stalls at the wicked amusement dancing in them.

He goes back to the contract and starts shaking his head. His hand ducks to the pocket of his denim jacket hanging on the chair behind him and he brings out a small stub of a pencil.

'No public displays of affection? What sort of boyfriends have you had? We're going to be staying with your family – presumably sharing a room. Surely they are going to expect some physical affection between us.'

My mouth drops open – he's seriously considering this.

He makes a quick scribble on the contract. I read it. What!

'I think we should limit them,' I say. 'Three kisses a day.'

'Ten.'

'Ten.' I shake my head. 'That's too many.'

'How is it too many?'

He's got me there. I have no idea how many is too many, or too few.

'Eleven. It goes up every time you disagree.'

'That is not how you negotiate.'

He grins. 'Who's negotiating?'

'I'm paying you, you're supposed to do as you're told.' My imperious stare does nothing even though I hate the words coming out of my mouth. They are not the words of a good manager in a transactional arrangement. I've never had to use those words at work. My team always does as they're told.

'And there should be stroking.' Again, his husky timbre sets a fluttering right where it shouldn't. He's doing this on purpose.

'I'm not a fucking cat,' I snarl and immediately regret the choice of words as it brings to mind our one and only night of fucking that is going to be indelibly printed on my mind for evermore. It's the blueprint of fucks. But, I tell myself, that's all it was; a fuck. I can move on from that.

'And hand holding.'

I glower at him. He's pushing it now. 'I don't do any of those things.'

'Dress code?' His mouth does that annoying quirk that tells me he's amused by this.

'Yes. Appropriate dress. You'll need a decent suit. Do you have one?'

'I have a suit.'

'That doesn't answer the question. Is it decent?' I've got visions of him turning up in something from the high street.

'I got it for my sister's wedding. I think it will fit the bill.'

'Good. And you're going to need a haircut.'

'I beg your pardon.'

'A haircut. My family aren't going to believe that I would go out with someone with long hair.'

He tugs at one of his glossy brown curls. 'This isn't long.'

'It's on your shoulders.'

He folds his arms. 'I'm not getting a haircut.'

'You have to.'

'I don't have to.'

'Why not?'

'Because I don't want to cut my hair.'

'You're just being stubborn.'

'*I'm* being stubborn? We're supposed to be in love. People in love don't give a toss about that sort of thing.'

I stop short. 'Who said we're in love?'

He lets out a half-laugh. 'You want to show your sister that you're not bothered about her engagement and that you've brought me all the way across the Atlantic – of course we're in love.'

'We don't have to be.'

'It would make it more convincing. Otherwise, I could be any old boyfriend. You want your sister to think this relationship is important and that you're indifferent to old Oswald.'

'Andrew.'

'Him too.'

'You're not taking this seriously.'

Hudson puts on a faux stern face which is so unlike his normal twinkly-eyed expression that I burst out laughing even though he's being so frustrating.

He turns to the last page and scribbles his signature on it. 'Looks okay.'

Every cell in my body freezes in horror at his casual perusal and I feel positively lightheaded. For a full minute I'm speechless. This is no way to treat a contract. I think I might be making goldfish motions with my mouth.

'Relax,' he says, looking at me, but I still can't speak.

He lays a warm hand on mine and now creases of worry line his forehead. I'm not going to hyperventilate, I'm not, but it's a close run thing. And this is why people get into such terrible trouble, they don't read the contract properly. I finally manage to exhale the breath that's been caught in my chest for an inordinate amount of time.

I snatch the paper from him. 'You need to pay attention to the other clauses.'

He shakes his head. 'Let's talk orientation.'

'What do you mean?'

'In the time-honoured tradition of fake relationships, we need to know a little about each other, you know, as if we were trying to pass one of those immigration tests to prove you haven't married for a visa.'

I stare at him but then I concede, he has a point.

'What sort of things?'

'Your favourite brand of toothpaste, which side of the bed you sleep on, the name of your first pet.'

'Colgate, right and Brandy.'

'Right, that's a bummer. That's my side too. We'll have to toss for it. What's your favourite colour?'

'How on earth is that relevant to anything?'

'Well, say your sister says her bridesmaids are all going to be dressed in green. Then I can say, good job that is/isn't Becs' favourite colour.'

'No one calls me Becs,' I point out.

'Except me.' He beams at me.

'No, not you. Not anybody.'

He picks up the papers. 'Not in the contract.'

I glare at him. 'I hate green. It was my school uniform.'

'See, that wasn't so difficult. I got two pieces of information there.'

'No one is going to expect you to know what colour my school uniform was.'

'No, but they would expect me to know that you hate that colour, if you feel that strongly. Brown is my favourite colour by the way.'

'Brown? No one's favourite colour is brown.' I study

him. Surely he's taking the piss, I've never ever heard of anyone whose favourite colour is brown.

'Mine is. I work with wood. Wood is brown, every shade, dark, light, golden, russet. Bark is brown. Brown's an amazing colour. It's the colour of nature. What's your favourite?'

'I don't have one.'

'Everyone has a favourite colour.'

'I don't.'

'Seriously?'

'Yes. I guess if I really have to say, I prefer subdued colours, navy blue, black, burgundy, grey.'

'What about food?

'I like all kinds of food.'

He shakes his head in amused exasperation. 'If you were on death row, what would your last meal be? Mine would be sausages and mash, proper Cumberland sausages, with onion gravy and loads of wholegrain mustard and a big glass of red wine. Actually I'd probably specify the whole bottle. And I'd have to have Yorkshire pudding with them.' He sits back closing his eyes, a dreamy expression on his face and inhales as if he can smell the meal, totally oblivious to anyone around him. Thank goodness no one is looking our way.

His eyes pop open. 'Now you.'

I take a delaying swig of wine. Food is food. Don't get me wrong, I've got a sophisticated palate, my mother and father entertained a lot when I was a kid. I ate sushi, curry, dim sum, caviar and salted fish from an early age. In front of guests we had to eat everything on our plates whether we liked it or not. I don't remember particularly liking anything. It was just food that had to be eaten.

There's that flicker of concern on his face again as he waits. He wants an answer and I have none to give. 'Food is food,' I say in a small voice. I feel stupidly inadequate. Why couldn't I have made something up, anything just to keep that bemused, are-you-an-alien-creature expression off his face?

'Favourite musical?'

I give him the 'seriously, do I look like the sort of person that likes musicals?' look. I'm not even going to deign to give that question an answer. The partners in the office have all been raving about the new David Hare play on at the Bridge Theatre.

No one, not even Mitzie, knows that I've been to see *Come From Away* three times on my own or that *Grease* is my absolute all-time favourite film.

'Okay.' He shakes his head in disapproval, which is fine by me because I'm not trying to impress him. This is strictly business.

'What about favourite book?'

Easy question, '*Persuasion*.'

He pulls a face and groans. 'So clichéd. Jane Austen, seriously?'

'It's a classic,' I retort.

'Tea or coffee?' he asks with a neat change of subject.

I breathe a sigh of relief. A question I can answer without worrying about how the answer sounds. When did I get worried about how I come across to people? 'Coffee. Black and very occasionally I might take sugar in it. Only half a teaspoon.' If I'm stressed and I need a sugar hit, but I never tell anyone that bit. Mitzie knows but that's because we've been colleagues and friends for the last ten years.

'I'm a tea man. Strong, two sugars and a dash of milk. Proper builders'. Yorkshire Tea is the best but, failing that, Marks and Spencer's Extra Strong.' He grins at me. 'There's nothing like a really good mug of tea first thing in the morning. I can't start the day without one. Are you a morning person?'

'I have to be but I'm not.' I usually get to work by seven-thirty, so that by nine o'clock I'm semi-human. I've chugged three cups of coffee by then which helps. Left to my natural body clock, I would happily stay in bed until nine which I occasionally do at the weekends but that's because I've been awake from two until five most nights. My brain doesn't do sleep. It keeps nocturnal rodent hours. I think in a former life I might have been a hamster.

'What about you?'

'I'm a lark man. As soon as it's daylight I'm raring to go.'

We are so different. I wonder for a second how we're going to carry this off.

'It's only a couple of days,' he says, reading my mind. 'What exactly are the dates?'

'Thanksgiving and the party are on the twenty-fourth so we'll fly out on the twenty-second and come back on the twenty-fifth, providing I can get the flights.'

'Four days for seven thousand pounds.' He lifts his shoulders. 'Seems fair enough.'

I'm glad that he's brought the money up. 'Once you've

signed the contract, I'll transfer the first half of the money into your account. Do you want to give me the details?'

'Sure.' He whips out his phone and texts me his bank details. 'Where do I sign?'

'You need to read it properly.'

He fixes me with a stern look. 'I'm going to be your fake boyfriend for four days for seven grand. That's the deal. It's simple. As long as you've got something in there about not falling in love with me and living happily ever after. I've seen *The Proposal*.'

'That hadn't occurred to me,' I snipe. 'But I can write an addendum.'

'Excellent. We're all set.'

I swallow. If only it were that simple. He has to spend the time with my family convincing them that he's my significant other and that he's madly in love with me. Oh God, am I mad? He has no idea what he's letting himself in for. What am I letting myself in for?

Suddenly I feel the warmth of his hand as he gently lays it on top of mine. 'Becs. It's going to be fine. We can do this. We both want it badly enough. I need that money and this is the only way I'm going to get it. I promise you I'll make it work.' He pauses, his eyes meeting mine, and they soften in a come-to-bed way that makes my heart flip in my chest. He lowers his voice so that I have to lean forward to hear and says in a husky whisper, 'By the end of the week, your mum will be thinking about buying a wedding hat.' The words hover in the air and I can smell the aftershave he uses, a woodsy lemony smell, which brings back a memory so sharp it stabs my brain. Him wrapped in a towel, fresh from the shower, water droplets dotted across his broad chest.

Oh shit, I think I might be in trouble. 'I don't think you need to go quite that far,' I snap, desperate to put some distance between us. 'And we won't be sleeping together again. This isn't about sex.'

He rears back. 'Whoa!' He holds up his hands. 'No. We won't. You've already put it in the contract and I'm not a fucking gigolo.'

Ouch! That's put me in my place. Of course he doesn't want to have sex with me.

## Chapter Six

As we board the flight I give his jeans a disparaging look. I'm of the 'you dress smartly to fly' school. It comes from my mother and I think it must be one of those Seventies things back when flying was a big deal.

Mind you, these days plenty of rock stars fly first class in their tattered jeans. Since we met at check-in and went through to the first class lounge, Hudson has been like an excitable puppy – despite our quick exchange about why he hasn't had a haircut. A conversation he managed to circumvent rather neatly when his attention was captured by the free bar. Apparently he's never flown first class before. He's never been to New York. His excitement is off the charts and a part of me finds it quite charming. All that wide-eyed enthusiasm is infectious. I can't remember the last time I felt like that about anything and it makes me a little sad. Hudson Strong isn't afraid to show his emotions.

'Hi there,' he says to the stewardess who welcomes us aboard.

'Good morning.'

'It is. It's great. I've already had a glass of champagne.' He beams at her with an unexpectedly goofy expression that has her brittle smile breaking into a full-blown grin.

'Always a good way to start the day,' she says with a little flirty wink.

This is Hudson, I realise. He makes friends wherever he goes. He doesn't do indifferent sophistication or cool froideur, he's pleased to meet everyone.

'I'd like to start mine by finding my seat,' I say as I push my ticket into her hand. We reach Hudson's seat first – I wasn't able to get them together. He looks at me.

'Whoa!' And he's actually speechless and then he slides into the seat and starts checking out all the buttons and features. 'This is like having your own little room.' He bounces up and down and he's reclined the seat down and back again before I've taken another step.

'Steak au poivre or pork medallion for lunch. Awesome. This is so cool. I've never been in first class before.'

'So, you said.' I think it's the fourth or fifth time he's said it. The other people around us smile. Normally when you travel at the front of the plane you keep your cool, making out you do this all the time.

'This is awesome, isn't it?' he says to the elderly lady in a mink jacket in the window seat.

Her haughty face melts into a smile. 'It is, dear. Your first time?'

'Yes. Where are you headed? We're going to visit Becs' parents in New York for Thanksgiving.'

I exhale loudly. I really need to wean him off calling me

Becs. I look down the cabin searching for my seat and frown; they all seem to be occupied.

Mrs Mink Jacket is still talking to Hudson. 'I'm going to see my daughter for Christmas. She and her husband have a place out on Long Island in Southampton.'

'Bit different from our Southampton, I'm guessing,' he says with a cheeky smile.

Everyone really does love him. On the two previous occasions we've met, we've not had much interaction with other people. I hadn't appreciated this eager-to-be-friends-with-everyone side of his personality. Suddenly I realise how little I know about him. Our orientation session in the pub just scratched the surface. I know basic things about him like both his parents are still alive, he has two older sisters and there's a five-year gap between him and them, and then there's a younger sister, who's five years younger than him.

'I don't even know where you live,' I suddenly gasp. How could I have forgotten something so basic? I thought I'd thought of everything.

'Clapham,' he says calmly. 'How about you?'

'Chelsea.'

'Have you got some swanky condo on the river?'

I have actually. It's embarrassing that he's nailed it so easily.

I move down the cabin looking for my seat. I check my boarding pass. Someone is sitting in my seat. A square-jawed bouncer-shaped man who looks rather settled and not the sort of man who's going to be gentlemanly and give up his seat. As I go to tap him on the shoulder, the stewardess who had greeted Hudson so enthusiastically stops me.

'Sorry, Madam, I'm afraid there's been a problem with our booking system and this seat has been doubled booked.

'I beg your pardon.' My tone could freeze over the Sahara.

'I'm afraid there's nothing I can do about it,' she says with an insincere smile.

Hudson offers to give me his seat, but the ever-helpful stewardess explains that it isn't possible to transfer first class seats to other passengers, quoting the Civil Aviation Authority with a smug smirk. I should have stuck to the golden rule: don't ever piss off the cabin crew.

All I can do is hiss at the stewardess that I will be making a complaint. I dig in my bag and thrust a folder at Hudson.

'Background information. I've put our history together to date.'

It contains a list of questions that have crowded into the wide-awake club of my brain cells over the last few weeks.

'You need to come with me,' says the stewardess, a touch impatiently.

I glare at her. 'Just a minute.'

I turn back to Hudson. 'You need to read all of this and let me know if you've got any questions. I think I've covered everything.'

'Chill, we'll go with the flow. It'll be fine, Becs.'

'It's Rebecca,' I grind out through my teeth.

'Are you sure I can't swap seats with her?' he asks the stewardess. 'I really don't mind.' I'm a little taken aback by his solicitousness until he adds, 'She's getting very stressed.'

I have the indignity of being escorted to premium economy, with everyone staring at me like I'm some kind of criminal or imposter trying to blag my way into first class. Even as I'm taking my new, sub-standard seat, I'm composing the email to customer service. The airline will most definitely be hearing from me – the statutory refund of double the cost of my fare is no fucking consolation whatsoever.

With angry, jerky movements I take out my laptop, completely ignoring the safety talk going on right beside me, much to the disapproval of the man next to me, who keeps giving me hard stares. I glare at him. 'Can I help you?'

'No,' he looks surprised by the ferocity of my expression but I think he's got the message. Leave me the fuck alone. Not long after that he dons his headphones and starts watching a film.

Fifteen minutes into the flight, Hudson appears in the aisle with two glasses of champagne and hands one to me.

'I don't see why you should miss out.'

I purse my lips. I can't quite bring myself to say thank you even though it is very thoughtful of him.

'Have you read the information I put together?' I ask in a low voice.

He laughs. 'We don't need to know everything about each other. Why don't we just talk? That's a good way of getting to know each other.'

'Because we might miss something,' I whisper furiously at him, looking round to make sure no one can hear us.

'So, we miss something, it makes it natural. I'm sure your parents don't expect you to know my inside leg measurement.'

I shake my head and raise my eyebrows and nod my head at the seats across the aisle.

'No one's listening,' he says.

'At least tell me you know where we met,' I whisper

He wrinkles his nose and takes a sip of champagne as he perches on the arm of my seat. The man next to me eyes us suspiciously.

'I prefer we bumped into each other at Costa and I spilled coffee all over you and offered to buy you dinner as an apology.'

'This isn't a romcom.' Then I sigh with childish exasperation. 'Where did we go to dinner, then?' I ask.

'There's this really great Sri Lankan place in Soho called Hoppers. Have you heard of it?' he asks hopefully.

It just happens I have. I'm the only person in my family who likes spicy food. 'I've been to the one at King's Cross.'

'Did you have a dosa? The masala dosa is amazing.'

I laugh at his enthusiasm because I did, and I agree it was amazing and it's much better if we both know the place. I probably wouldn't admit it to anyone ever, but of the two places I actually prefer the cosy darkness of the little Sri Lankan restaurant to the members-only club I'd suggested in my notes. 'OK, so we went to dinner at Hoppers.'

'Cool. We had a great meal, maybe drank just a little too

much and we went back to my place. The rest is history. There, job done.'

'I don't sleep with someone the first...' I run out of steam as I realise that, one, I'm talking at normal volume and the woman across the way is eying me with interest and two, yup, I did exactly that the first time I met him. It might not have been a date but that's splitting hairs.

'Pardon?' he says, those vivid blue eyes dancing with mischief. I squirm in my seat.

'Not usually,' I whisper, widening my eyes to indicate someone is listening.

'Ah but we had chemistry.' He lowers his voice in that way that gets me every time; it's almost like a cello bow that plays my strings to produce the perfect vibration.

'I won't be telling my parents that,' I say, fighting the little glow inside. We did have chemistry, we certainly did, but chemistry is not the foundation of a relationship. 'What are my parents' names?

He beams in quick triumph as if to say, 'See, I have been paying attention.' 'Jonathan and Jennifer. Jon and Jenny.'

'Never Jon and never Jenny. Only her best friend, Traci with an I, is allowed to call her that.'

'Really? My father is Geoffrey, he's only ever known as Geoff, mum is Micky and my sisters are DD – Doris Day, PP – Catherine, cat urine, and my younger sister is CC.'

I blink. 'Run that by me again. "Cat urine?"'

'Crazy, eh? That's my family. My sister was called Catherine but DD was quite young then and thought it was cat urine. My dad thought that was hilarious and shortened it to Pussy Pee and then it got shortened to PP, because we already had a DD. So Cecily became a CC.' He says it as if it's all perfectly obvious.

'Right.' I nod, grateful that I never have to meet his family. They sound alarmingly bonkers. I type the names quickly into my laptop at the bottom of the document I was working on.

'Excuse me, sir,' says one of the cabin crew, 'but would you mind returning to your seat? You're blocking the aisle.'

'OK, see you later, Becs.' He lifts his champagne glass in a quick toast and disappears back through the curtain with a cheeky wink.

Bugger, I have a list of questions that I'd planned to ask him on the flight. When the seat belt light goes off again, I quickly scribble a couple down.

Where did you grow up?

Did you go to university?

Where was your last holiday?

Are your grandparents alive?

None of these questions seem very personal. What can I ask him to show that I know him? What do I know about him? He wears jersey boxer shorts, has a mole to the left of his belly button, his second toe is longer than his big toe (I noticed that when he was on the phone) and he has chest hair and is completely uninhibited in bed. I'm not sure I can share any of this with my family.

I fold the paper and rise to my feet and head towards the curtain.

'Excuse me, Miss, you can't go through there.' It's my friendly stewardess again.

'I'm just going to see my friend, give him something.'

Her face morphs into icy disdain. 'Really?'

I huff out an irritated sigh. 'Would you mind giving him this note?'

She raises an eyebrow and her mouth curls. She takes the piece of paper and with a toss of her head goes to find Hudson.

An hour later there's no sign of Hudson and I am sitting stewing. Where the hell is he? Why isn't he taking this seriously? Periodically, I peer down the aisle trying to get a glimpse through the curtain to first class.

Finally, he appears. 'Wow, the food is really good. I had the steak and a really nice glass of red wine.'

'Good for you,' I say. I've just had an extremely sad omelette with a half-hearted salad that would have been better going straight into the compost bin. Complete with a warm glass of an extremely dubious chardonnay which had so much fruit, I'm surprised I couldn't see the bunches of grapes sitting at the bottom of the plastic cup.

'Did you get my note?'

'Yes.' He's kneeling by my arm rest when another member of the cabin crew reminds him that he's blocking the aisle and should return to his seat.

'For fuck's sake,' I mutter under my breath.

'Sorry,' says Hudson to the flight attendant, who stands there waiting for him to move.

Hudson tilts his head down the aisle, his eyebrows telegraphing some indecipherable message.

'I'll just go to the loo,' he says, giving me another look and walks away down the aisle towards the back of the plane.

A few seconds later I rise to my feet. The man next to me gives me a knowing smirk. I shoot him a withering glare. I follow Hudson's route down the plane to the toilets. He's waiting in line with one person ahead of him. But, sod's law, as I reach him, the doors of both toilets open making them both vacant. The other man goes in one. Hudson looks round, grabs my arm and pushes me into the other, stepping in behind me.

'Hudson!' My outraged whisper is lost in the tiny compartment. 'What are you doing?'

Our bodies are pressed up against each other. I have to tilt my head to look up at him. It's far too close for comfort. I can smell his aftershave and feel the warmth pulsing from his skin.

'You wanted to talk.' He grins down at me. I can see the darker blue flecks in his irises and the faint crinkles around his smiling eyes. As usual he looks full of fun and mischief.

'Yes, but not in here.'

'It's fine.' His grin widens. 'People will think we're joining the mile high club.'

'That's even worse,' I squeak, mortified.

'Just hold your head up high and own it,' he says with a wink.

I think I might just kill him. 'I don't want to own it.'

'You really do need to relax, Becs. You'll give yourself a heart attack one of these days.'

'You'll give me a heart attack.'

'You don't mean that.' He looks around at the confined space and plops himself down onto the toilet seat, looking up at me. 'I know that you went to Cambridge to do a degree and a Masters of Law, and then straight to Carter-Wright, where you've been for the last ten years. You were made a partner two years ago, the first female and the youngest person in the company to do so. You're a trustee for two charities, head of the female legal network organisation Prudentia and have lectured at both Oxford and Cambridge in recent years.'

I blink at him as he smiles at me. 'So what do you want to know about me?'

This wasn't quite how I envisioned this conversation. 'You got the list of questions.'

He sighs. 'Degree at Nottingham Trent with a Masters in Applied Design at the HDK-Valand Academy of Art and Design at the University of Gothenburg. But how does that tell you anything about me? About the person I am. I still might be a serial killer.' He stands up and gently puts his hands around my neck, leering with mock villainy which makes me giggle. The gentle touch of his hands tickles and I feel my insides heat up.

'You're not a serial killer.' I can't help smiling at the ridiculousness of the statement.

He strokes my neck. 'Are you sure?' he asks in a low voice that sends a shiver through me but it's not fear that makes the hairs on the back of my neck stand up, it's his closeness and the sudden desire for him to kiss me. Even though it's the most clichéd thing I can do I look at his mouth, a small involuntary breath puffing out of me.

We're so close he must be able to read me and then he dips his head and his lips caress the corner of my mouth. I close my eyes, my heart thudding with relief at the touch of his mouth on mine.

'Hey.' There's a hammering on the door. 'Some of us need to pee. Are you going to stay in there the whole flight?'

I flush bright red, jumping back and banging my head on the door. 'Shit!'

'Busted.' He winks and puts his hands on my waist, shuffling us round so that he is now in front of me.

He opens the door and holds up his hands. 'Sorry, folks. My girlfriend isn't feeling very well. I didn't want her to be on her own. Come on, hon, let's get you back to your seat. Morning sickness is a bummer.'

# Chapter Seven

Immigration always takes for ever at JFK but we finally get through and retrieve our bags and head out into the arrivals hall. The tension in my shoulders is starting to build and I can feel a headache nagging at my temples. I rub at them as Hudson pushes the trolley with our luggage.

'You okay?' he asks.

'Yeah, a little bit apprehensive.'

'Don't worry. We'll be fine.'

How do you know that? I want to ask. I wish I had his supreme confidence.

I scan the row of drivers holding up iPads or mini clipboards with names on them and there it is: *Madison R and guest*.

I nudge Hudson. 'There's our driver.'

'Driver!' He gives me a strange look but I'm already walking up to the man holding the sign.

'Miss Madison, please follow me.' He takes the trolley from Hudson and leads the way to the car park.

Once we reach the sleek Mercedes, he opens the back door and ushers me in. Before he can open the other door, Hudson has already scooted round the back of the car and opened his own door and got in.

'What the hell?' he asks. 'Where are your folks?'

'My step-dad will be working and my mom and sister will be busy.'

Traffic is heavy and the run into the Upper East Side seems to take for ever. We finally pull up outside the thirty-six-floor tower block at a little after six p.m. and I heave a big sigh. This is it. My palms are clammy despite the biting chill in the air.

The concierge in the foyer greets us as the driver unloads the luggage. He's new and I have to tell him who I am.

'Ah, the penthouse,' he says as he consults the computer screen to make sure I'm on the list of approved names that are allowed access to the lift that goes all the way to the top floor.

'The penthouse?' murmurs Hudson, obviously impressed. 'I don't think you mentioned that before.'

The lift is one of those supersonic high-speed ones that leaves your stomach behind. I'll never get used to the fairground sensation and it gives me a thrill every time.

When we emerge from the lift, Hudson immediately goes to the bank of windows on the right.

'Wow! That's what I call a view.'

'That's the Hudson River,' I point out. 'Central Park and, on the other side of the river, New Jersey.'

'Cool eh? Having my own river?' He puffs out his chest and gives me a cheesy wink.

I laugh because only he would say that. 'Come on, time to brave the lion's den.'

He stops me, taking hold of my arm. 'It's going to be fine. We've got this.'

Can we really carry this off? I ring the doorbell with a slightly shaky hand. This has never been my home. We lived in New York until I was about five and then we moved to London and lived in a Regency terrace in Knightsbridge.

'Rebecca, you're here.' My mother opens the door and her smile is heartfelt as she pulls me into a fragrant hug. She always smells lovely; she's worn Shalimar for as long as I can remember. I melt into her arms, surprising myself by how pleased I am to see her.

'It's been too long, darling.' She steps back holding my shoulders. 'You're looking a little pale. Are you eating properly? You're very thin.'

Great. I feel like a child again. I know she's not really being negative, just observational, but why can't she say something nice, like 'Your hair looks lovely. Those highlights really suit you'? At least that's what Mitzie says.

'Mum, this is Hudson.' I step to the side to introduce him as he's standing on the step below me. It's quite gratifying to see my mother's eyes widen in a comically unsubtle double take. Yes, Mother, isn't he gorgeous?

'Hudson. That's an … interesting name,' she says.

'Hello, Mrs…' He pauses, and I realise I never told him

my mother's married name but he's realised that she's not Madison any more. Rookie error. So much for my dossier.

'I'm Rebecca's mother, Jennifer Adler. Welcome.'

'Pleased to meet you, Mrs Adler.' He holds out a hand. 'Rebecca's told me so much about you.'

Even my mother looks surprised at this. We are not a close family. 'It's so great to be here for Thanksgiving and for your other daughter's engagement.'

She gives him a regal, nod accepting his thanks as her due, but then he adds with one of his trademark twinkly, warm smiles. 'You must be so excited. I know my mum spent months deciding on her mother of the bride's outfit when my sister, DD, got married. It's such a big decision and a delicate balance when you're going to be centre stage but you don't want anything to detract from your daughter being belle of the ball.'

Now it's my turn for my eyes to bug out. He's seriously smooth and my mother laps it up.

Her eyes light up and there's real warmth in the smile that she gives him. She gives a little laugh. 'Tell me about it, I'm already stressed. Come in and meet the rest of the family.' And just that like Hudson has charmed her, thawing her usually chilly hauteur. My mother is actually quite shy but she hides it well with a standoffish, cool demeanour.

We leave our bags in the hallway at the bottom of the stairs and follow my mother down the hall to the door of the main reception room, which runs from the front to the back of the building.

'Did you have a good flight?' She stands at the door to

usher us in.

'Excellent,' says Hudson reaching out and taking my hand. 'Didn't we, Becs?'

'Y-yes.' He's taken me by surprise, even more so when he drops a kiss on my cheek.

My step-dad, sister and Andrew are all standing in the room with flutes of champagne in hand. They both do a comically visible double take at Hudson's shortening of my name.

'This is Hudson, Rebecca's—' My mother pauses and she's floundering a little.

'Boyfriend,' says Hudson, diving straight on into the murky water of my mother's hesitation.

There's an awkward collective gap in conversation as everyone stares at Hudson, his casual elegance, his smiling face and his extreme handsomeness. Even though I find him dazzling, I've kind of got used to it now. I know he's good looking, so I don't get that sudden *wow* jolt when I look at him, but I realise the rest of the family are getting exactly that now and they're struck dumb. I can't decide whether this is insulting or not.

My sister, also one of the beautiful people, recovers first and sashays across the room on high, peep-toe courts. Laura must have come out of the womb with geisha girl attributes embedded into her DNA.

'Hi,' she murmurs and gives him a rather blatant once over, her approval registering in her feline smile. 'Nice to meet you. How long have you been dating my sister?'

My hackles rise. I want to say, 'Not long enough for you to have got your claws into him', but I refrain because I'm a grown-up now. Andrew is not the first of my boyfriends to have defected to her side. She always claimed she had nothing to do with it and my mother defended her because how could she help it if men found her beautiful? And she is. Beautiful. She has a swathe of glossy brunette hair with natural highlights of red, the Barbie figure and a perfect oval face with luminous creamy skin and large dark eyes that would give Bambi a run for his money. When we were children, people would stop in the street to tell my mother what a beautiful little girl she had. Laura got her first modelling job at age two, a stumbling cutie-pie toddler in a nappy advert, after a modelling scout followed us home from the park one day. Not creepy at all.

'Six months,' says Hudson and he tugs at my hand pulling me to his side where he kisses my cheek again. 'Six wonderful months.'

Wow, he's really going for it.

'Funny she's never mentioned you before.' Trust Laura to go straight in for the kill.

He raises an eyebrow and grins at her. 'I've kept us on the downlow where my sisters are concerned too. I know I'd get the Spanish Inquisition and they'd want to know where we met, how we met, is it serious?' He covers my hand with his other hand and smiles at me, a for-your-eyes-only, intimate little smile.

In that moment I have the strangest realisation. I don't think he likes my little sister very much. This shocking revelation almost floors me. Everyone likes Laura.

Andrew slimes his way over. I'm surprised he doesn't

leave a trail behind him like a slug or snail. It's quite mortifying. What the hell did I ever see in him?

'Hi, I'm Andrew. Laura's fiancé. Nice to meet you.' He reaches out to shake Hudson's hand and Hudson has to drop mine. Andrew's slim hand engulfed in Hudson's looks effete, almost boyish. In fact, Andrew looks like a pale shadow; he's not as tall or as broad, and in his smart suit looks constrained and shoe-horned in, whereas Hudson looks tanned and happy in his own skin.

Jonathon steps forward. 'Welcome to New York. I'm Jonathon, Jennifer's husband and step-father to these two young ladies.' I've always liked Jonathon, he's a tanned, vital man who plays a lot of golf and likes to be outside when he's not working. He sold his company a few years ago but he's a non-exec director on dozens of boards and still knows a lot of people. He and my mother seem happy together. They're not particularly demonstrative but they're solid, they make a good team and seem to agree on just about everything. I sometimes wonder if my mother has settled a little, after Dad died, gone for companionship rather than love. It seems to work though and she's fond of him but she's not the way she was with Dad. They have lots of friends, socialise frequently and generally seem happy with life, which I guess is a pretty good win. They're a good partnership, which I guess in marriage is the best way. It must be pretty exhausting to be swept away by passion all the time. And my brain turns on me. Reminding me just what being swept away by passion feels like, as the memories of the stomach-dropping, knee-trembling sensations induced by Hudson's kisses pop, pop, pop back into my head, exploding like balloons full of confetti.

'Nice to meet you, sir,' says Hudson. He does have impeccable manners.

'Let me get you a drink. Champagne?'

I hold my breath for a tiny second but Hudson simply says, 'Yes.'

We all sit down on the formally arranged sofas on either side of the coffee table, with Jonathon in the armchair at the head. Hudson's next to me while my mother, Laura and Andrew sit opposite.

'So where did you two meet?' asks Laura, with a toothy smile about as friendly as a shark's.

Hudson and I look at each other, sharing a quick conspiratorial smile. I nod giving him permission to answer.

He pulls a face. 'At Costa. I thought she was going to kill me.'

'Hudson!' I splutter realistically because it's absolutely not what I was expecting him to say.

'Yeah, she was as mad as a wet hen. Well, she was wet because I just spilled a whole cup of coffee over one of her schmancy pants suits.'

I don't believe it. I am going to kill him for going off script and taking the piss out of me at the same time. He's not even taking this seriously. I nudge him in the ribs with a sharp elbow.

'You know what she's like when she's angry. I thought she was going to melt my face off with "that" look.'

At this my mother claps her hands together, with a peal

of laughter. 'Oh yes, Rebecca has the fiercest expression when she's cross. You know her so well.'

At the same time my sister quips, 'Her famous resting bitch face.'

'Oh no,' said Hudson. 'She was so mad, with coffee dripping everywhere, it was kind of cute.'

Jonathon's lips twitch and he winks at me.

'So I just had to ask her out on a date.'

'You asked her on a date?' asked Andrew in disbelief. 'Rather than offer to pick up her dry cleaning bill?'

Hudson grins. 'It was a black suit, although the shirt was toast and I offered to buy a new one. Big mistake. Who knew shirts were so expensive?'

I glower at him. There's no way I would have let anyone buy me a new shirt and everyone here knows it. They all know I'd have shrugged the incident off in my desperation not to make a scene or bring further attention to myself.

He laughs. 'She told me, in no uncertain terms, I couldn't afford it.' He turns to me, and picks up my hand, lacing his fingers through it. 'So, I told her I could afford dinner.'

'And she let you take her to dinner?' drawls Laura, her mouth twisting in disdain.

'Of course she didn't,' says Hudson, in a long-suffering tone. 'I had to kidnap her.' Everyone stares at him. 'Not literally of course but I felt so bad that I followed her back to work, begging her to let me take her.'

I roll my eyes because it is exactly the sort of the thing Hudson would do, and while he's making our meeting into a much bigger drama than the more civilised cute-meet I'd have described, he has nailed our personalities perfectly and he talks as if he knows me.

'And the rest, as they say, is history,' I say sweetly, desperate to curtail the conversation.

'Where did you go for dinner?' asks Laura, with the finesse of a NYPD detective in interrogation.

'Hoppers,' we both say at the same time.

Hudson picks up my hand and kisses it before saying. 'It was love at first bite of the Masala dosas.'

'What kind of food is that?' my mother asks.

'It's Sri Lankan,' I explain. 'Quite spicy.' She and Laura shudder.

'It was definitely hot,' says Hudson, his voice lowering with double entendre.

Andrew eyes him with distaste as if he's too vulgar for words, which irritates me because Hudson might not be my type but he's worth a hundred of Andrew.

'Not just the food,' I quip, surprising myself. Did I really just say that? I want the ground to swallow me up. Andrew, my mother and Laura are all staring at me.

'Definitely a night to remember,' Hudson murmurs, loud enough for everyone to hear, pretending it's for my ears only as he slings an arm around my shoulders, pulls me towards him and gives me a kiss on the mouth. In front of everyone. PDA are not a thing in our family but Hudson has just made a very public statement.

But my mind goes back to the night we really did meet. It was hot. Superhot, and I'd be lying if I said I hadn't relived those heated kisses over and over again. I have a sudden memory of him touching me, my muscles clenching around his fingers and that hot, sweet, burst of the first orgasm.

He beams at everyone. 'And that's how we met.'

I can feel the blush staining my cheeks. Yup, he's just declared that we slept together on the very first date. Laura's lips are pursed, I'm not sure whether in disapproval or disbelief. My mother is smiling benignly, clearly completely charmed by Hudson, while my step-dad is looking a tiny bit taken aback but hiding it well because he could have had a career in the diplomatic service. Andrew's lips curl with superior gentlemanly disdain as if he would never do anything so uncouth as sleep with someone on a first date.

'Enough about us,' says Hudson, surprising me by taking charge. 'It's all about you guys. Tell us about the proposal, just in case I want to get any tips.'

I stare at him in astonishment. Our faux relationship is nowhere near this stage, which he should know. In the world of dating stages, we're mere babies, not even crawling yet, let alone up and running towards the aisle. He winks at me and leans in and kisses me again.

'It was so romantic,' gushes Laura. 'Andrew took me to Momofuku Ku.' She breaks off and smiles at Hudson. 'It's *the* most expensive restaurant in New York. You have to book months in advance to get a table.'

Of course you did. I refrain from rolling my eyes. It was so Andrew, it was textbook.

She holds up a princess cut Tiffany diamond ring the size of a small chandelier. I think I'm supposed to leap across the table and grab her hand to admire the thing. 'It was a complete surprise. And he chose the ring.'

'Very nice,' I say because I have to say something but what I'm actually thinking is that if I were getting engaged, I'd want to pick the ring out with my fiancé and have something that was a bit more meaningful. I might be a cynic but a Tiffany ring sounds a bit clichéd and a bit too easy. But then Andrew isn't known for his imagination.

After a twenty-minute blow-by-blow account of the proposal, from the waiters clapping, the champagne, the cost of each course and a wide-eyed, hand-over-the-heart-clasping repeat of her emotions, my mother says, 'I'm sure you want to get unpacked before dinner.'

I close the bedroom door and sag against it. I stare at the super king-size bed opposite. Of course I knew we'd be sharing a room – it would look a bit odd if we weren't – and I wrote in a clause about sharing a bed and being adult about it. But now the difference between writing the clause and the reality of it hits me. Sharing the bed with Hudson and how we're going to choreograph getting undressed and coming and going in the bathroom is suddenly far more intimate than I'd anticipated.

He's by the window, peering out, not the least bit fazed by the bed dominating the room, and it irritates me – this tied-up, knotty feeling in my stomach when he's the wide-eyed tourist gazing down at the street.

He turns round. 'That wasn't so bad. I told you meeting at Costa was a much better idea than at a posh hotel.'

I put my case on the bed and start to unpack and he comes to sit on the bed watching me. It unnerves me so I go on the attack.

'You have to stop with the public displays of affection,' I say. 'The kissing.'

'That's not kissing,' he says lowering his voice and taking a step towards me as if he's about to show me what kissing is.

' I don't do PDAs,' I say quickly.

'Ah but I do.' That knowing, wicked glint in his eye makes me want to clench my thighs to stop the bud of warmth blooming between my legs and I have to resist the desire to cross them like some prim virgin putting up the barricades, even though some insane, crazy part of me wants to open right up for him.

'People expect us to be affectionate with each other. That's what people in love do.' I think of his lips grazing my neck and I can't help but remember the small shiver that raced across my skin. Then I remind myself, it's science. The stimulation of skin receptors that send signals via bundles of nerve fibres to neurons in the spinal cord and then onto the thalamus and then the brain.

'We're not people in love. We're people pretending to be in love.'

He leans back on his elbows, looking comfortable and at ease, that wry smirk on his face as if he pities me. Bastard.

'The old you doesn't do PDAs but don't you want to show old Archibald down there that you're a changed woman and that you're not missing him?'

'It's Andrew,' I snap for something to say. Shit, he's got a point but still I fight it because what if I get used to those things? I push that thought away. 'No one's going to believe I've turned into a complete sap overnight.'

He shrugged. 'It's your show but you want me to be convincing, don't you?'

I huff out a sigh, because he's got yet another bloody point. 'The occasional touch and hand holding only when it's imperative.'

'Imperative hand-holding.' He nods solemnly but despite that, I know he's taking the piss. 'Do you want to write that down?' He nods to my notebook. 'In case you forget.'

I draw myself up with a haughty sniff. 'I'm not likely to forget. And while I remember. Perhaps we can go through your wardrobe options for the next few days.'

He opens his case and throws back the lid. 'Knock yourself out.'

Several pairs of jersey boxer shorts are on the top of the case and they immediately bring to mind the feel of him through the fabric. I almost shake my hand as if the memory burns me. I am not going to touch his underwear.

I fold my arms and he grins at me. 'Not touching my unmentionables?' There are times when I think he might be telepathic.

'No, I am not. But I need to see what else you have to wear.'

I guessed right about the selection of Henley T-shirts. He's brought the navy one, a pale aqua one and a red one. He's also brought a suit, a crisp shirt and a tie and I'm surprised by the labels. Armani suit. Hermes tie and Turnbull and Asser shirt.

'I borrowed them,' he says as my eyes narrow in suspicious surprise. The feel and quality of the fabrics are not those that I associate with him and suddenly I want to see him in a crisp white shirt and imagine feeling the warm skin on that broad chest through the fine cotton. It's a fantasy that springs to life with a mind of its own and already my fingers are slipping buttons through button holes and smoothing the dark silky chest hair.

'Rebecca.'

'Mm?' I ask almost dreamily and then realise that I'm staring at his chest and he's said something that I missed.

'Are we going to toss for the bed?'

'You don't have to sleep on the floor, we're both adults and this is purely a business arrangement.'

'I've no intention of sleeping on the floor but as I recall we both sleep on the right side of the bed and if we're both adults, that isn't going to work.'

I swallow as we both look at the bed. He takes out his wallet and opens up the coin section. I'm close enough to see the foil packet of a condom in one section. It brings back another memory which I push down smartly as he tosses the coin.

'Heads or tails?'

'Tails.'

'Bad luck.' He holds out his hand to show me the coin.

• • •

I head downstairs feeling much better after a shower but that's relative as it's seven-thirty New York time and my body clock is operating on British time, which makes it half past midnight, so I'm starting to flag. Despite this I'm feeling a lot happier. Hudson and I have just successfully managed a bathroom routine without any embarrassment. He let me use the shower first and I took my clothes in and then did my make-up in the bedroom while he used the bathroom. Not an ounce of awkwardness. See, this was all going to be fine. Leaving him in the bathroom, I yelled through the door that he should join me downstairs as soon as he was ready.

I glide down the wide staircase, thinking of my mother's effortless style. The walls are half-covered in pale cream wainscoting, with a striped stair carpet in hues of pale green and cream held in place by brass rods. Tasteful Victorian botanical prints grace the walls, co-ordinating with the sage green painted walls above the panelling. Except none of this is effortless; it might look it but, knowing my mother, I can guarantee the paint will have been matched from some authentic source in a museum and she will have spent hours tracking down the prints.

My heels tap on the marble floor and I cross into what is referred to as the salon, which is a small room just off the dining room. It has an art deco drinks trolley filled with a range of bottles of spirits, which I suspect have been chosen for their aesthetic appeal as much as their taste. We usually congregate here for a pre-dinner sherry before moving through to dinner. I'm the first to arrive which is reassuring in one way because I don't have to talk to anyone, but it means I'm left alone with my thoughts and how these next few days are going to go. So far so good.

The rapid-bullet-fire taps of heels signal the arrival of my sister and I steel myself for whatever attack she's about to launch.

She wastes no time. 'Nice work, Rebecca. How did you pull that off?'

I smile thinly at her. As always she looks immaculate. She's reapplied her make-up, her eyeshadow now smoky grey to match the body-hugging silk dress that emphasises her bust and tiny waist.

'Pull what off?' I frown at her. Is she talking about my last contract negotiation? It wasn't that spectacular and since when has she been following my career?

'Mr Hottie.'

'Who?'

She rolls her eyes with painful disdain at my patent stupidity but I still don't get what she means.

'Hudson. Strong. What sort of made-up name is that?' She laughs derisively. 'How much did you pay him?'

'Pardon,' I say with as much icy disdain as I can manage, although my heart is thumping.

She can't possibly know that Hudson is a fake. The best defence as anyone knows is to feign complete ignorance.

'Nice try. I know you.' Her eyes bore into me with malicious glee. 'Come on, sister. There's no way you would sleep with a guy like that, let alone date him.'

'What's wrong with him?' I ask, stung by her dismissal of Hudson. In a cross examination the logical questions would have been to ask her why she would say that and on what grounds would she base that statement. Where's her evidence? But no, I went on the defence. Slipped up. Showed my weakness.

Her face sharpens with a feral gleam. 'There's nothing wrong with *him*, in fact there's a lot right with him. I bet he looks even hotter without clothes on, but he's so not your type. Come on, Rebecca.'

I open my mouth but she interrupts.

'You're a bit on the uptight side. And young Hudson Strong, if he's even called that, doesn't look the least bit uptight.'

I suck in a breath, she's bluffing. Even so I need to come up with a snappy come-back. 'Oh, he's not uptight at all. I can vouch for that.'

# Chapter Eight

Despite my confident tone and outward appearance, a solid iceberg settles in the base of my stomach and my blood freezes in my veins. She's right, Hudson isn't the uptight one. I take in a tiny breath and catch my lip between my teeth remembering his steady gaze on me and clamping my legs together when he started to kiss his way up my thigh. I'm the uptight one. Buttoned up.

Hudson's voice booms from the hallway behind me. 'Becs.' Has he heard any of the conversation?

I hear his footsteps stride toward me. Before I can turn around, he lifts the hair at the nape of my neck and places a gentle kiss that has goosebumps erupting all over my skin. The barely-there touch makes me close my eyes and shiver.

'Mmm,' he growls and puts a hand on my waist to spin me round. 'Have I told you how much I love kissing your beauty spots?'

My eyes widen and he gives me a wicked, wicked grin.

Oh God, he's going to mention the birthmark on my inner thigh.

'Especially the one – maybe we should go to Sydney one day.' He nuzzles my neck and then glances up at Laura and winks.

I blush bright scarlet, with an incongruous mix of pleasure and embarrassment, while my sister looks as if she's been slapped. 'Hudson,' I whisper, as if I'm admonishing him when inside my head he's being awarded the Queen's Gallantry Medal, an Olympic gold and my everlasting gratitude.

'Sorry,' he says in the most unapologetic way, smiling broadly at Laura. 'But you know how it is, we're still in the honeymoon period. I guess that wears off when you've been together a while.'

Laura nods but slowly as if she's trying to compute a difficult sum or do two things at once, like rub her tummy and pat her head. I feel an absolute thrill of victory shooting through me, a flamethrowing burst of delight that Hudson has so clearly demonstrated that we have indeed slept together.

When Hudson comes in to sneak yet another kiss, I can't help but turn to kiss him back. It's supposed to be a quick peck of gratitude, a thank-you kiss, except it catches him right on the lips and they immediately soften and he holds me tighter pulling me towards him. Every nerve ending in my body leaps into action and I find myself kissing him back.

'Ahem.'

Oh God. I spring back. Jonathon and my mother are

standing at the doorway looking vaguely amused. In fact, my mother even looks fondly at me. It's not something I can recall seeing on her face for a very long time. Laura's eyes narrow and she tosses her hair.

'Where's Andrew?' she asks with the sort of snap that could take a small child's hand off.

'I believe he's in Jonathon's office making a call,' volunteers my mother.

'I'll go and find him.' Laura disappears without making eye contact with me or Hudson.

Jonathon sorts out drinks, providing beer for Hudson and a gin and tonic for me.

'Do you play golf, Hudson?' asks Jonathon, when we've settled into the leather club chairs.

I fully expect him to say no, because he doesn't look like any of the men at work that congregate on the golf course, in that 'my putt is longer than yours' business, so I'm surprised when he says yes.

They start talking about courses they've played and Hudson seems to have played at many of the same places in the UK as Jonathon, including the Royal and Ancient at St Andrews, which even I know is extremely prestigious.

'You must play with us on the morning of Thanksgiving, Hudson. Andrew and I have got a tee time booked for eight-thirty. Just nine holes.'

Hudson looks over at me and I realise he's checking with me.

'Go ahead,' I say because I figure by then I might want a break from him.

'He seems very nice,' murmurs my mother. 'What does he do?'

Much as I would have liked to say that Hudson was a banker or a lawyer or something corporate in the city, we'd both agreed that where possible we should stick to the truth.

'He's a furniture designer,' I say.

'Really?' My mother's voice pitches and she tilts her head, studying me with sudden interest as if I've grown a second head or announced I'm off to find myself at an ashram in India.

'Yes, he's very good,' I say, which may or may not be true because he has the worst website in the world and the photography on it is so bad that there's no way of knowing if the furniture is any good or not. 'He went to the HDK-Valand Academy of Art and Design at the University of Gothenburg.' The name trips off my tongue with pleasing familiarity.

My mother nods as if she knows exactly where it is. 'It's in Sweden,' I add for further authenticity. In fact, I looked it up. I suddenly realise that perhaps I'm being a little bit too precise – would I really know the name of a foreign university and be able to say it with so little difficulty? I must watch my step, there's a fine line between knowing someone and knowing too much about them. At this rate, it will sound as if I've been stalking Hudson rather than dating him. My sister has already voiced her disbelief. I need to be on my guard from now on. She'll be looking for any clues to prove her theory. Will Hudson's quick save be enough?

Dinner is full of Thanksgiving and engagement party plans. I can blame my constant yawns on jet lag but after my fifth yawn in quick succession, my mother takes pity on us.

'I think you two need to get some sleep. What is it your time?'

'Four in the morning,' I mumble through yet another yawn. It's been a very long day.

Hudson and I both stand and say our goodnights as we trudge, heavy-footed, to the stairs. There's absolutely no pretence at affection between us as we both lurch like a pair of drunks up to our room. Sleep deprivation is a form of torture for a very good reason.

'Do you want to use the bathroom first?'

I nod gratefully at Hudson's question and clean my teeth almost swaying on the spot. We swap places and while he's in the bathroom, I peel my clothes off and drop them on the floor, sliding into bed in my bra and knickers because I haven't got the energy to try and find my pjs and it's not as if he hasn't already seen everything. It's only as my head drops onto the pillow I remember I'm on the wrong side and I shuffle over to the right side, or rather the left side. A minute or so later, I'm only vaguely aware of Hudson sliding in beside me. I think he mutters 'goodnight' but I've lost all motor control and I can't even manage to slur a response. Lying back into the pillows, I congratulate myself: despite the minor hiccup with my sister, which Hudson saved beautifully, all in all our first night has gone off extremely well.

. . .

My bladder is bursting and I'm just about to sink onto the loo for blessed relief when I realise I'm dreaming and I'm not actually on the loo at all. I fight my way out of the thick down duvet, vaguely aware that I'm not at home. New York. Parents. Bathroom. With my eyes still closed I pad to the bathroom, arms outstretched, feeling my way, too desperate to worry about finding the light switch. I'm on a mission and the toilet is my sole goal. I find the cool porcelain under my skin and manoeuvre into place, sinking down with a sigh. I keep my eyes closed because I don't want to wake up, I don't want to lie in the dark for hours waiting for the morning, which is what normally happens at night.

I stagger back to the bed and hop in, happy to find it is still warm. Closing my eyes, I nestle in, aware of a musky male smell. I breathe in and smile to myself. Hudson. Nice man, Hudson. Then my nose collides with warm skin. Hudson.

Sleepily I smile. Nice man, Hudson. Gorgeous man. Hudson.

Then just as awareness is dawning – I've climbed into the wrong side of the bed – a hand heavy with sleep slides across my waist, the touch of his fingers on my skin immediately setting my nerve endings on fire. He nuzzles my hair and in my sleepy haze I melt against him, my body some way ahead of my brain which is still trying to come to terms with what is happening. Skin to skin, he's soft and strong and some instinctual part of me craves the feeling of his body against mine. My leg is slipping between his, my hip meeting the rock-hard erection. I want him. My body wants his, my muscles soften and relax in anticipation. I feel loose and free, in the twilight between sleep and awareness. Real life doesn't exist, just feelings, and I give in to the need to kiss him. I press my lips against his skin, my mouth taking a lazy inventory of the landscape of his chest, the gentle prickle of hair, taut muscle and… oh! Oh, yes, hard nub of nipple. Tasting it very gently sends a lick of desire through me, a hot flame of instant need. It elicits a groan from him. I freeze. My brain is wide awake now, it's battling with my body, which is supine and cat-like in its warm cosiness, wrapped around Hudson's body. I can't move. No, that's a lie, a big fat lie, I don't want to move. Not ever. I want to stay here and be consumed by him. I'm awake now. Very awake.

Is he? Is he aware of this? There's a chance I could just slide back out and perhaps he'd never know I was here. Just as I'm wriggling towards the edge of the bed, his hand wraps around my wrist.

'Going somewhere?' he asks in a soft whisper and leans in to kiss my mouth before dropping his head to nuzzle my neck. I freeze for a bare second but he's so warm, I can't resist giving myself a minute. Soaking up and absorbing the feel of him. I can feel the rise and fall of his breath. I can smell him. I can feel the beat of his heart beneath the skin on the inside of my wrist. My eyes have adjusted to the dim light and I risk lifting my head to look at his beautiful face.

His eyes are open. Watching me, almost unfocused, as if he's just coming to. My fingers freeze in that caught-with-my-hand-in-the-cookie-jar way, as if I might get away with it if I stay very still. Our eyes meet and the moment stretches out in the silent night. I'm holding my breath as if the very sound of it would disturb the moment. I go to pull my hand away, but he grasps it and places a kiss in the palm before his other hand makes a slow sure sweep down my back before cupping my bottom and pulling me towards him. He lowers his head and kisses me, his lips soft and slow, nuzzling sleepily. This softness is a turn on, it feels tender and gentle and so different from the driving hunger of our first night together. I sigh with pleasure. I love kissing Hudson.

The thought pings in my head like an alarm. Kissing Hudson. Kissing is allowed. Ten kisses. What counts as one kiss? Do these long drugging delicious kisses count as one kiss?

His hips nudge at mine and I soften again, my body ready for him. He's still kissing me, his soft mouth on mine.

'We shouldn't,' I murmur even though I really want to.

'We should, you feel so good, Becs. So good.' He sighs and it's the use of my name and the sigh that pushes me over the edge. I feel good to him. He feels good to me. I can't fight it, this delicious softness that has invaded every part of my body. I feel like a woman, like a woman should.

When he nudges his way into me, pausing for a moment before pushing in slowly, slowly, I let out a long sigh of pure pleasure. Thank fuck. I lift my hips to his and the rhythm is slow and languid, each slide in bringing shooting stars and each slide away that panicked ache and need to hold on. 'Don't stop,' I whisper, gripping his waist as if I can pull him in deeper. His hips sink in the cradle of mine and we fit. I hold him tighter, knowing I need to hang on. I push against and with him.

'Becs,' he murmurs against my lips. 'Fuck, this is good. You feel, fuuck. I can't…'

The muscles in his arms go taut. I feel him come as he groans, 'Fuck, Becs, fuck. Oh fuck.'

The words, said like a litany, again and again in desperation, make me come too. That sheer thrill that he's beyond control now, that he's lost in the moment. I hold on tight to him as if I'm anchoring myself in place and I feel a sense of peace as we both float back to earth.

# Chapter Nine

I burrow into the warm bed as I wake. I love being in bed. I love it when I don't have to get up and … my leg is draped across another warm leg. A hand is wrapped around my waist. Warm breath fans across my face. I open my eyes. Hudson is lying on his side, facing me, his eyes are open and there's a small smile playing on his face.

'You're just like a hamster, you know?' he whispers as I snuggle into the pillow. His mouth curves into a much bigger smile and his fingers stroke my waist.

I sleepily smile back at him and close my eyes again, I'm not ready to face the day yet and amazingly I drift back off to sleep.

Hudson is tapping away on his phone when I wake up, propped up against his pillows, bare-chested, with dishevelled hair. I'm lying on my side and furtively watch him for a moment, keeping still so as not to draw his attention.

'I know you're awake,' he says, a grin lighting up his face, although he hasn't taken his eyes from his phone screen. Does this man miss nothing? He exudes cheer and I'm-completely-refreshed vibes. God, he really is a morning person. I've probably got the remains of yesterday's make-up smeared around my eyes and my hair will already be rebelling into its perennial curls. I sigh and roll onto my back, pulling the duvet up to my chin because I'm suddenly very aware of my nudity and oh … Oh. Oh. Oh. Last night. Oh God, it really happened.

'What time is it?' I mumble, trying to surface through the fog in my head and work out how I'm going to behave. With aplomb. With dignity. Pretend it didn't happen? Pretend it did happen and it's all perfectly normal. Why am I such a klutz about sex? With a flash of insight, I realise it's because deep down I've always believed in the fairy tale, that sex and love go together.

'It's six-thirty.'

'What?' I groan. That's far too early. But I know it's best to force your body to work with the new time zone.

'It's eleven-thirty in the UK. So you've had a lie-in really.'

'Mmm,' I mutter, not convinced by his Pollyanna logic.

'So what are we going to do today?' he asks me, putting his phone down, a smile hovering around his mouth as if he knows something I don't. Is he waiting for me to refer to last night?

There are no family plans today which suits me perfectly

as I'm desperate to get out of the house and spend as little time around Laura as possible. Actually, bringing Hudson has proved a smart move. He's my excuse for escaping.

'How does playing tourist sound?' I ask.

'I hoped you'd say that. Empire State Building?'

I groan.

'Don't be a tourist snob,' he says.

'It's not that,' I explain. 'The queues will be hellish.' And full of tourists, milling about like directionless sheep, oohing and aahing about everything, instead of moving sharply and quickly to where they need to be. If I were in charge, I'd whip them into shape.

'Ah but we've got plenty of time. Look,' he shows me the picture on his phone screen, 'it opens at eleven.' He beams at me. 'And I've just booked tickets online, so we can go and have breakfast first. I want to have proper American pancakes and blueberry muffins.' Then he grins down at me. 'Why don't I go and get you a coffee? Where's the kitchen?'

For coffee alone, I could kiss the man. Instead, I just nod, impressed whether I like it or not by his ability to engineer the situation to get his way. Not that I could have deprived him of a visit to the iconic tower. I have to play the good hostess and solicitous girlfriend. Not doting, mind. That would be a dead giveaway.

More importantly I'm impressed by his casual acceptance of last night, it makes me feel a gazillion times better. No big deal. Nothing to talk about. Two bodies coming together to do what bodies do. All perfectly natural.

Who am I kidding? Why hasn't he mentioned it. IS he

going to mention it? And shit – I'm paying him. We agreed no sex. Does he think I'm assuming he's okay with this? I need to say something but before I can, he throws off the duvet and strides across the room, his backside slightly paler than his back and legs. There's a ripple of muscle down his back and I recall stroking the indent of his spine. My mouth goes dry and I feel sparks firing up again. He grabs one of the white waffle guest robes that my mother always makes available. There'll also be posh toiletries in the bathroom, she's a brilliant hostess. It wouldn't surprise me if there were spare razors, pairs of tights and tampons in the cupboards under the sink in there.

He disappears and I lie there for a moment, allowing myself to revel in the post-sex glow down below. I squeeze my thighs together, there's still a remnant sensation. I wonder if there's time before he comes back to see if I can tease that feeling into full-blown orgasm. I know I'm wet already or maybe I'm still wet.

Shit. We didn't use anything last night. I mean, I'm on the pill, so it's not a disaster but … is it a conversation I want to have, along with the paying for sex?

Forcing myself up, I get out of bed and snatch up one of the robes and go into the bathroom to survey the damage. Oh dear God, I'd like to say I look like a thoroughly well used sex-kitten, but no, I'm rocking the rampant hamster look, with mascara streaks around my eyes and my hair sticking up in every direction.

I grab my clothes and dive in the shower because I want to be dressed when he gets back. My hair is going to take some work to get it back to its smooth curtain. I hope

Hudson isn't one of those men who complain constantly about how long it takes for a woman to get ready. That really pisses me off. They want you to look good on their arm but they're not prepared to put the yards in themselves, i.e. a bit of patience.

The rest of the family are going to lunch with Andrew's parents. I wonder what they think about him marrying Laura. I always got on quite well with his mother. She was a lawyer so we'd had something in common. I bet he never told her the real reason he dumped me. Laura had yet to find her niche, although I guessed if she was getting married, charity committee member, lady who lunches and gym bunny would become principal elements of her job description.

'Here you go.' Hudson appears with two steaming mugs, one coffee, one tea, clearly having found the kitchen himself, and places the coffee in front of me on the dressing table before settling into one of the plush armchairs.

'So, last night…' Hudson pauses.

I clutch my coffee cup – what is he going to say?

'It went quite well. I told you the spilling coffee angle was a better story.' He shoots me a triumphant smile. 'Your sister's quite a piece of work. And what the hell did you ever see in your ex? What a stuffed shirt! Was he born in a suit and tie?'

I laugh because he's summed Andrew up perfectly but I still have to defend my own taste. 'What's wrong with looking smart?'

'Nothing but there's smart and there's…' He pauses and there's a sly cat-like gleam in his eye. 'Buttoned up.'

I blush scarlet as I remember my whispered words. *Unbutton me.* Taking a quick sip of coffee, I head into the bathroom, even though I've done everything I need to. I just need a break from him. From his gorgeousness. 'If we want to do the Empire State Building *and* you want pancakes, we'd better head off early.'

Hudson licks his lower lip, the one I really want to suck on right at that very moment. I'm developing a mild obsession about his mouth and yes, it's every cliché in the book but his pure, unadulterated enjoyment is so sexy. I've never seen anyone take as much pleasure in a stack of pancakes as Hudson does. We're at the iHop about ten blocks from the Empire State Building.

'Go on, Becs, try some.' He holds a fork out towards me, the syrup glistening and inviting.

'It's Rebecca,' I insist, shaking my head. This man is far too tempting.

'Go on, you know you want to.' His eyes dance, his mouth curving into a wicked smile as if he knows me inside and out.

He doesn't, I remind myself, and I retort, 'I don't.' Even though my mouth is watering, I want a taste and I want him to watch me as I taste. 'I don't eat breakfast.'

He gives me a sorrowful look. 'You're missing out,' he says before adding, 'Nice things in the morning make the day start well.' His eyes widen in pretend innocence. He takes the mouthful himself and closes his eyes before moaning. 'Oooh that's soo good.' The pitch of his voice throbs through me, reminding me of his words last night and how I'd climaxed to them. What is wrong with me? I can't seem to stop thinking about sex or, more accurately, sex with Hudson.

'You should let yourself go a bit more,' he observes, swiping his finger around the syrup on the plate and popping it into his luscious mouth. 'What do you do to enjoy yourself?' He takes another swipe but this time he pauses for a moment before leaning forward and pressing his finger onto my lip. Like a baby chick I immediately open my mouth and lick his finger, a rush flooding through me at the feel of the calloused tip which then strokes its way across my lip.

'Enjoy myself?' I echo more as a delaying tactic because I'm still adjusting to the feelings jumping inside me like a fistful of Mexican jumping beans.

'Yes, you know. What do you do to have fun? You do have fun, don't you?'

'Of course I have fun.' My voice is sharp, because I'm fighting an internal battle between trying to appear cool and not wanting to dip my finger in the syrup and feed him. 'I go to restaurants. For drinks.'

'Who with?'

I shrug. 'You know, work colleagues. Friends.'

'Interesting. She says work colleagues first. Friends second.' He pops a strawberry in his mouth and chews, watching me. A tiny bit of juice spurts out and rests on the skin just beside his mouth. I want to lick it, taste the berry sweetness, taste him. Instead, I focus on what he's just said.

In that brief sentence he's laid bare the truth of my life.

But I have nothing to apologise for. 'So I'm a workaholic. I enjoy my job. I'm good at it.' And it's my safety net, but I don't tell him that.

'It defines you,' he says with startling alacrity and a touch of empathy. 'I envy you that.'

Now that has surprised me. Given his carefree, happy-go-lucky approach to life, I'd have expected him to disapprove.

'Why?' I frown, still trying to figure him.

'People respect you. They know who you are, what you do. It counts for something. You're successful.'

I lift my chin. He's nailed it. I'm proud of what I've achieved and I know my dad would have been too. He loved me for my achievements and I'm never going to let him down. I've earned the respect. I've worked damn hard for it but it's Hudson's last word that makes me wonder. What does success mean? Yes, I've made partner, I have an amazing flat... But where do I go next? What do I do next? Do I stay at Carter-Wright? There's no chance of being made Managing Partner – not with an heir and a spare waiting in the wings – even though I can run rings round the pair of them. I could move to another firm, and I've been headhunted plenty, but there'll just be more of the same glass-ceiling bullshit. Marriage has never appealed, or rather the marriage and 2.4 children. I want a partnership, with someone as strong as me. Not someone who sees me as competition or a threat to them because I earn more than them. I want someone who won't expect me to do the hoovering or cook dinner just because I happen to have two X chromosomes, which is why I also don't intend to have kids, I'd be the one that would have to take a 'career break' – AKA professional suicide.

I realise, when I look up from this silent rumination, that Hudson actually looks disconsolate for once. There's no sign of his usual high energy, bright smile and sunny expression. His mouth crumples and for the first time, with sudden, unexpected insight, I appreciate the depth of his worry. There's an odd pang in my chest. I'm a little concerned on his behalf.

'This exhibition is important to you, isn't it?'

He nods. 'Yeah.'

'Why?' I ask, unsure how I feel about this different view of Hudson.

He puts both elbows on the table in an apex over his clean plate, propping his chin on his hands, and sighs. 'It's make or break. If I don't get noticed with this exhibition, I never will. Why do think I agreed to your crazy contract?'

I catch my lip between my teeth. The contract that specifically said no sexual relations. I've broken the terms of my own contract. Shit. I need to bring it up with him, but … where do I even start?

'But why is *this* exhibition so important?' Why did it make him agree to this mad idea of mine?

'It's a small exhibition, but it's *the* exhibition. The London Contemporary Arts and Crafts Exhibition. You have to be invited to exhibit. Only twenty people, each year, get the call – it's the equivalent of winning the Wimbledon ticket ballot. I heard I'd got the place last year, so for the last twelve months I've been working my balls off to create two collections.' He gave a self-deprecating shrug. 'And I'm pretty pleased with them. They're innovative but work with the natural grain of the wood. I've been using ash from … from an estate, a couple came down in a storm, and also reclaimed weathered wood, it gives a great effect.' His whole face lights up and I'm reminded of the time in the pub when he'd said that brown was his favourite colour. It occurs to me, for the first time, that his work is important to him, in a way I hadn't appreciated. Unlike me, it doesn't define him, yet he's passionate about it. I'd been coasting along with the impression that being locked out of his studio was a matter of male pride and he needed the money to reclaim what was his. Now I understand, it's so much more than that.

'It's my best work. I know it is. I just need people to see it. This is the best showcase.' His hands clench on the table.

'What made you want to make furniture?' I ask. I've never met anyone who works with their hands. Well, of course I've met them, but I don't know anyone who has a physical or creative job. People I know are lawyers, doctors, insurance underwriters, bankers, marketers or management consultants; they're professionals, with smart minds, smart jobs and smart clothes.

'My grandad always whittled. When I was a kid he would make these tiny animals. Little birds, woodland creatures. Me and my sisters had an entire menagerie. I was always fascinated by his process. Why a frog? Why a wren? He used to say the wood spoke to him and then he'd show me the grain or a knot in the wood. After that, whenever I saw a piece of wood, I'd be looking to see what secrets it held and what it could say to me. But I wanted to do bigger pieces and as soon as I started woodwork at school, I knew I'd found my thing. I was in my element and luckily for me, old Mr Dobson, who must have taught hundreds of utterly indifferent kids, latched onto my enthusiasm. He encouraged me. More than that, he had a wonderful understanding of wood, he taught me what it could do, how I could work with it, what I could create.' Hudson's eyes are dreamy and soft with happy memories as he talks, his hands talking for him, shaping imaginary pieces of wood. I remember them gliding over my body, like a master craftsman, sure and strong. He's mesmerising. Passionate. He feels things. I'm fascinated. The men I know, they enjoy the pace, the challenge, the hunt in their careers but I never imagine that they feel things or that they can search and tease out a shape from something else entirely. It seems at once both alien and incredible. After I've closed the negotiations on a big contract, there's the buzz of adrenaline but then I move on to the next thing. I'm not sure anyone will remember my stamp on a contract or think, *That was created and designed by Rebecca Madison*. What must it be like to create something that can last for hundreds of years, that will be used for a lifetime?

'So, are you going to take me up this tower or not?' he asks, breaking the moment, his face lapsing back into its usual handsome happy-go-lucky smile.

There's already a queue despite us being there before eleven a.m. Hudson immediately engages with the Canadian couple in front of us. I listen with half an ear, taking the chance to check on my emails and listen to a voicemail. I might be on holiday but it's an unwritten company rule that none of us ever switch our phone off.

'How long are you staying?' he asks, once he's established that they're in New York for their tenth wedding anniversary, live in Toronto and have three kids who are at home with his parents. By this time I've deleted a dozen emails and quickly responded to five others.

'Just three days,' says the woman. 'Today's our last day but we've had a blast.'

'Same here. We only arrived last night and go home on Friday. What's your top recommendation?' he asks.

'Oh, you have to go to Ellen's Stardust Diner, don't they, hon?' she says. 'All the waiters and waitresses are Broadway stars in waiting and they are sooo good.'

'Yeah, it's such a great atmosphere,' her husband adds. They start telling us all about it. Of course I've heard of it but even if I hadn't, it sounds truly hideous. Singing waiters. I can't imagine anything worse.

'That sounds brilliant,' says Hudson. 'We should go.'

I look up from my phone and stare at him as if he's grown two heads, no, make that three. 'Seriously,' I mutter to him as the Canadian couple talk to each other about their favourite number, 'it's the biggest tourist trap in Manhattan. The food is overpriced and of average quality. If you're going to eat out in Manhattan, the city has some of the best restaurants in the world.' Quite frankly I'd rather die than go there.

'There you go again, being all buttoned up,' says Hudson. There's that wicked hint of a challenge in the lopsided smile that lifts one corner of his mouth. 'It sounds fun. Have you actually been there?'

I purse my mouth, refusing to dignify the question with an answer, because I hate that I'm going to come out as the bad guy in the 'I don't like it but I've never tried it' scenario that is about to ensue. I glance at my phone screen but he shakes his head and covers it with his hand. 'You haven't been.' He says the words both accusing and triumphant at the same time.

I glare at him. 'I don't need to go, to know that on balance of probability I'll be correct.'

'I love it when you go all lawyerly on me,' he says. My heart has one of those slip-sideways moments as his eyes telegraph that he remembers me not being lawyerly at all.

He shakes his head and turns back to the couple. 'What do you reckon? Shall I insist on Ellen's?'

'Definitely,' chorus the couple in unison.

I glare at Hudson. How dare he make this a spectator sport? And encourage said spectators to join in?

'There,' says Hudson, with a satisfied smile on his face. 'That's decided then.'

As the couple's interest is diverted by something else, I hiss. 'No it isn't. We're not going there.'

'You'll have fun. I guarantee it.'

I give him a withering look. He really doesn't know me. 'I won't and we're not going.' That's final. It's the tone I use at work and everyone knows then to back the fuck off.

'Yes we are,' he says, his eyes brimming with amusement. 'If we don't I'll take your phone away.'

I jerk back and cradle a protective hand over my heart. 'You wouldn't.'

He takes a step forward and we're almost nose to nose. 'Wouldn't I?' he teases.

I look into his eyes. My heart feels a bit lighter and I smile back at him, because in this mood he's irresistible.

He stares at me, his mouth curving with the familiar naughty smile, the one where I know he's got something up his sleeve. I toy with kissing him, just to see what his reaction would be but then I chicken out because I know that he'd probably take it on the chin and push it up to full throttle even though we're in public.

'Or I could tell your sister I was mistaken about that mole and about the you know what.'

'I'm not sure she's going to believe you – you sounded like you knew what you were talking about. Besides, I could sue you for breach of contract faster than you could take your next breath. There's a confidentiality clause in our agreement.' I give him a faux smile. 'And that is why you should always read the contract.'

His eyes gleam. He loves a challenge. I've miscalculated. And badly. This man is a winner too. He's just more subtle about it, not a bulldozer. It's not a tactic I'm used to. At work the men force their way through everything and I've had to match up.

'What if we break up?' he asks.

'We're not supposed to break up until a week after we get home,' I remind him and my heart does a funny little dip at the thought of it. Not seeing Hudson again.

'Is that in the contract?' he asks frowning.

'No but it's the scenario in my head for when my family ask later on. They will, you know.'

He nods. 'You've got all the bases covered. Just out of interest, why do we break up?'

'Irreconcilable differences.'

'Isn't that for a divorce? I think I prefer that I caught you cheating on me, punched his lights out and you only just got me off an assault charge.'

I laugh. 'I'm not a defence lawyer.'

It's his turn to laugh. 'And that's what worries you, not that you were cheating?'

He has a point. 'Because hello, I'd never cheat.'

'Never?'

'Never,' I say. It's one of those unbreakable rules.

'Did you put that in the contract?'

'You know, you really should have read it,' I tease.

He shrugs and gives me a smile. 'I trust you. The fact that you didn't put it in the contract says it all.'

'How do you figure that?' This conversation is escaping me, unravelling faster than a ball of wool with a litter of kittens. One minute we were talking about going to a restaurant – or rather not going – and now we're talking … God knows what we're talking about but it's straying badly towards things that I don't want to talk about.

'Because it didn't occur to you that you could cheat. I like that. Not that I think you couldn't but that you're so sure you wouldn't.' He smiles at me and I think it's sincere. 'You are a woman of strong principles and incontrovertible belief in herself.' He pauses and then adds with a slow grin, 'I find it very sexy.'

I roll my eyes but seriously, what else am I to do with this maddening but quite charming man? 'We are still not going to Ellen's Stardust Diner.'

'You wouldn't want your sister to know that you cheated on me once, would you?'

'What! You wouldn't?'

'It's just a restaurant. Besides, you wouldn't want to disappoint my sisters.'

His sisters. Oh dear God, I do not even want to go down this latest side alley. I am not going to ask. 'Fine, we'll go to the fucking restaurant but don't blame me if you can't stop singing "Summer Nights" for days on end.'

'I won't,' he says and tucks an arm through mine and kisses me full on the mouth. 'Thanks, Becs.' And all I can think is kiss number one, there are still nine more to go.

By the time we get to the final elevator, I've taken a couple of calls and Hudson has befriended half the queue. Okay, a slight exaggeration, but he has chatted to lots of people, all of whom 'love' his accent and love him even more when he tells them, yes, he's met the late Queen but not the King.

'Have you really?' I mutter to him as I answer another email. He gives me one of his grins but doesn't answer, so I'm none the wiser.

'You know this building is an Art Deco masterpiece,' he tells me, prodding me with his elbow. I look up from my phone. Can't he see I'm busy? But he seems oblivious. If he were a real boyfriend, he'd have earned an oven load of brownie points for not nagging me about working all the time.

He points to the sharp vertical and horizontal lines of the windows and the marble and metal finishes inside as we go and by the time we reach the observation deck, I feel like I'm the tourist and he's the guide. He's been doing his research and is very knowledgeable. On the plane he'd looked me up. I need to remember he's more thorough than he lets on.

It's a cold crisp November morning, the visibility is perfect and Hudson is entranced. 'My God, it's like toytown down there.' Far below you can see the iconic yellow taxi cabs, which look like toy cars. 'It doesn't look real. Everything is so square. Straight lines everywhere. This is amazing. What a view.' We're on the south side looking down towards the tip of Manhattan with Brooklyn over to the left. His first-time enthusiasm is infectious and I point out a few landmarks to him.

'It's very blowy,' he observes as my hair whips him in the face and he has to keep swiping at the curls escaping from his beanie hat.

'Did you know that originally they planned to have zeppelins tethered to the top but apparently the wind is caused by the updrafts funnelled along the skyscrapers. They had to scrap that plan because it wasn't safe, which is a real shame. It would have been so cool.'

He gazes upwards and I stare at his profile, suddenly consumed with an urge to kiss the smooth column of his neck. Who said the kissing had to come from him? We've still got nine to play with. He's just so vital and energetic, interested in everything. It's surprisingly refreshing.

'I bet coming up here never gets old, does it? It's quite awe-inspiring. What man can do.' Several floors below, he'd pored over the pictures in the exhibition of the workmen working without safety equipment.

I nod, although I've never thought of it like that before. Now that I really look I can see the city spread out before me. Looking down at buildings that are skyscrapers in their own right. The tiny water towers decorating the tops of buildings. And marvel at what man can achieve.

'It's so different from London,' says Hudson with a sigh, busy snapping pictures with his phone. 'My sisters are going to be so jealous. They love that film *Sleepless in Seattle*.'

I quite liked the film, although I haven't watched it in years.

'I wonder how many people arrange to meet up here,' he muses, looking round.

'I didn't have you pegged as a romantic,' I say.

'With three sisters, I'm in touch with my feminine side. I can be very romantic when I want to be.' He raises his eyebrows at me and gives me a suggestive smile.

'Romantic doesn't always include sex,' I tease him.

He frowns with mock disappointment, 'Doesn't it?'

We walk around to the east side of the observation deck, where it's even windier and my hair whips into my eyes and across my lips leaving lipstick drag marks around my mouth. I try to push it away but with the frequent gusts you'd need to be an octopus to hold it back.

'Here.' Hudson whips off his beanie hat and carefully pulls it down on my head with both hands, smoothing my hair backwards. His fingers graze the skin around my mouth, stroking away the stray lipstick trails. I look up at him. He's laughing, his eyes crinkling, and I feel that funny thud in my heart again at the sight of him so close to me. It would be so easy to reach forward and kiss him. How would he react? Would he kiss me back? In our agreement there are ten kisses per day. I think of last night's accidental kiss and how quickly I wanted more. That's not a good road to travel.

'Thank you,' I say, turning away quickly and looking out over the East River, trying to school my face into calm indifference. I need to remember that there is an agreement between us, one set up for very good reasons, and that this break will be over in a matter of days. Going forward, we need to stick to the rules otherwise it's not going to work. But the rules do allow for ten kisses a day, an insidious voice in my head reminds me. But they're public kisses, I think. For show. Not for us.

But you could have another one, I think.

Honestly I'm like someone on a diet promising myself just one chocolate, even though I know I probably won't be able to stop there. There. I've admitted it to myself. Hudson's kisses are addictive. I want to kiss him, for him to kiss me. Would it hurt? But I know, even as a curl of lust winds its way through my system, that it would lead to more. But so what? We're both adults, we both know the score. It's just sex. Fucking. That's all. Consensual sex. We've done it twice now. And I can't help it, I close my eyes and think of last night. My thighs clench with remembered desire. No, we can't do it again, we mustn't.

'You all right?' asks Hudson. 'You're not frightened of heights, are you?'

I open my eyes to find kind eyes checking my face. 'No, not at all. I'm fine.'

'Good. My hat suits you. Makes you look cute and a lot less frosty.'

'Frosty?'

'Yes, more approachable. You're very intimidating when you want to be. No wonder your sister and her fiancé Albert are a bit scared of you.'

'Scared of me? What are you talking about? And his name is Andrew.'

'They're scared of you. The whole family, yesterday. They were walking on eggshells around you.'

I snort. 'You're joking, aren't you? It's the Princess Laura show all the way.'

He frowns and stares at me, serious for once, before shaking his head. 'I don't think so.'

With an exasperated toss of my head, I mutter, 'Yeah, because after all of a couple of hours, you understand the family dynamic.'

Unfortunately, despite the strong breeze rushing around us, his hearing is keen. 'It's easy to spot something that you've all grown so accustomed to, you don't even notice it. Familiarity and all that.'

I shake my head vehemently. 'You're definitely wrong.'

'Am I?' he asks with that determined quietness I'm becoming accustomed to. Hudson Strong can be quite stubborn and tenacious when he wants to be. There's steel running through that delicious body and I've underestimated him, sucked in by that easy charm. He's not as happy-go-lucky and easy-going as he first appeared and that worries me. I don't want him analysing me and my family's relationship. I don't want him probing beneath the surface, putting those observations into well-framed words. He's here to be arm-candy. That's the total extent of his role. Maybe I should have spelled that out in the contract. Views and opinions not welcome. Perhaps I should add it as an addendum – yeah right, Rebecca, because that would really work. I close my eyes because I can imagine it all too clearly – it would suggest to him that those views count for something – which they definitely don't.

## Chapter Ten

We arrive back at the house and just as we're greeted in the penthouse foyer by the housekeeper, Mrs Makepiece, I snatch the beanie hat from my head and push it back into Hudson's pocket. She's English and stuffier than my mother but on this occasion she gives me a faint smile.

'Miss Madison, will you be dining in this evening?'

I shoot Hudson a resigned look. 'No, we'll be going out, thank you.'

'Your mother is in the drawing room, I'll bring tea and coffee,' she says, nodding her head before turning away.

'Wow.' Hudson stares after her incredulously. 'Mrs Danvers in the flesh. She was much nicer this morning.'

'This morning?'

'When I made the tea and coffee, although I did have to give her a bit of a tickle. Quite stuffy to start with.'

I dread to think what he means by giving her a bit of a tickle but it would seem no woman is impervious to the Hudson Strong charm. 'She's not that bad,' I say, despite her

119

giving us the implicit order to join my mother, and the fact that I've never seen her smile. 'Do you want to go up to the room? Have a rest or something?'

'A rest?' He grins. 'Why would I need a rest? Or do you mean a *rest* rest?'

I immediately realise where his mind has gone. I also immediately think that I've never had sex in the afternoon, as in not specifically gone to bed in the afternoon, but I can't let him know that I'm thinking that. Instead I give him a withering look. 'I thought you might like a quick break.' Also it's as much for me – being under scrutiny from my family is harder than I'd expected.

'And leave you unprotected,' he says, and he tucks a hand under my elbow. 'Lead me to the drawing room.'

I take him with me because after all that is why he's here.

'Rebecca, Hudson,' my mother greets us and waves us to the white leather sofa opposite her. Andrew and Laura are sitting with her with a laptop. 'We're just talking wedding plans. We're thinking England actually. June next year. Laura's found this darling barn place in Oxfordshire.'

'Hudson's from Oxfordshire originally,' I say, delighted with this opportunity to prove to Laura how well I know him.

'It looks perfect.' Laura says with a beam and turns the laptop screen towards us.

Hudson leans forward. 'Murcott Manor,' he says

'Yes,' said Laura, surprised. 'Do you know it?'

'Yeah,' he says and I realise I know him well enough to know that he's being evasive. Well, he's not being expansive, which is unlike him. Normally he'd say something about the venue, the design of the building or the grounds, but he says nothing. It's curious.

While I know very little if anything about planning a wedding, even I know this sort of venue is booked up years, let alone months, in advance and I can't help blurting out, 'Won't they be fully booked for this June? At the weekends anyway.'

My mother closes her eyes. Laura purses her lips and turns towards me with a dramatic swivel. Okay, I might just get a small kick out of winding her up.

'Why can't you just be happy for me, Rebecca?' she asks. 'Instead, you have to be mean about it, don't you? You've always been so jealous of me.'

'I was just pointing out the obvious fact. Big fancy weddings take years to plan. Unless of course you're in a hurry.' I shoot a quick glance at her stomach.

She draws herself up, like an indignant chicken with very ruffled feathers. 'We're not in a hurry. I just don't want to wait.'

'Would you like some tea?' my mother asks hurriedly, as Mrs Makepiece brings in a tray, the china cups clattering faintly on the saucers.

Hudson looks at the tray and sends what I now think of as his puppy-dog smile her way. 'I don't suppose I could have a mug of tea, could I?' He holds up his big, elegant hands. 'I think these beautiful tea cups were built for delicate ladies, not for the likes of me. I'd hate to break one and ruin the set, when it looks so lovely together.'

Andrew, mid sip of his tea, his pinky finger held out at

an angle, glowers at Hudson and I bite back a smile. Hudson, without even trying, has cast aspersions on Andrew's masculinity and what's more, his blend of flattery and practicality has cracked Mrs Makepiece's chilly froideur; she actually breaks into a smile. 'Of course. A working man like you needs a proper mug of tea. Just one moment.'

Andrew almost chokes on his tea. I smile at him.

Between us we're really doing well at upsetting Andrew and Laura this afternoon.

A minute later she's back with a tray with a mug and another pot of tea which she places carefully on the coffee table in front of him, as if presenting a gift to the king. 'I've made an English Breakfast for you, a bit stronger than the Earl Grey.' I don't fucking believe it. I've had to put up with insipid piss water in this house on every visit and bloody Hudson in less than twenty-four hours has got her eating out of the palm of his hand. I've become accustomed to strong tea at home, always Yorkshire tea.

'How did you manage that?' I murmur, as my mother makes a big deal of pouring his tea.

'I told you, we had a nice chat this morning when I went and made the drinks. Her dad was a chippy and we got chatting. I mentioned I liked a decent brew.'

'So what are your dinner plans, this evening? Laura and Andrew are meeting friends at Balthazar.' It sounds wonderful; spending the evening with Andrew and Laura, less so. My mother continues, 'I'm sure they could squeeze two more in, if you don't have reservations anywhere. With the holiday it's going to be busy.'

My heart sinks. You can't make reservations at Ellen's Stardust Diner, we'll be queuing for hours. I glance out of the window. The clouds look very grey, snow-laden. We're going to freeze to death. It was cold enough up at the top of the tower this morning.

'Becs is going to take me somewhere special…' I close my eyes waiting for the shoe to fall. They'll all be horrified at us going somewhere so touristy. 'It's a surprise but she says I'll love it. She knows me so well.' He brushes his lips across my cheek in a soft kiss that should be friendly, platonic, but it reminds me of other soft kisses, the slide of his lips across my collar bone.

My mother beams approval across the table. 'Ah, that's the sort of thing Jonathon does for me, even if it's not his cup of tea at all.'

'Becs is very thoughtful like that.' He takes my hand and squeezes it. I'm not thoughtful at all. There's only been me to think about for such a long time. Occasionally I'll surprise Mitzie in the office with flowers, because she loves them and her husband is allergic to just about everything. And I did buy my PA, Hester, who is currently on maternity leave, a pamper day at a local spa because everyone else had bought presents for the baby, which I didn't think was fair. But that is the sum total of my thoughtfulness.

Talk turns back to the wedding and Laura's ideas for her big day. I notice there's been no mention of bridesmaids. Not that I'm expecting to be one. I'm just interested to find out how Laura is going to handle this hot potato diplomatically and moreover what our mother will have to say about it.

'Have you had any thoughts about where you'll go on honeymoon?' asks Hudson and I could kiss him (again) for asking exactly the right question. Laura beams at Andrew. 'We're thinking a month in Europe, a week in Paris, a week in Rome.'

I'm not going to point out that this is only two weeks.

'But then we could go to the Caribbean. There are so many places to visit.' She looks at me. 'We all know Rebecca would want to go to Paris and visit every museum and art gallery available. Which is so dull.'

Hudson takes my hand. 'We should totally do Paris together. The Musée D'Orsay, the Louvre. Have you ever been to the Musée Marmottan? It has the largest collection of Monet paintings in the world including some stunning Giverny and waterlily pictures there.'

My mother clasps her hands. 'You two are so well-suited. I remember taking you to Paris when you were teenagers. Laura wanted to spend her whole time on the Champs-élysée and at Galleries Lafayette while Rebecca was quite happy wondering around Montmartre and the museums.'

I give Hudson a wary glance. Is he being sincere or is this part of the doting boyfriend act? Either way he is absolutely nailing the romance between us.


'Jeans?' my mother asks when we come down at five-thirty p.m.

'Yes, the place we're going is very understated.'

'Oh.' She looks doubtful.

124

'They pride themselves on being uber casual,' I improvise. There's no way I'm wearing my Max Mara Weekend trousers to Ellen's Diner. Waiters who are too busy singing and showing off are not going to be particularly good at serving without spilling. That's my view and I'm sticking to it. Hence the jeans, though still Ralph Lauren, which won't be ruined when someone gets carried away hitting a high note or something.

Hudson is wrapped up in a North Face down coat, with jeans, boots and a scarf wrapped several times around his neck. It looks vaguely familiar but I can't quite place it.

'Dr Who,' he says cheerfully, tucking the very long scarf tail into his coat.

I frown. I still have no idea what he's talking about.

'Dr Who scarf. My nan knitted it for me when I was seven.'

'You've had a scarf since you were seven?' I hope he's washed it since then.

'That's so sweet,' says my mother. I stare at her; this coming from the woman who has a new wardrobe every season?

'It was the first thing my nan ever knitted. She was so proud of herself. It's practically a family heirloom. Do you knit, Jenny?' I wait a full two seconds for my mother's eyes to narrow and for her to give him a withering look, but no, to my utter amazement, she laughs.

'I don't, but perhaps I should take it up and start knitting family heirlooms.'

I stare at her. My mother sends out my step-father's shirts to have buttons sewn on.

125

He turns to look at me. 'Don't even ask,' I say.

My mother laughs again. 'Rebecca…' and trails away into peals of giggles at the very thought. Okay, she doesn't need to rub in my inability with craft things so much. Laura's home-made Christmas decorations always made it onto the tree, back in the day when she decorated our own tree. Mine went to Daddy's office at work. To be entirely fair, she does have an eye for that sort of thing. I never had the patience, there was always something else I'd want to do, and I guess judging how good something like that is is purely subjective. In law you know where you are, all the time. There's black, white and shades of grey but not a whole rainbow of possibilities.

'Like Mum says. Not my thing.' Not ever. I wouldn't be seen dead with a pair of knitting needles. 'Shall we go?'

'Have a nice evening. I hope it's a lovely surprise wherever you go.'

I nod, grateful that I've still not had to say where we're going.

'Before we go…' Hudson holds up a white envelope and gives it to my mother. 'Can you put a cross on the back of this for me to prove that the seal has been unbroken?' I eye him. What is he up to and why is he involving my mother?

Somewhat unpredictably, she smiles at him, her eyes crinkling properly at the corners, and says, 'You're so romantic, Hudson,' as if that's a good thing. Who is this person? Romantic? I've never seen her and Jonathon show a single PDA. I would have laid bets on my mother not knowing what romance was let alone indulging in it.

• • •

We take the subway to Times Square. It's not too busy but Hudson, as always, stands behind me and places a hand in the centre of my back whenever we get on or off or as we're standing. It's a barely-there touch but it's a constant. I find it reassuring, despite the fact that I've been using the New York subway quite happily on and off for the last fifteen years. It's so Hudson. I'm sure he'd do it to any woman he was with but there's something about the gesture that says a lot about him. He's innately considerate.

The queue outside Ellen's is predictably long but Hudson isn't the least bit daunted. He rams his hands deep in his pockets and rewraps the scarf, which seems to have a life of its own, around the lower part of his face so that only his nose is poking out. He's wearing a different beanie hat; I still have his. I'm reluctant to give it back because … I've no idea why I don't want to give it back and he hasn't asked for it.

Behind us a man grumbles. 'The line is fifty minutes, honey. Are you sure you don't want to go someplace else?'

Fifty minutes. In November, in New York.

'Let's play a game,' says Hudson. 'It'll help pass the time.' He stamps his feet on the sidewalk.

'What sort of game?' We're both a bit old for I-spy.

'Snog, marry, avoid.' He grins at me.

I raise an eyebrow. 'Seriously? How old are you?'

'I'm twenty-nine and nine twelfths,' he says.

I swallow as if I've just tasted something unpleasant. He's younger than me.

'I'll be thirty in March,' he adds. 'The big three O.'

'It was a rhetorical question,' I say.

'What do you want to play, then?'

He's serious. 'Nothing.' I want to get out my phone and check my emails. I haven't checked them since this morning. That's unheard of and a knot tightens in my belly. I pull out my phone.

'Becs, you're on holiday. Come on, I let it go earlier but *you* need to take a break. Hand it over.' Although there's a teasing glint in his eye, there's also that odd sympathy again. Does he feel sorry for me? Because I can't leave my phone alone. I lift my chin and hand it over to him. See, I can do this. Hudson takes it from me and puts it in his jeans front pocket with a gentle smile that takes the sting out of his high-handed action. 'I'm doing it for your own good.' He reaches up and strokes at the spot between my eyebrows above my nose. 'You get this little line right here, when you start checking your emails. You need to take some time for yourself. You're on holiday.'

'I'm never on holiday,' I say before I can stop the words. There's a tiny touch of panic in them. Because I *have* been on holiday. I haven't checked my emails since first thing this morning. It's not like me at all. I'd forgotten about work, distracted by what I've got myself into, that's all.

'You should try it some time, you might enjoy it.' He nudges me and his smile is warm and matey as if we're on the same side. I'm so used to being on my own, I feel a strange sense of happiness.

'Where else have you been on holiday or not holiday?' he asks and we spend the next half hour talking about the places we've travelled to. He seems to have been to every corner of the UK and a fair bit of Europe.

'How come you've been to so many places?' I ask intrigued. My mum and dad took Laura and me on a European tour when we were in our teens and we did Paris, Rome, Dubrovnik, Prague and Berlin. Since then, aside from Cambridge, I've spent most of my time in London.

'My parents had a camper van, and we used to set off every summer at the beginning of the six-week holiday and just travel anywhere and everywhere. If we were in the UK, my grandparents would meet us with their caravan and my uncle and aunt.' He grins at the memory. 'The Stronghold, my dad used to call it, because we'd usually take over an area of the campsite.'

I've never been camping in my life, or in a camper van or caravan, and I'm not sure I ever will.


Finally we're at the front of the queue and an extremely smiley man greets us with on-stage enthusiasm. 'Welcome to Ellen's Stardust Diner, I'm Rushton and I'm going to be your server this evening. Now what's your favourite musical?'

'*Come from Away*,' says Hudson and the man immediately bursts into song.

I take the menu and stare hard at it, wanting to curl up with embarrassment. Eventually I realise no one is looking at us. Hudson is beaming from ear to ear and joining in as Rushton dances on the spot or rather stomps. I can't help smiling when I study the menu; it's one of my favourite songs from one of my favourite shows. Not that Hudson – or anyone – needs to know that.

'And how about you? What's your favourite show?'

I lift my shoulders, about to give my stock answer. I don't have one, in particular, but this time I check myself and answer, '*Grease*.' I still remember the very first time I watched it, when I had glandular fever and had to stay off school for a week. My mum's neighbour brought round a basket of DVDs for me. I watched it seven times that week. My dad caught me one afternoon singing along word-perfect to 'Greased Lightning'. I froze with embarrassment. I smile at the memory of him in suit, shirt and tie, immediately morphing into John Travolta, singing along and mimicking all the moves, even knocking his knees together in a most un-Dad like way. Not long after that he took the whole family to see the stage show. I remember, sadly, that Laura too had loved it. Somewhere along the way, I'd lost her as well as Dad.

We order burgers as Hudson looks round the restaurant. 'This is so cool.'

It's anything but cool but everyone around us appears to be having the time of their lives. The next table are singing along to 'Mama Mia', their server leading them in a beautiful high pure voice. She's really talented and she looks like she's having a really good time. Looking round, everyone appears to be having a wonderful time. Their faces are flushed, eyes bright and all singing their hearts out. The servers seem to be having a whale of a time too.

Our burgers arrive but I'm too distracted to eat. Our server has launched into 'Summer Nights', along with another female server, and they're doing a fantastic job. His falsetto at the end has me applauding enthusiastically. John Travolta, eat your heart out.

Hudson grins at me. He's obviously loving it and there's absolutely no sense of an 'I told you so' coming my way.

As we're eating one of the amazing desserts, two of the staff get up on the narrow platform between our banquettes and the tables next to us and start to sing one of my favourite songs.

As the opening words are sung, my face lights up in instant recognition. It's the finale from *Grease*, the duet between John Travolta and Olivia Newton-John. It still makes me want to cry that she's no longer with us. As the first voice starts, it gives *me* chills.

When it comes to the refrain, 'You're the one that I want,' I can't help singing along. Hudson joins in with the ooh ooh oohs, shimmying his shoulders along with me. We're both singing now, our faces bright with happiness. We're so in sync as our eyes meet, not just with the words but with our shared joy. It's a wonderful moment, euphoric, as the voices in the restaurant reach a crescendo. Hudson's beaming at me and I'm beaming back. I'm buzzing and I can't remember a time when I felt like this with someone else. Not since my dad died. He would have loved this place.

As the final chorus of 'You're the One That I Want' goes up, Hudson grabs my hand, really hamming it up as he sings to me. *You're the one that I want.*

With the happy atmosphere all around us, I can almost believe he means it for real.

## Chapter Eleven

'If you were to make a bet, what would you bet?' asks Hudson, as we're walking in the chilly night air, which feels as if we've stepped into a void after the warmth and raucous joy of Ellen's.

I'm not drunk but I'm filled with a sense of well-being and ... happiness. I smile up at him. What silliness is he plotting now? He's grinning from ear to ear and I can't help but grin back at him. I've not felt like this ... in a very long time. For once, my brain has finally shut down, it's not racing onto the next thing. I'm in the moment and staying there.

A gust of wind swirls around us, lifting the ends of his ridiculous scarf and whipping my hair about my face.

Once again, he takes his beanie out of his pocket and pulls it down over my ears, pushing back my hair from my face. A few stray bits have started to curl and he wraps a finger around a curl, toying with it. 'Why do you straighten it?' he asks so softly I have to strain towards him. I look at his mouth. I shouldn't look at his mouth. I lift my eyes to his, deliberately away from the soft lips.

'It looks more…' Me, I want to say but after this evening, I'm not quite as sure as I always am of who me is. 'Professional. Neat. Tidy.'

'The curls are pretty.'

I raise an eyebrow. Pretty? That's girlish, cute, charming. Not smart, sophisticated, glamorous. Pretty is not a look I've ever aimed for.

His grin brightens, like a firework lighting up the night sky, as if he's had the most brilliant idea. 'If I win the bet, you don't straighten your hair for the party tomorrow. I'd like to see it curly.'

'You are weird, Hudson Strong,' I say. Because that is weird. 'Why does it matter how my hair is?'

'Exactly, why does it matter?'

Shit, I walked into that one. 'Anyway, what bet?'

He pulls the white envelope out of his pocket and waves it like a flag in the air. 'This bet.' His eyes are dancing with pure devilment; in fact he's dancing on the pavement, swirling the envelope above his head out of reach.

If he wants me to make a grab for it, I'm not going to … oh what the hell, he's clearly enjoying himself and I'm still on a high, so I go up onto my toes and make a lunge for the envelope. He wraps his arms around me, still grinning like a loon as he pulls me in for an exuberant hug.

'Too late, I already won the bet.' He kisses the tip of my nose and releases me, ripping open the envelope and holding a sheet of paper in both hands like a banner.

I BET THAT BECS WILL HAVE A BRILLIANT TIME AT ELLEN'S DINER.

'Not fair, I wasn't party to the bet,' I say with a laugh because his triumphant expression is so full of mischief and he's so pleased with himself. Besides, what else can I do? He's right. I did have a brilliant time.

'Doesn't matter. I win.'

'That would never stand up in court,' I tease him. 'Plus where are the terms and conditions?'

'You, Ms Contract Lawyer always with the terms and conditions.' He wraps an arm around my shoulder. 'What are you like? Where's your sense of honour?'

'Honour!' I squawk in mock outrage, enjoying the game. He's so easy to be with.

'Yes, I won the bet. You have to honour the outcome.'

'But I didn't lose the bet,' I protest, unable to stop myself smiling at his childish glee.

'That's not my problem.' He pulls me in for a hug. 'You snooze, you lose.'

I shake my head. His logic, or skewed logic, is unassailable.

'Curls tomorrow at the party.'

I smile at him because what else can I do? There's no point arguing, I let him think he's won. My hair will be ruler straight at that party but tonight I'm happy to let him have his victory because he's right. I did have a good time. A really good time.

• • •

As we near the house, my steps slow because it feels like once we pass the threshold, the magic of the evening will snap out, extinguished as thoroughly as a flame denied oxygen. It has been magical and I don't want it to end but end it has to.

'Wecan'thavesexagain.' I blurt the words out.

It takes Hudson a couple of seconds to extract the words. He doesn't say anything. Just looks at me. I catch my lip in my teeth. Now I need to make sense of them. Explain, although surely it's obvious.

'We shouldn't have slept together last night.' Which is a dumb thing to say because of course we were supposed to *sleep* together, as in, in the same bed. 'I mean we shouldn't have had sex.'

'Okay,' he says, his face completely bland.

*Is that it? Just Okay?*

'Because…' I prompt. Has he even thought about the payment side of things? Is he okay with it? I want a response from him. I need a response from him. I hate that I'm suddenly so needy, even though he doesn't know that. But was it good for him? Does he want to do it again? It. Ugh! What am I, sixteen? Is he totally indifferent that we had sex again? What does he think about it? The not knowing is making me slightly crazy.

He still doesn't say anything.

'Because we agreed we wouldn't,' I say, adding to the crazy.

'Okay,' he says again.

My stomach twists and turns with frustration.

'Just okay?' Oh God. Is that a slight whine in my voice? What is happening to me?

He lowers his mouth to my ear. 'It was pretty hot, actually. You coming on to me like that.'

Indignation at him saying that wars with the huge sense of relief that he found it hot. I go for indignation. 'I came on to you! I did not,' I cry, while my mind is savouring 'hot'. He said 'hot'.

'I didn't mind. It was a *very* nice way to wake up. One of my fantasies, actually. You know, being woken to have sex.'

For fuck's sake. I walked right into that one. 'I did not wake you to have sex, I got into the wrong side of the bed by accident. I was half asleep.'

He shrugs. 'The subconscious is a powerful thing. Some say it just obeys the commands from your conscious mind.'

'Bollocks,' I say because it is. I didn't plan to have sex with him. I didn't want to have sex with him. Well, not consciously. I mean my body was quite keen but … oh God, I'm tying myself in knots here.

'It won't happen again,' I say and I mean it because … why do I mean it? It was hot. He makes me feel amazing in a way that I've never felt before. That's why we shouldn't do it again. Because it's too good. That's a good reason for not doing something, isn't it?

'Okay,' says Hudson.

He's agreeing with me far too easily again. I give him a suspicious look. The corner of his mouth is quirking as if he wants to break into a smile.

'We can't have sex again.'

'So you keep saying.' The smile wins.

'We're not.'

'Okay.'

'We agreed, we wouldn't. It was in the contract. I'm paying you, for God's sake. That makes it very different.'

He nods again. 'Exactly,' he says.

'What?' I frown.

'The sex was/is outside the scope of the contract.'

'Sorry.'

He looks steadily at me and there's no sign of his usual amusement. He's deadly serious. 'Sex is not included in the contract, so you're not paying me for sex. I wouldn't have had sex with you if I thought you were paying for it.'

I gape at him, impressed by his slipperiness. How did I not spot this particular loophole?

'It would only be paying for sex if you stipulated we had to have sex. And it only breaks the contract if the clause stipulates we can't have sex but then again, contracts can always be renegotiated.'

## Chapter Twelve

I stare at myself in the downstairs mirror. My cheeks are flushed and my eyes look over bright. Temptation fizzes and bubbles over, like a shaken bottle of champagne. I'm alight with possibility. Contracts can be renegotiated.

I swallow. They can. But only if you need to compromise. If you need to change the terms and conditions. In my world it's a weakness, a sign that the first contract wasn't strong enough. There was a loophole I hadn't spotted, a flaw in the terms.

I look at myself in the mirror. Really look at myself. That contract was designed to protect both of us. This is supposed to be a one-off business transaction. Money an agreed purpose. Sex was not the agreed purpose. I need to stick to that because if I don't ... I might want more. More sex. More intimacy. More of everything. And I don't need that in my life. My life is full, busy. I do not need a man to be fulfilled. I don't have time for one. I don't want one.

My mirror image stares back at me as together we

acknowledge the truth. The sex is amazing and I do want more. But can I afford it from an emotional point of view? Can I keep letting go with Hudson Strong and not let a little piece of me slip out each time? I'm like a hot air balloon and he's loosening the guy ropes. I'm in danger of floating out of my well-ordered life, where I know what I want, how to get it and how everything works.

What if it's just here, though? For the next two days. Two nights. He flies home on the 25th. Now I'm negotiating with myself. What if I make an addendum to the contract? As soon as we get back to the UK, no, as soon as we step on the plane, I can revert to being Rebecca Madison. Maybe here I could be Becs just at night, in private.

Why not?

Decision made. Negotiation complete. So now, how the hell do I broach this one? I can stand up in a roomful of corporate executives and demand that they make changes to a contract, I can ball-break with the best of them, but what do I say to Hudson Strong? 'OK, I've had a rethink, yes, we can have sex the next two nights.' It sounds bald and blunt. And then how do we go about it? It suddenly feels very clinical and unsexy. And what about the financial side of things? I really am tying myself up in knots.

I glare at myself. Why am I suddenly so fucking clueless? Seriously?

Just undress the guy and have done with it.

My brain is hurting now. It's as if a racing greyhound has been given a real rabbit to chase and it's taken off over the hills and far way.

. . .

When I come out of the cloakroom, Hudson has disappeared but I can hear him talking to Mrs Makepiece down the corridor. I follow the sound of the voices. She's smiling and he's telling her all about dinner.

'Hey Becs, Maddie's just making us a hot chocolate.'

Mrs Makepiece, or rather Maddie, smiles at me. 'I hear you had a great time.' I nod, again suddenly in unchartered waters. The housekeeper has been a fixture off and on for as long as I can remember. She came when I was about five and then left when I was ten, to have her own family. She returned twelve years later to our house in London, just after my dad died. 'My niece worked there for a while. She has a wonderful voice. She's in England now and she's been in the chorus of *Les Miserables*, *Phantom of the Opera* and *Mama Mia*.'

I've seen all of those shows. Perhaps I've seen her.

'Becs can sing. Did you know that?' pipes up Hudson. 'She's really good.'

'Oh yes, I did know. My niece used to babysit for her and Laura when they were tiny. Mr and Mrs Madison used to go to the theatre a lot back then.' She turns to me, 'Do you remember?'

'Gosh, sorry, no.'

Her stern face is relaxed, her eyes warm with nostalgia. 'You would sing together, you both loved *Mary Poppins* and *The Sound of Music*. Laura didn't like it because she couldn't hold a tune like you could.' Mrs Makepiece shakes her head. I can't think of her as a Maddie. 'That girl could throw a tantrum.'

A memory darts like a small fish in the sunlit shallows,

me being picked to be in the musical at school and Laura being upset because she wasn't. I must have been about eight. 'But I'm the pretty one. I should have the part,' she'd wailed. 'It's not fair.'

Memories surface like stitches that have come loose. If I tug on them, I know other things will follow.

'Do you want marshmallow and cream on top of your hot chocolate?' asks Mrs Makepiece and she's briskly efficient again, pouring hot milk out of a pan into two tall china mugs.

'Yes, please,' says Hudson.

'That would be lovely, thank you,' I say.

'We'll take them up to bed. Nothing like snuggling in bed with a hot chocolate,' says Hudson.

Mrs Makepiece gives him a fond look and turns to me. 'He's a keeper.'

Is there any woman that he can't bloody charm the socks off?

'I haven't had a hot chocolate in years,' I say as I take a sip, my lips touching the froth of cream and marshmallows. Mrs Makepiece has added a dash of brandy to the hot sweet liquid, and it warms my throat as I swallow.

We're in bed, sitting next to each other on a pile of pillows, the bedside lamps on. It's so ridiculously domesticated I want to laugh. I could be in a sitcom.

Hudson gives me a reproving look and shakes his head sadly. 'You need to live a little, Becs. Good job I'm here.' He drains his hot chocolate and leans back against the pillows.

I could remind him that he's here for the money but it would be churlish and we have had such a lovely evening, I'd like to bask a little longer in this contented glow. I'm starting to feel sleepy as the hot milk and brandy hits my system. I can hardly keep my eyes open, my body is still in a different time zone.

'Night, Hudson,' I murmur.

I'm just drifting off when I think I hear, 'Night, Becs. Sleep tight, little hamster.'

I smile. Becs. I can be Becs for the next two nights.

When I wake in the morning, I'm alone. There's no sign of Hudson.

## Chapter Thirteen

M y body sparks with awareness when I hear the bedroom door open and close.

'Honey, I'm home,' calls Hudson.

I'm naked in the shower, with water cascading down me. 'I'm in the bathroom.'

Perhaps I should have qualified it, because Hudson breezes in.

I swallow a mouthful of water but outwardly manage to keep my cool.

'You're in the shower,' he says, coming to a rapid halt.

'So it would appear,' I reply, turning my back on him and looking at him over my shoulder.

Without shame or embarrassment he stands there and grins at me. Of course he does. This is Hudson, there's no situation in which he ever finds himself nonplussed.

'Do you want me to come and scrub your back?'

I laugh at what I'm assuming is a rhetorical question. But when I say, 'What would you do if I said yes?', my voice comes out in a husky undertone. Since he left this morning I've been trying to wonder how I broach the subject that I might just have renegotiated the contract in my head. The simplicity of this exchange is breathtakingly easy compared to the imaginary conversations I've been having.

His eyes meet mine and his hands stray to the hem of his T-shirt. I swallow and turn my head reaching for the shampoo bottle. I don't dare turn around now. What will he do?

As I'm lathering the shampoo into my hair, I feel him stepping in behind me. My breath catches in my throat, my nipples peaking. His hands cover mine and he starts to massage the soap into my hair, his fingers firm as they rove over my scalp. Each touch sends an electrical charge through my body. His hands are heaven. I close my eyes and sigh, lifting my shoulders and rolling my head back. With my back still facing him, he guides me under the water to rinse my hair. I love the feel of his body against mine and I want his hands to circle in front of me to cup my breasts. But all he does is gently run his fingers through my hair. I can bear it no longer and I turn around. He smiles and I step into his arms and kiss him. His mouth is gentle and his body warm as he wraps his arms around me, pulling me against him. We fit and I sigh with instant relief. I can feel him jutting up against me, his penis hard with eagerness. I take it in my hand and stroke him.

'Becs,' he whispers and moves his lips to my neck. 'If you start that we're going to be late.'

'So?' I return. He kisses his way up my throat and pulls away, smiling down at me.

'So,' he responds, 'sometimes things are worth waiting for.'

With that he turns me round and gives me a playful slap on my arse and pushes me gently out of the walk-in shower. 'Later, Becs. Later. We've got a party to go to.'

Annoyingly he's right but I still pout at him.

'You're so cute, you know that?' he says with that irrepressible grin. He grabs the shower gel and starts soaping himself. It's a dismissal so I leave him to it.

When he comes out of the bathroom, I'm wrapped in a bath sheet sitting at the dressing table. My make-up, hairbrushes, hair dryer and straighteners are all laid out ready for business and so is every nerve ending in my body. I try to focus on the job in hand but it's difficult when certain parts of me are thrumming and pleading for attention. Focus, Rebecca. Tonight it's important I look perfect. Everyone should know that I don't give a flying fuck about Laura getting engaged to Andrew. And tonight is also my last night with Hudson.

'Just in time,' says Hudson. Thankfully he's put a robe on because if he was just wearing a towel tucked around his waist, I'm not sure I could stop myself ripping it off. A belted robe sends its own signal – hands off.

'Just in time for what?' I ask. He has that familiar, triumphant look of delight on his face that spells trouble with a capital T.

'To help you get ready, of course,' he says as if it's completely obvious and only an idiot wouldn't know it.

I frown and give him a cool don't-mess-with-me look. 'I don't need any help getting ready.'

'Oh, but you do. That's why you brought me, remember.' He shoots one of those effortlessly winsome smiles. Honest to God, I think he's part puppy.

'No,' I say in my best reproving, behave-yourself tone, which is hard in the face of that hopeful expression of his. 'I brought you to look adoringly at me, to show how indifferent I am to my sister's engagement to my ex and to stop the "when are you going to find a man" insanity.'

'Exactly,' he says. 'So you need to be more strategic.'

'What are you talking about?'

As usual he grins. 'Not trying too hard.'

'Still no idea.' I'm sooo tempted to stick my fingers in my ears and hum loudly.

'You plan to go out there, Rebecca Madison at her finest, full armour wardrobe and resting bitch face.'

'Yup, that's the plan,' I agree because he's not wrong. It has served me well, why deviate?

'It's the wrong plan. Trust me.'

I raise an eyebrow.

'Wrong?' I drawl. I'm not even going to touch the 'trust me'.

'You need to be relaxed, happy in your own skin. That resting bitch face doesn't say happy, I don't give a crap about what anyone thinks. What you need to be...' he pauses and his mouth curves into that familiar wicked smile, 'is unbuttoned.' He's dropped his voice, the bastard, he knows damn well what that word does to me. Every fucking time. A Pavlovian response. Instant wetness between my thighs.

I stare him out, as if I'm completely unconcerned even

though under the towel my nipples have gone hard again and I want to squirm on the stool I'm sitting on, grind myself down to relieve the intense ache that has come from nowhere. Actually, that's a complete and utter lie, it's been building for the last twenty-four hours.

'You need to be mussed, that just-got-out-of-bed-after-an-eyeball-rolling-fuck look.'

I loosen the towel from my hair and start tugging a comb though the wet curls, avoiding looking at Hudson's reflection in the mirror.

'Here, let me.' He takes the comb from my hand. 'Gently does it.' Rather than start at the crown and dragging the comb through the full length of my hair, he starts at the bottom, teasing out the tangles, working his way up. I watch him in the mirror. He works methodically, his head bent, his mouth slightly open and his focus drilled down to the one job. He's so gentle, his hands feel soothing as he gathers the hair at the nape of my neck and his fingers stroke the soft skin

Then he picks up one of my hair clips and with the comb sections my hair in two and clips up half and then calmly unplugs the cable of my GHD hair straighteners before picking up my hairbrush.

'What are you doing?' I ask, although I haven't moved. I'm not sure I could.

'I'm going to do your hair for you.'

'You?' My eyes meet his in the mirror.

He nods. 'Three sisters, remember. Only boy. Their favourite game was hairdressers. What's a guy to do? If I hadn't taken turns at being hairdresser, I'd have been scalped, shaved, braided, you name it. It was survival. I'm quite good, you know.' He strokes his own curls.

'No,' I say. 'No, no and no.' Like I'm going to entrust my hair to him.

'If you don't like it, you can straighten it afterwards. Promise.' He turns those beseeching eyes on me. I roll my eyes.

'That doesn't work on me.'

'You're hard.'

'Yes,' I respond but he's already taken the hairbrush and lifted a strand of hair. I haven't moved a muscle or made any attempt to stop any of this. I'm not hard. We both know he's won. I've turned soft and pliable and while I would deny it with my dying breath, I've relinquished control.

He turns on the hair dryer and starts to blow dry my hair into soft curls. He's absorbed in the job. I close my eyes enjoying the warm heat of the dryer and the lovely surprise every now and then as his hands brush my skin or lift my hair. I'm in a cocoon and I want to stay here, just savouring the shivers of pleasure at his touch, the gentle thrum of my body's longing for more. I sink into the slow build-up – we are going to have sex tonight and the thought fills me with a secret warmth. When I open my eyes, he's watching me and he smiles, that slow only-for-me smile, full of promise, cockiness and confidence – he's on the same page.

Without saying a word we've come to an unwritten agreement – the where and the when has yet to be decided. The thought, the knowledge, the awareness, is illicit and alluring. There's a hum of desire fizzing away and we're going to leave it to build.

I look at him and quirk an eyebrow. Who will break first?

He raises an eyebrow in response. The challenge is there, simmering between us.

When he's finished, my hair is a symphony of curls, lying around my shoulders like sleek coils, but then he digs his hands into my scalp and pulls his fingers through them, ruffling them up.

'There you go.'

I stare at myself. I look softer, feminine. Is it the hair or are my revved up hormones showing?

'Not bad,' I say because I do not need to pander to Hudson's ego.

'Gorgeous,' he says and drops a kiss on my bare shoulder, holding my gaze as he does. The simple gesture loosens a storm of butterflies in my stomach. My eyes widen and he sees it.

He strokes his heavy bristle. 'I need to tidy this up, if we're going to be ready on time,' he says and saunters off to the bathroom. In the mirror I watch him go.

While he's in the bathroom, I put on the smart shirt dress I've chosen. It's Ralph Lauren and fits perfectly, flaring from the waist in a full skirt. I do my make-up, keeping it lighter than usual. Hudson is right, I need to look like I'm not trying too hard. I flick my hair back over my shoulder. It swishes and I like the feeling of the soft cloud settling.

I look at my watch; we're going to be late. Only a few

minutes but it's unforgivable in this household, unless you're Laura.

Hudson emerges from the bathroom in black trousers, his shirt unbuttoned as he tries to do the buttons at the cuff. Holy moly. The tan skin beneath the white cotton makes my mouth dry. I want to touch him.

'Do you need a hand there?' I ask.

'Would you?' He holds out his arm. 'Bloody hate getting these things on.'

He's trying to thread the button holes with dark onyx and gold cufflinks. I give them a passing glance and notice there's some sort of engraving on the surface of the dark stone.

I focus on the cufflinks and not the smooth chest in front of me or the delicious smell of pine and lemon. I want to press my nose up against his neck and inhale him. I want his mouth on mine and I'm looking at it and he sees me. Our gazes lock. There's another of those frozen-in-time moments when we just stare at each other, the silence weighted with heavy anticipation.

'We need to go down,' I murmur. One of has to be sensible, although I wish he'd just sweep me off my feet, to hell with crumpling my dress, push me down on the bed and come into me.

'We do,' he murmurs back. His hand lifts and traces my lips. 'How many kisses are we up to today?'

'Not enough,' I reply because it's the truth and in this moment, there is only honesty.

'We need to rectify that,' he says leaning in closer and

brushing his lips over mine. It's the most exquisite, soft kiss and it's like a terrible punishment because we have to stop.

'Later,' he says.

I haul in a deep breath and nod, realising I'm a bit shaky.

'Shall we go?' I say, trying to sound normal and jolly.

'Yes.' He does the rest of his buttons quickly and shrugs on his jacket. The fine wool fabric smooths over his shoulders; he's broad but the suit fits like it's been made to measure. There's something about him, trussed up in a suit, that hints at the masculinity beneath. It can't quite bind his vitality and presence.

Just as we reach the door, he leans forward and, with great deliberation over each one, he undoes two more of the top buttons on my dress, his fingers straying beneath the fabric to stroke my skin. 'That's better,' he says with a guileless smile.

## Chapter Fourteen

'So you're based in London,' says William, the dinner partner my mother had obviously invited before I'd told her I was bringing a plus one. 'What is it you do?'

'I'm a lawyer.'

Talking to William is like a cold shower after I've been basking in warm Mediterranean seas, not helped by the fact that my gaze keeps straying across the table to Hudson sitting opposite me. He's next to my fifteen-year-old cousin Amy. I can guarantee she will retreat to Jonathon's study the minute she can, along with the ever-present Kindle tucked in the side pocket of her backpack and her Bose noise-cancelling headphones. Laura calls her The Dork. I wonder why my mother changed the table plan at the last minute to put Amy next to Hudson.

'Interesting. I work in real estate. Central Manhattan. I've currently got the new Rochester Tower development on my books. Three billion square metres of luxury retail premises.'

'Wow,' I say. Where the fuck is Rochester Tower, am I supposed to know? My mother should have given me York exam revision notes.

'So do you own a place in London? Or rent.'

'I have an apartment although over there we call them flats.' Hudson looks over and gives me a slow, dangerous smile as his gaze dips to the buttons on my dress. Heat rushes through me. I feel like a cloth being twisted tighter and tighter; with each look he's wringing a response out of me. I'm velvet fabric, the nap stroked the wrong way. I need his touch to smooth it back down,

'I didn't realise you were British. Whereabouts in London are you? Covent Garden? Notting Hill? Primrose Hill?'

I laugh politely. It sounds as if his knowledge of London is gleaned from romcom films.

'No, I live in Chelsea.'

'So how much is your place worth?'

'Pardon?'

'The value of your property. What did you pay? You got a mortgage?'

I realise in a crass way he's trying to work out my net worth. The words 'None of your damn business' curl on the edge of my tongue.

'I've been looking at a place in Williamsburg. It's not Manhattan but you get more bang for your buck and these days it's pretty bougie.'

He drones on about property values in New York. I look over at Hudson, hoping for one of his secret smiles, but he is chatting away to Amy. I've never seen her so animated. Is there any woman he can't draw out of her shell? He's smiling and nodding as they talk, pointing to something on her phone and then laughing. She laughs back and then nudges him with her elbow. Fast friends already.

I know what it's like to be the recipient of that lighthouse beam of Hudson attention. I'm struck by a pang of envy and then a twist of something darker. Unease and uncertainty. Hudson is everyone's light; it doesn't matter who you are. I have to remember that. He might make me feel special, he's good at that, but it doesn't mean I am, not to him.

At last dinner is over and my mother is rising to her feet, tapping her wine glass. Other guests have started to arrive, we've heard them in the hall and being ushered into the salon with its sparkling night-time view of Manhattan. The distant skyscrapers on the other side of Central Park glitter like scattered diamonds.

'Thank you all for coming,' she says. 'There'll be plenty of opportunities to toast Laura and Andrew later but I wanted to say a special word now to you, our closest friends and family. It is with great joy that we are welcoming Andrew into the family and we're thrilled for our daughter Laura that she'll be in such safe hands. We know that he will look after and keep her in the manner which she deserves. I'm delighted that you could all share this special day with us.'

I catch Hudson's eye. He winks at me. It sounds as if Laura is the bride's bouquet that's been caught and is going to be stuck in a nice glass of fresh water. It doesn't sound like the sort of marriage I would want, if I were to get married. Far too much like a chattel. I happen to know that Jonathon is giving the happy couple a down payment on their first penthouse flat two blocks away. Laura is quite a catch.

The salon is full of smart, elegant friends of Laura and Andrew's and I don't know a soul but it doesn't matter because Hudson is at my elbow the moment we walk into the room.

'Wow, swankee,' he says catching the full view. We've not been in here before. 'Jonathon and Jennifer really are loaded, aren't they?'

'They are.'

'No wonder old Algernon is so keen to marry your sis.'

I smile and wonder how many more names he can come up with for him.

'Where's Amy?' I ask.

'She's got a hot date with Colleen Hoover, whoever that is. Sweet kid.'

'She is. Normally she's very shy.'

I look up and realise that Andrew and Laura are approaching.

'Rebecca. This is a new look for you. Don't you think the Rubensesque look is a little young for someone in her thirties?' She eyes my curls with a sneer.

'Thirties,' gasps Hudson, feigning horror, slapping a hand to his chest before he grins at her, pure glee sparkling in his eyes. 'I've always wanted to be a toy boy.'

Laura narrows her eyes. She can't tell whether he's taking the piss or not. Then he frowns. 'Do you mean Rubensesque? I thought that was women with voluptuous figures. I think you probably mean Millais or Waterhouse. Ophelia or the Lady of Shallot.' He wraps a finger around one of my curls and tugs me towards him to kiss me on the corner of the mouth. 'Although of course,' he lowers his voice, 'Becs is a lot sexier.'

He's incorrigible and I love it. He was right. This loose, free look has completely confused my sister. It's pushed her out of kilter, she doesn't know who I am, she can't relate to this me.

'Rebecca,' a querulous voice comes from behind Laura and for a brief moment we exchange a rare moment of shared panic. It's Great Aunt Maude. 'Why aren't you engaged yet? Laura is two years younger than you. I blame your father. He wanted you to achieve more than he could. He was far too hard on you as a child.'

I lean down and kiss Maude's powdered cheek. 'Hello to you too. How are you?'

She pats my cheek as if I were three instead of thirty-three. 'All the better for seeing you.' Laura looks as if she wants to make a hasty retreat but manners dictate otherwise as Maude smirks. 'You're the only one in the family that has the chops to put up with me.'

Laura scowls and threads her arm through Andrew's as if to underline that in the partnering up stakes, she is winning.

'Let me introduce you to Hudson,' I say. 'Hudson, this is Maude.'

'Nice to meet you,' he says with his impeccable manners. You really can take him anywhere.

'Why have I not heard of you before?' she asks with a

frown. All her wrinkles scrunch together and she looks like a less cute and a lot more grumpy Shar Pei.

'Because Becs didn't want you frightening me off.' Hudson's conspiratorial grin has Maude cackling with delight.

'I like him. He might be worthy of your eggs. You know she's thirty-three.'

Laura actually gives me a sympathetic look.

'I. Am. Here. And Hudson isn't interested in my eggs, thank you very much.' Maude just beams at me.

'Now, I didn't say that, Becs,' says Hudson, looping an arm around my shoulder. 'I just said, I thought we should wait a while. I want to enjoy being with you before the kids come along.'

For the first time in my life, I swear I feel my womb twinge. That has never happened before. It shoots fear into me, like a spike driven home. It's just his robust defence of me, that's all. My womb can go do one. Children are not part of my plans for the time being.

In that moment, though, I realise that Hudson is the sort of man who will want kids. Of course he will. And he'll be great with them – look how easily he tuned in with Amy. I can imagine him with small boys and footballs, carrying fishing rods along the riverbank, parading a mini-him princess on his shoulders. Doing her hair for her. Behind him is a mist-softened image of a woman. His wife.

'Well, if you'll excuse us, we need to circulate,' says Laura, making her escape bid. She takes Andrew's arm and glides away.

'Well, that's spoiled my fun,' says Maude. 'Where's your

mother? I need to speak to her.' Before I can answer she's striding away, hunting down her next victim.

'How was the golf?' I ask once Laura and Andrew are out of earshot.

'Okay,' he says guardedly. 'Jonathon can play. Alfred not so much...' He screws up his face and looks after the retreating back of Andrew. 'Seriously, did you go out with the guy? Yes, Jonathon, no, Jonathon, really, Jonathon, can I lick your balls for you, Jonathon?'

I snort champagne out of my nose and he grins delightedly.

'Golf balls?'

'Of course.' Irresistible naughtiness shines in his eyes.

'You've had a lucky escape there, Becs. You deserve a lot better than that.'

Pursing my lips, I give him an implacable, dismissive look but inside his words light a little glow. I deserve better. Has anyone said that to me before? My mother setting me up with William is clearly expecting me to settle.

I give Hudson an impulsive hug. 'Thanks for coming.'

'My pleasure.' His eyes dance and I know he's talking about something completely different.

'Ah, Rebecca and Hudson.' My mother's sister sails up. 'What a handsome couple you make. Rebecca, you're looking gorgeous. Positively blooming. Must be love.' Although I don't miss her quick sidelong glance at my stomach. 'Have you seen Amy?'

'No.' I shake my head. I know perfectly well where she'll be but I'm not going to give her up.

We circulate through the room, Hudson's arm linked through mine. Occasionally his fingers will stroke my inner wrist, just enough to remind my system that it's on a slow boil.

Every now and then he discreetly lifts my wrist and checks the Cartier watch on my wrist. 'Why do you keep doing that?' I eventually ask because each time he does it, I get another one of *those* smiles, the ones full of promise.

'Don't you know?' he asks.

Of course I know. I give him a reproving look despite the fact his words send yet another thrill through me. You'd have thought I'd have reached my limit by now. How many thrills can your body take before it spontaneously combusts? It's got to the point where every look, word, touch is revving me up.

I can't wait for the moment when we can go upstairs and rip each other's clothes off. Will those shirt buttons survive? Because I want to get it off him so badly. Will my dress make it? I've not missed those sly looks at the buttons, as if he's already imagining slipping each one open.

'It's only nine o'clock.' There's a faint whisper of a whine in my voice. God, I want this party to be over. We can't go upstairs yet, it will be too obvious and it would be seen as an insult to my sister.

'Hudson.' My mother swoops. 'There's someone you must meet. She's in retail at Bloomingdales but knows the furniture buyer at Nordstrom, she's dying to meet you.'

I'll say one thing for my mother, she's a genius at networking.

Hudson gives me an uncertain look before mouthing, 'Okay?' It's such a simple gesture but it means so much to me. This is a golden opportunity for him to make a potentially useful contact and instead of jumping at it, he checks back with me. I think in that moment, I might just have fallen in love with him, if I was the falling in love type.

I give his arm a reassuring squeeze. 'See you in a while.'

I watch him walk across the room and already I miss the low-level electricity that buzzes between us. Can anyone else feel it?

Across the other side of the room, I catch my sister studying me. She's been watching me like a hawk, keeping me in her sights all evening, almost as if she needs to reassure herself of her triumph. She got the boy but she wants to make sure that I know it. Until I got here with Hudson, I hadn't truly appreciated how over him I was. I thought this weekend would be much harder than it is. I don't even give Andrew a second glance because I'm too busy looking at Hudson.

I give her a gay wave and turn away, snagging a fresh glass of champagne and heading over to the full length glass windows to look out at the night skyline of Manhattan.

I'm not alone for long. My mother appears behind me; I see her reflection in the glass.

'There you are, darling,' she says, as if I've been hiding all evening.

This is a typical mother preamble for a 'serious' talk. What's she going to say?

'If you're going to tell me that Laura has chosen someone else to be her chief bridesmaid, it's no surprise and I really couldn't give one.'

Small lines appear on my mother's forehead, not quite a frown but yup, the serious talk is en route. 'I'll just be grateful if you turn up,' says my mother with astonishing honesty.

I stare at her.

She takes a glug of champagne. My mother is a sipper, not a glugger. It's like she's been building up to this. She sighs. 'I know she's difficult.'

Well hello, understatement of the year.

'You've always been the easy one.'

'Me?' Well, no one's ever said that to me before. Every last boyfriend I've ever had has made some comment about high maintenance and it's not been a compliment.

'Although I do worry about you.'

I stare at her. She's never said anything like this to me before.

'Although I loved your father, he wasn't an easy man to love. His affection had to be earned. He lost interest in Laura when it became obvious that she didn't have your academic brain. I worry that you're still trying to please him. You are allowed to be happy, you know.'

I stare at her. What is she talking about?

'That's why Laura has always been so jealous of you. I'm really hoping that...' I can see her dancing around the words.

'You hope that because she gets a man down to the altar before me, she'll see it as a victory and it might make her happy,' I finish for her because suddenly it's obvious that Laura has always been jealous of me, I just never understood why. Dad was often dismissive of her in my hearing. She didn't work hard enough, she didn't care enough. It makes sense now why she went out of her way to try and get his attention. A knot of uncomfortable realisation ties itself in my stomach – I was always his favourite because I put the work in.

My mother fixes her gaze on my face and she shakes her head. 'I'm so glad you've got Hudson. Work isn't everything, you know.'

I stare at her. What's she trying to say? What's coming next? I feel a prickle of alarm.

'I'm really happy for you, he's perfect for you.'

I take a slug of champagne, almost choking. 'P-perfect?'

'Yes.' My mother beams at me. 'The two of you just fit. When you walk into a room together, you're a couple. And he's such a lovely man. I mean Andrew is exactly what Laura needs, he has money, status and will give her the life she wants. Hudson is kind. That's why I put him next to Amy. I knew he'd look after her. And he'll look after you, even though you don't think you need looking after.'

I'm still having trouble swallowing my champagne, let alone being able to speak.

'When I married Jonathon, I fought really hard to keep a shell around me. After your father died, I didn't want to feel again.'

There's a lump in my throat. I understand that all too well.

'Jonathon gave me financial security and a future. That's why I married him.'

I nod because no surprises there, but then – then my mother drops the bombshell.

'But along the way, I fell in love with him and it's wonderful. Unconditional love is very liberating. Your father...' She sighs, as well she might because she knows I'm not going to accept any criticism of him. He always encouraged me to be the best I could be.

'You can survive a marriage built on mutual respect and wanting the same things. That will be Andrew and Laura. But it's so much better when love comes along too.' Her eyes shine with unshed tears. 'You deserve more, Rebecca. Let love in. I know you adored your father and since he died you've buried yourself in work. You are more than just your career. Give Hudson a chance, he's one of the good guys.'

My heart twinges at her words. Hudson is one of the good guys. If I was in the market for a good guy. But I just can't bring myself to risk the pain and hurt all over again.

She's got it so wrong. What would she say if I told her I paid him to come? Never in a million years did I think she'd approve of him. He's got long hair, for God's sake. He wears ratty jeans. He talks to the help. And where's the brittle socialite that's been my mother for the last thirty-odd years? Why hadn't I noticed her softening? Is this what love does to someone?

I've stepped into a parallel universe. Any minute now, my sister will turn into a human being.

Just then Andrew slimes up and the world reverts back to normal – or so I think.

'Jennifer, Rebecca. Lovely party, Jennifer, thank you so much for hosting. My parents are about to leave, they wanted to thank you.'

And that is typical Andrew. He's summoning my mother to bid her guests goodbye.

'Of course, excuse me,' she says and disappears, leaving me with Andrew. It's the first time I've been alone with him since I arrived, since the engagement was announced. I have nothing to say to him.

'You look lovely tonight,' he says in a low, urgent tone and I shoot a startled gaze his way. 'I'd forgotten how beautiful you are.' He puts a hand on my arm.

I scowl at him and give his hand a pointed look.

'Oh, Rebecca, don't be like that. I'm just being friendly. We're going to be family, after all.'

'Unfortunately,' I snap. What a horrible thought.

'You think I owe you an apology?'

Dear God, I really have fallen through a hole in the space-time continuum. What is going on tonight?

'I couldn't give a shit,' I say, brisk and brittle, and I realise I mean it. If anything I feel sorry for my sister settling for someone so vapid and insubstantial.

His laugh is bitter and his eyes glitter with the tell-tale of too much alcohol. 'No, I know you were always more interested in your career. Some nights I'm not sure you even remembered you had a boyfriend. Laura notices me.'

It would be easy for me to point out that of course she did, she thought she was getting one over on me, but I refrain. I cannot be arsed.

He sighs. 'She's everything you weren't. Chilled, easy to be with, and she has time for me. She isn't too *tired* all the time.' And there it is, the crux of the matter. He comes first.

'Oh, poor Andrew. So, it's my fault,' I say, rolling my eyes.

'She's into me,' he says and I know exactly what he's getting at. Sex.

'I think we've had this conversation before. Are you going to tell me I'm frigid again? Crap in bed?' I grin at him. 'Hudson doesn't think so but then Hudson is dynamite in the sack.' The inference is clear. I don't need to say another word. His mouth is hanging open as I turn on my heel and walk away.

Hudson is leaning against the door jamb on the other side of the room and he's seen the exchange. He's grinning at me.

'I can lip read, you know,' he says.

I look at him sharply, not sure if he's telling the truth or not. 'You can't.'

'I got the gist. Did you tell him he's crap in bed?'

I gape at him.

He uses a finger to lift my chin to close my mouth and then kisses me on the lips.

I smile up at him and whisper in his ear, 'I want you. Now.'

# Chapter Fifteen

I push Hudson through the salon door into the empty hallway and a few metres down, I open a door and pull him in. We stumble against a box and there's the tinkle of glass. Then a crash as something else falls off.

Hudson goes to pull away and my grip on him tightens on him in quick reassurance.

'It's fine,' I murmur against his lips which are scorching their way across my throat.

We're in the supplies cupboard. It's where Mrs Makepiece and the cleaners keep the spare china, the linen, the floral arrangement accessories and that sort of thing.

His hands plunge into my hair, holding my head as he kisses me. I kiss him back. Open-mouthed deep kisses, that I could sink into and die.

He pulls away with a heavy sigh, resting his forehead against mine. 'Fuck, Becs. I might have to do you, right here, right now. My balls are turning every colour of the fucking rainbow.'

It's hot, how much he wants me. His hands are already sliding my skirt up, stroking my arse. I grind against him, against his erection. He groans, and it sounds like he's truly in pain.

My hands are at his belt buckle. Outside a burst of laughter passes.

Shit. We're in my mother's cleaning cupboard.

Hudson grasps my arms and our breathing sounds loud in the dark cupboard.

There's the sound of conversation outside and I swallow, need and sense at war with one another.

My heart is thudding so loudly, it's a wonder the people on the other side of the door can't hear it. Their words are inaudible but there are at least three people outside holding a conversation.

I feel Hudson's hand on my leg, his fingers skirting my knicker elastic. I grip his shoulders but I'm too turned on to push him away. I let out a small breath of encouragement in his ear. 'Yes,' I whisper. A second later he's slipped another finger inside me and my hips urge him on.

'You're so wet, Becs.' He's kissing the tender skin between ear and throat, nipping at the sensitive flesh. I make an involuntary squeak and Hudson's hand stills. I swallow, desperate for him to carry on. He makes me wait several seconds. I nudge at his hand.

I feel his lips curve into a smile against my ear as he asks, 'What do you want?'

'You,' I whisper.

'Are you going to be quiet?'

I lean my head against his chest, biting my lip.

'Are you sure?' he asks, pushing his other hand into my bra and pinching my nipple hard. I bite harder on my lip, swallowing my gasp. He's going to torture me. I nod so that he can the feel the movement of my head against his chest.

He slides his fingers out of me and I want to grab his hand but then in a fluid move he slides them back in. I can't make a sound. I press my lips together. He's going to make me come and I have to be silent. I'm hanging on to him, gripping his shoulders. He's released one of my breasts from my bra and is sucking hard at the nipple through the cotton of my dress. The friction of the wet fabric against me is twisting me tighter. I'm not sure I'm going to make it. There's a burst of laughter on the other side of the door. The guests are mere inches from me. I close my mouth over Hudson's bicep trying to bury the breathless pants that are escaping from me.

The intensity is building but I fight against the orgasm, terrified I'll put voice to it. I pinch my lips together, my eyes scrunched so tightly closed that tears are forced from them. It's no good, I'm not going to hold it.

'Hudson,' I make a desperate whispered plea, gripping his arms so hard I'll probably leave a bruise.

His hand stills and I almost cry out with disappointment.

In the gloom of the cupboard, the only light seeping in under the door, I feel disassociated from real life. Thankfully the voices have moved away but I'm not sure I can walk. My legs are trembling and my heart is pumping so hard, it might beat its way out of my chest.

When my pulse has returned to near normal, I peep

through the door. The corridor is empty. 'Upstairs. Now,' says Hudson, when we've straightened our clothes.

No one has ever wanted me this much. I've never wanted anyone this much.

He opens the door and pushes me out. 'You've got two minutes tops and you'd better be halfway to naked when I get there.'

I leave the cupboard and look back over my shoulder. I've made it as far as the foot of the stairs when Jonathon catches me. 'Ah, Rebecca, are you all right?'

'Yes. Bit of headache. I'm just going to get a couple of Tylenol.' I don't turn around. I'm too conscious of the damp patch over my nipple where Hudson has sucked me through my clothes.

'Excellent,' he says genially and before anyone else can come along I race up the stairs.

I get to my room. In the mirror, my cheeks are flushed and my eyes glitter.

Halfway to naked, Hudson said. But I'm not sure I want to deny myself the pleasure of him peeling my layers away.

A second later he comes through the door and he locks it.

He turns to me. 'Fuck, what is it with you? I'm so fucking hard.'

Then there's no time. We're both so turned on. He peels my dress straight over my head, as I'm undoing the buttons on his shirt, fumbling, tugging, kissing his bare skin where I can reach it.

He moves his hand and the withdrawal leaves me bereft. 'Please, Hudson, please.'

He pushes me on the bed, kissing me hard. Both our hands are fighting to undo his trousers, frantically scrabbling, and I undo the zip as he pushes them down.

He kisses me again and looks into my eyes. We stare at each other and the fullness in my chest, in my heart, is quite terrifying. In that moment, I've no idea what to do with this feeling. I have to close my eyes because I don't want him to see all the way inside me.

When he slides in, my pants are round my ankles, I still have my shoes on and I'm lost to the waves of hot, white heat that are coursing through me. I'm coming and coming around him and in only seconds I feel him tighten, then groan in a long guttural moan.

I cry out at the sensation as I feel him come. It's too much. Too intense. I clench around him, lost in a haze of desire and sheer joy. But there's more, so much more. There's the longing to hold on tight to him, to not let go, to stay in his arms. It frightens the crap out of me. I don't need other people. I'm self-sufficient. My life is ordered. I have everything I want. I should roll out from under him, go into the shower, but I can't bring myself to move. Just a minute. Just a minute lying here, limp, half-dressed, just feeling. With him.

Gradually I'm coming to.

Hudson is sprawled across me. I welcome the weight of his body pinning me to the bed. It grounds me because I'm floaty and dreamy with post-sex endorphins. It also means I don't have to look at him because … I might have made the most terrible mistake.

He nuzzles my neck. 'Shit, Becs, you're amazing. That was amazing.'

It was. And it was so much more and I can never tell him because this has to be it. I'm starting to feel something deeper for Hudson. Feelings I can't allow myself. The only thing I can rely on in this world is myself.

Thank God he's getting on a flight tomorrow. The car is booked to pick him up at seven-thirty. After that we have no reason to ever see each other again.

His hand is grazing my breast with lazy almost involuntary strokes as if he needs the skin-to-skin touch and I realise I'm doing the same. My fingers skimming the muscles and dips of his back because I can't bear not to. I need to trace each contour and commit it to memory. I'm taking possession of each inch of him while I can. My fingers feather across his waist to his hips and I dot small kisses along his collar bone.

He sighs and slides his hand down my stomach. I arch and stretch under him.

This time, we're leisurely. We have this last night to tease and explore. Hudson pins me down, his mouth working the length of my body and when he goes down *there*, I don't stop him. I don't want to, he tastes every inch of me, the rasp of stubble across my thighs. Fingers, tongue – he's teasing out the pleasure and I let go over and over. When at last he stops, I want to make him helpless, I want him to be mindless too. I push him onto his back and rise to my knees, leaning over him.

He looks at me, watching me, I see on his face the tiny agony of waiting for what I know he wants. He swallows. I smile and slowly lean down, and behind the curtain of my hair take him in my mouth. He groans my name. He gathers up my hair, so that he can watch my mouth on him. I revel in his breathless groans and pants, the chant of my name, 'Becs, oh, Becs.'

Then he pushes me away, fixing my mouth with a desperate kiss, moaning into my mouth, 'I can't take any more. You're driving me crazy.'

He pulls me up and flips me onto my back, easing my legs apart. Our eyes lock as he pushes inside me. I'm tight, so tight and he fills me up and then pulls back and then surges again. For a few strokes, it's slow and tortuous. It's heaven and hell. My muscles are clenched, every part of me straining to hold on, to hold on to this feeling. To keep control. I'm sweating. It's too much and not enough.

Then he drops his forehead to mine, his teeth gritted. 'I can't, Becs, I...'

The power of his desperation lifts my hips and urges him on. And then it's as if neither of us can stop ourselves. He sets a frantic rhythm but I'm with him, racing towards the end. Our bodies are slick against each other. Our breath harsh in the silent night. There's just us.

Suddenly he stiffens, his back arching, his face lost in oblivion. I feel it deep inside me and with a rush, I come too. Aftershocks rippling through me.

He kisses my temple.

'Becs,' he murmurs. 'Fucking A.'

'Mm,' I murmur back. He pulls me into his side, my head on his shoulder, my leg between his. I start to drift off. I fight it, I want to savour the feeling of him beside me, stitch it into my memory, like a jewel sewn into a pocket, so that I'll never lose it.

'Set alarm,' I say drowsily, stroking his chest, listening to the rise and fall of his breathing.

'Already done.' His words are spoken into my hair.

I fall asleep and when I wake, he's gone. The only sign that he was ever there is his beanie hat left on top of my suitcase.

## Chapter Sixteen

I drag myself through sleety rain which glistens in lamplit puddles and the dark, dank, cold morning to the tall office block of Carter-Wright. It's half-past seven in the morning but it feels like midnight. Jetlag's a bitch. I give a brief wave to security, the same guy that has been here for the last ten years … and I have no idea what his name is. I walk past him but just before I reach the lift, I change my mind and go back to the front desk.

'Excuse me.'

'Yes, Miss Madison.' He casts me a quick uncertain look.

'How long have you worked here?' I ask.

'About ten years.'

Nearly as long as I've been here. A touch of shame nudges me. 'What's your name?'

'Ed Williams,' he replies noticeably nervous now.

'Morning, Ed. I'm sorry I never asked before. I hope you have a good day.'

Leaving him doing an excellent impression of a

recently landed fish, I take the lift up to the silent fourth floor. I walk through desks, all the wastepaper baskets empty and the chairs straight, and into my office. It feels as if I've been away for weeks rather than just a few days. I discard my damp wool coat and hang it up, toss the damp beanie hat onto my desk. I'm lethargic and slow today. My limbs heavy and unresponsive. It was a hard job getting out of bed but there's so much to do. My inbox, despite my working through it last night, still has a hundred unread emails and it's going to take me all morning to get through them before I can start work proper. This in itself is a very good argument for not taking vacation time.

Mitzie bounds into my office at eight-fifteen, bearing coffee.

'Thank you, there is a merciful God,' I croak as she holds out the take-away cup. It's cappuccino. 'You are an angel.'

'I know,' she says and props her hip on my desk. 'New hair. I like it.' She indicates the messy bun with curls escaping around my face. 'Cute.'

I take a sip of coffee and close my eyes, shuddering. Normally I drink espresso but today I need the soothing froth and comfort of milk. Coming back to work isn't usually so hard.

'Please don't ever say cute again.' Hudson called me cute. 'I overslept. Severe jetlag. Didn't have time to do it properly. It was messy hair or pjs. I thought I might get a few looks on the tube.'

'Good choice, then.' She takes a sip of her coffee and then tilts her head to one side. 'And is that all there is to it?

Not new hair syndrome.' There's a bird-bright beady look in her eye as she assesses me. I refuse to prompt her.

'New one on me.'

'New hair, new you. New man?'

'Nope,' I say. 'Where do you get these ideas?' I give her a disapproving look. She's so wrong. The hair was the lesser evil this morning. That's all.

'So, have you got anything to tell me?' she finally asks.

I deliberately put down my coffee and stare her down.

'Nope,' I say again and pick up a manila folder and open it.

'Nothing?'

I shake my head. What is she getting at? I didn't tell anyone that I was taking Hudson to New York. Unless she has a hotline to my mother or sister, there's no way she could know anything.

She rolls her eyes and gets out her phone and shows the screen to me before clicking on TikTok.

'Tell me this isn't you,' she says and scrolls for a second before selecting a video which shows a camera panning across the skyline of New York until it hits a couple. The man is stroking the woman's hair from her face before he pulls a beanie hat on her head.

The song is 'Meet Me at Our Spot' by Willow Smith, which magnifies the inconsequential footage, feeding the *Sleepless in Seattle* and *Affair to Remember* trope. It looks a very romantic, tender moment. It isn't.

'Who's the hottie?'

I stare at the video. What the fuck? Who took this? It's me and Hudson at the top of the Empire State Building.

I shake my head. Who else has seen this? My eyes widen. Maybe I can pretend it's a doppleganger.

'That's not me, Mitzie.' The words slip out easily but even to me they don't sound that convincing. I turn away and open the file on my desk and attempt to read the paperwork inside, although the words are swimming in front of my eyes.

'Rebecca Madison,' says Mitzie, putting her hands on her hips. 'That was the most pathetic lie this side of the planet. Besides, I have proof.' She lets out a triumphant cackle and pounces towards my desk. 'It is you.'

Proof? I glance up at her, wary now. How can she have proof?

She's holding up the khaki beanie hat between her thumb and forefinger, waving it like a flag she's captured.

'Exhibit A, m'lud.'

I groan and snatch the hat from her. It's still covered in beads of moisture from my short walk from the tube.

'Come on. Give it up. Who is he? You took him home to meet your folks and you never told me about him?' With this she pouts.

'He's no one,' I say, waving my hand as if Hudson was a minor irritant like a moth or a mosquito. If only. I haven't stopped thinking about him since I woke up alone in Manhattan.

Which is stupid because we had an agreement. I transferred the rest of the money to him before I left New York and then I deleted his number. It felt the right thing to do. A finite ending. Or maybe, says that insidious little voice, so you wouldn't ever be tempted to make a booty call.

'No one?' she echoes and plays the video again, waving it in my face like an annoying sibling. She's outdoing Laura, which is saying something. 'He doesn't look like a no one. He looks really into you and, if I may say, Ms Madison, you look into him. Miss dreamy lips. You look like you want to kiss his face off.'

'I do not.

'Do too,' she says in a teasing high pitch.

I throw down my pen. I do not have time for this. 'His name's Hudson. I took him home for the weekend. My sister was having an engagement party. I took Hudson to keep my family off my back.'

'Hudson. Nice name. Where did you find him?'

I open my mouth but nothing comes out and she catches me.

'OMG. It's him. Mr Shag. That's Mr Shag, he's gorgeous. You didn't tell me you were still seeing him.'

'I'm not, it was a … a thing.'

'A thing and you took him home. Sounds like more than a thing to me. Spill, Rebecca. You've got that guilty-as-all-hell look on your face.'

I look down my nose at her. 'Mitzie, calm down. I needed a date for the weekend. He was free, that's all it was.'

Her face is incredulous. 'He went to New York with you for the weekend.'

I shrug my shoulders.

'Nice work if you can get it. So when are you seeing him again?'

'I'm not.'

'Why the hell not?' She holds up her phone and plays the fucking video again. Like I need to see it again. I remember every damn moment a bit too well. Hudson touching my face, his dancing eyes when he tugged the hat down over my hair. His fingers skimming my cheeks. I pray no one in the office has seen it.

'Rebecca,' she points to the screen, 'exhibit B, he's freaking gorgeous, and exhibit fucking C, he's clearly so into you.'

Like she needs to point it out. I do know about B but C?

'Don't be ridiculous. He's not my type and I don't want or require a man in my life.'

'The lady doth protest.' Again, she plays the video. 'It gives me shivers just watching it. Sooo romantic.' I want to snatch it out of her hand and toss it out of the window. It looks exactly like a scene out of a romcom.

'And you're sooo annoying. He was just a fuck buddy for the weekend.' The words turn acid on my tongue, their crudity suddenly offending me. We had awesome, amazing, once-in-a-lifetime sex. I shouldn't belittle it. But then again I shouldn't be making such a big deal of it. Hudson probably has sex like that all the time. He knows his way around the female body. I almost sigh. He certainly does – but I'm not kidding myself that I'm anything special. I made it easy for him. I was available and despite my good intentions I didn't say no. And I'm not going to apologise for that.

'Doesn't look like that to me. And not just me. Do you

know how many views this video has had? Five and a half million. That's how many.'

'Shit!'

'I know. Awesome, isn't it?'

'No,' I snap. 'And it's not what it looks like.'

'What? A hot man is doing something nice for his girl.'

'I'm not his girl. It was a hook-up. Like I said, a one-time-only thing.'

She folds her arms in that I-don't-believe-a-word-of-it fashion.

'This is all your fault,' I say, exasperated.

'What's it got to do with me?'

'Remember I told you about Andrew getting engaged to my sister.'

'Yeah, weasel dick with warts on.'

I laugh because Mitzie does do a fine line in insults.

'And you suggested I get a fake date…'

'No way. You're fucking kidding me. Mr Hat!' Her eyes brighten.

'Exactly.'

'Nice move, he's way better looking than dick weasel. What did your sister think?'

I giggle and tell her about my sister accusing me of paying him. 'I nearly wet myself, thought she'd worked it out.'

'What a bitch.'

'An astute bitch, though.'

She took a step back and examined me and scowled. 'So how come you don't have that shagged-brains-out afterglow?'

'Give me a break. I've got the most horrendous jet lag probably and because we didn't get much sleep on our last night.' I can't help smiling at the memory. As last nights go, it went out with a bang.

'And there it is, right there.' Beaming she points a finger at me. 'Happy, shagged little face. So, when are you seeing him again?'

'I'm not.' The words come out tighter than I meant them to. They're supposed to sound casual, indifferent. Mitzie jumps right on them.

'Did he dump you?'

'No.' Now I sound defensive, as if I've got something to hide. 'It was a business arrangement. Pure and simple We've got nothing in common. He's a furniture designer, for crap's sake. He's not my type. It was always a casual thing.' The excuses tumble out.

'That doesn't look like a business arrangement to me.' She holds up her phone. 'And you like him.'

'Mitzie, what are you? Fourteen? Yeah I liked him. We had fun. But I. Don't. Want. Any. More.'

'You're weird, you know that?'

'Because I don't believe in pots of gold at the end of the rainbow and love and marriage. I've got everything I want.'

'Yes but you could have more.'

'How many women do you know who have it all? Seriously. There's always a compromise between their job or their partners. It's the same story every time. Andrew was bad enough. Remember Josh?'

'He was a rat bastard. He used your job as an excuse to justify sleeping around.'

Apparently my job meant more to me than him, so he slept with other women. He had a point – it did.

'What about Miles?' I ask, dredging up another relationship attempt. I'd thought we were quite compatible. He was a lawyer too.

'You were asking for trouble with him. Stupid name. It's not your fault his ego was bigger than his dick.'

I shrug.

'You've summed it up, Mitz, it's just not worth the hassle and I don't need it.'

And I can't risk it with Hudson. What if I fell in love with him? One day things would have to end. And where would I be then?

Her face twists. 'Well, I got some bad news. I thought I'd give you the heads-up before you hear it elsewhere, although Marcus is bound to call you in today.'

I slump momentarily. 'He's retiring.'

'Fuck, Rebecca!' She slaps her hands on my desk. 'How did you know that?'

'Easy guess. Come on, it was only a matter of time.' I lift my shoulders. 'Who's replacing him, Dick or Dom?'

Now she rolls her eyes and slumps down into the chair opposite my desk. 'It hasn't been announced yet. But they're both wandering about like puffed-up despots with a chest full of medals. I'm waiting for them to start trash talking like a pair of boxers before a big fight.'

'Oh God, in the left corner we have Richard Billy Big Balls Carter Wheeler and in the right we have Dominic my-gonads-are-bigger-than-yours Wright.'

'John Fredericks is running a book.'

'Who's favourite?'

'That the firm will be run into the ground by next Christmas.'

Our laughs are tinged with the tiniest bit of hysteria because it really isn't a laughing matter. Neither of them is qualified to run a bath let alone an entire legal company. Everyone knows their executive assistants do all the work. Both of them are equally incompetent and woefully lacking in leadership skills. They belong to the politician school of ethics: why bother with the truth when a lie is so much easier.

I shudder. At least the current MD has good people around him and he listens to them.

'I'd better get to work,' says Mitzie. 'Glad you had a good break and welcome back to the madhouse.'

'Thanks for the coffee.'

'No problem. The barista guy needs something to do before nine.' She leaves the office, waving with one hand, without a backward glance.

I look at the hat on my desk and quickly snatch it up and stuff it in my bottom drawer. I have no idea what made me wear it this morning – it was there, because I was tired and running on autopilot.

The rest of the morning passes in a blur of allocating work, meeting with my team, none of whom appear to have seen the damn video, or if they have, don't connect me with it.

At one o'clock I'm summoned to Marcus Carter-Wheeler's office on the sixth floor.

## Chapter Seventeen

'Ms Madison,' his secretary of twenty years greets me, in her low respectful tone. She's in her early sixties and incredibly glamorous, with ash blonde hair and a wardrobe full of neat shift dresses that show off her trim figure and killer legs. She's always pleasant but I guess she's party to too many secrets to develop any friendships with anyone else in the office. 'You can go on through, he's expecting you.'

'Thank you, Mary.' I walk into the inner sanctum which takes up a third of the whole floor and has a panoramic view of the Thames.

'Rebecca. Good to see you. How was your holiday?'

'Very good, thank you.'

'New York, wasn't it?'

'Yes.'

'Flying visit?'

This is remarkably chatty for Marcus. Normally he'd be straight down to business by now. I'm a bit thrown.

'Thanksgiving with my family.'

'Aren't you related to Jonathon Adler?'

'He's my step-father.'

Marcus nods as if this is a very good thing. 'Excellent. He's a very good golfer, I hear. Plays off a single figure handicap.'

'I believe so.' Where on earth is this conversation going? I thought he'd just tell me about his impending retirement, which would take all of a minute. Instead he seems to be making a song and dance out of it.

'Do take a seat.' He invites me over to the corner where the glass panes meet and a pair of leather tub chairs are arranged opposite one another across a small glass coffee table. This is the informal chat space. I've only sat here once in ten years, when I was offered the partnership.

I sit in the seat, my hands primly on my knees.

'I'm sure you've already heard on the grapevine that I've announced my retirement. I shall be finishing at the end of the financial year.'

'Yes, Marcus. We'll be sorry to see you go.'

He raises an eyebrow. 'We.'

I smile because despite everything I'm quite fond of the old fart. 'I will be sorry to see you go.'

'So, I bet like everyone in the building you're agog to know who will be taking over.'

I shrug. 'Not particularly.'

He stares at me and looks nonplussed for a second. 'Why not?'

'Well, it will be either Richard or Dominic.' I sound indifferent even though, inside, my eyes are rolling with the best of them. The Dick and Dom Show – seriously, a pair of comedians could do a better job.

'And you don't think they're the right choice.'

Now he has surprised me. I stare back at him. 'I didn't say that,' I say carefully.

He laughs. 'You didn't have to.'

I touch my face involuntarily.

'It's all right, the poker face is still holding fast but I know you, Rebecca. The fact that you're not giving anything away says it all. Who do you think should be my successor?'

I look at him levelly. 'Not Richard or Dominic.'

'Reasons?'

We're back on safe ground. Marcus has always respected my opinions, even if he doesn't always agree with them.

I tick them off on each hand. 'Richard – too impetuous, easily swayed, not strategic enough.'

'And Dominic?'

'Too greedy, too ambitious, too egotistical. He won't do what's best for the company.'

He nods but doesn't comment. Instead, he goes on to talk about a new litigation case that has landed on my desk. It's between a multi-national supplier and an international retailer. A very public spat that is going to take some delicate negotiation.

'I'm sure you'll do an excellent job as usual, Rebecca. Be aware that there'll be some very public interest in this one.' He frowns and squints at my hair. I lift my chin. We both know what he means. There'll be lots of pictures of outside the court with the client and me. I'm representing the company. I have to look the part. It's never been in question before.

I'm not going to justify my hair to him. He's bald with a comb-over, it doesn't get more ridiculous than that. Men's ability in court is never judged on their appearance.

We start discussing a couple of other clients when my phone vibrates. It's on silent but as we all have to be available for clients, no one in the company ever switches them off in meetings. It's an unwritten rule that if it's a client, you can duck out and answer it.

I take a quick peek at the number. It's not in my contacts. I refuse the call and set the phone back on the table, picking up where I'd left off. Seconds later it calls again. The same number. I refuse it again.

I haven't even put it down when it buzzes in my hand.

'Someone wants to get hold of you,' says Marcus frowning.

'No one I know. It's probably one of those ambulance chasers, asking if I've had an accident.'

'Bloodsuckers. They give us all a bad name.'

He shakes his head in disgust.

When my phone rings for the fourth time, I switch it off altogether. If it's a genuine call, they'll leave a message.

Marcus gives me an approving nod and we continue our conversation.

After ten minutes, Mary knocks on the door and then pokes her head through as she opens the door. 'Sir David Nightingale is on the phone for you.'

'Right. Sorry, Rebecca, I've been trying to get hold of him for days.'

'No problem.' I rise and walk out as he goes to his desk.

'Thank you for your time and your input today,' he says, his brow scrunching thoughtfully.

I nod because I don't for a minute imagine that he's going to take a blind bit of notice.

When I get back to my desk, I switch my phone on. A little red dot tells me I have a voicemail message.

I listen to the message.

'Rebecca, it's Hudson. I need to talk to you. Call me back.'

He sounds business-like. Direct. And a tiny part of me is disappointed. Does he want more money? I can't think of a single reason he would want to talk to me. Not in that tone anyway.

I want to slap myself hard. Because for a few brief seconds, when I heard his voice, I had this stupid hope that perhaps he wanted to see me. But surely if he did, he would have sounded different, less clipped, softer. Like he sounded in bed.

Not going there. Over and done with.

He phones twice that afternoon. Both times I'm too busy to answer and he doesn't leave another message.

My phone is on fire today. My mother calls to tell me that with the wedding plans and everything else going on, they've decided not to come back to London for Christmas but I'm welcome to use the house if I want to. 'I don't feel so bad because I know you've got Hudson and I'm sure the two of you will want to spend lots of time together, so you won't even miss us.'

I even said 'Sure' to her. Then she babbled on about

getting together with Andrew's family over the holiday period. It sounded as if it were going to be The Andrew and Laura Spectacular, which I was more than happy to forgo.

Even though I'd have only spent Christmas Eve and Christmas Day – just two days – at the family home in Kensington it feels like the news has left a big hole in my Christmas. I've always liked Christmas. I'm big on present buying. I like the challenge of trying to find the most perfect present for people, the thing they wanted but didn't know they wanted or the thing they hankered after but never spoiled themselves. Now with Christmas overseas posting dates long gone, there's no desperate imperative for me to go shopping, which had been how I expected to fill my weekend. Even if I sent parcels off, they're unlikely to get to the States in time. My weekend plans are in tatters and I'm scared by the odd hollow feeling that brings with it.

I'm loading up my laptop and a dozen files for the weekend. It's only five-fifteen on a Friday night and the weekend stretches out before me but I'm calling it quits early. Maybe it's the lingering hangover from last night – Mitzie and I sank two bottles of Prosecco plus an ill-advised farewell cocktail before we called it quits – but the next two empty days loom like a Dementor sucking all the happiness out.

Just as I'm about to put my coat on I hear Mitzie's voice in the corridor. She's talking unnaturally cheerfully. She appears in my office doorway.

'Hello, you have a visitor. I was in reception, I thought I'd save you a trip and bring them up.'

As I'm staring in astonishment at her, because this is not normal behaviour and I'm not expecting a visitor, Hudson steps into view.

Mitzie beams at me as if she's presenting me with a gold medal while I'm frozen to the spot, my tongue superglued to the roof of my mouth.

'Hey, Becs,' says Hudson, smiling at me, as if I'd seen him a day ago instead of three weeks before.

'Becs?' mouths Mitzie behind his back, her eyes widening with what I'm guessing she thinks is comic effect. I glare at her but she refuses to take the extremely unsubtle hint and stands there as if her feet have taken root and it's going to take a tree surgeon to remove her.

'Hudson,' I say.

'How are you doing?'

'Aren't you going to introduce us?' asks Mitzie, infusing the cliché with the perky mockery it deserves. 'Although of course I've seen you on video. I'm Mitzie by the way. Rebecca's office bestie.' My lip curls. We have never ever described each other as besties.

'Hi, I'm Hudson. A friend of Becs.'

'She's still got the hat, you know,' says Mitzie.

I am going to kill her and it's going to be a long, painful, drawn-out death.

'Mitzie. Does your husband have any idea how much a Dior handbag costs?' The blackmail threat makes her shake her head.

'That's low. Even for you,' she says. 'Sorry, Hudson,

apparently I have to go. Have a great weekend, folks.' With that she walks out of the office. A second later she's framed in the doorway with both thumbs up.

Hudson laughs and I look behind me at the window. Mitzie's reflection is perfectly visible to him in the glass against the dark winter evening.

'See ya.' She laughs too and vanishes. 'Have a good weekend,' she calls from further down the corridor.

I roll my eyes.

'She's fun.'

'Mm,' I reply.

'So, Ms Corporate Lawyer, this is where you hang out.' He looks around the room.

'It's my office, yes,' I reply stiffly although inside my heart has developed arrhythmia. It's not quite sure where it's at.

'You're a hard woman to get hold of.' He looks at the big plate-glass window behind my desk and the lights of London. 'You really are important, aren't you?' There's a touch of awe in his voice which throws me. I've always liked that Hudson doesn't take what I do too seriously. He's the only one.

'Not really,' I say, my voice sharp because I don't want to feel the way I'm feeling inside right now – ridiculously shy and pleased to see him.

I study him as if I'm as cool as an iced cucumber in the arctic, but actually I'm drinking in the sight of him. Those bright blue eyes, the lopsided smile and the damp curls. He's wearing a denim jacket over a navy hoody and black jeans and he looks so familiar and dependable, which is an odd choice of word in the situation but that's Hudson.

'What do you want?' I ask. My brain has developed octopus tendencies with thoughts pulling off in at least eight different directions and I'm having a really hard time reeling them all back in.

'Ah, Ms Corporate Lawyer is back,' he says with a typical Hudson grin. 'I wondered when you didn't return my calls.'

'What's that supposed to mean?' I'm not sure I want to hear his answer to that, so I follow up quickly with 'And you didn't get the message?'

'I knew you didn't mean it,' he says with a cheerful shrug.

'Your arrogance is breathtaking.' I start walking again, more because I have no idea what else to do. That's a lie – I do. I want to hug him, squeeze him tight to me, feel that muscled broad chest up against mine. Tell him I've missed him. Be held by him. I'm absolutely scared shitless.

'I know,' he says and I start wondering how he knows, then I realise he's responding to my comment. I don't respond, wrestling with the silence for as long as I can, but then I burst out, 'What do you want, Hudson?'

'I need to talk to you. I did say that on the phone.'

'There's no reason for us to talk. You got your money. You did what I asked.' Brilliantly, I could add, but I don't because his ego is already quite big enough.

'Houston, we have a problem.' He stops and puts a hand on my arm. 'I do need to talk to you. Come for a drink with me. It's important.' His eyes plead with me.

I sigh and look at my watch as if I've got some place else to be, which is utter bollocks as the only plan I have is for yet another ready meal and yet another repeat episode of *Friends*. 'I can give you half an hour,' I say because time is money and in my business it's precious. As I think this, I think how much of it I squander when I'm at home. I kill time in between work instead of doing something positive with it. I hate the way I think of this stuff when I'm with Hudson.

With another one of his full lighthouse beams, he grabs my arm and steers me towards the lift.


I find a seat as Hudson sails up to the bar. It's another typical London pub but it's near the office and I'm unlikely to see anyone I know in here. The post-work crew will have moved onto bougier places. Hudson engages the barman in quick cheerful conversation because that's him all over. I watch him enviously. Everyone seems to like him. Even my mother.

Hudson hands me a large glass of wine. If I neck this in half an hour on an empty stomach, I'll have a job walking.

He takes a sip of the beer he's ordered and then puts the glass down, getting out his phone. He taps the screen and then slides it across the table towards me.

I glance down and see the now very familiar TikTok video. I push it back towards him, suddenly very glad that I'm not wearing his beanie hat today. I put it on this morning, even though it doesn't really go with my Stella McCartney scarlet wool, ankle-length coat but it's better than an umbrella at keeping my hair curl-free away from the damp air. It's currently tucked in my laptop case.

'I've seen it,' I say flatly, which is quite something because even though I've seen it so many times, it still gives me a pang of longing. If only it was as real as the five million TikTok viewers seem to think.

Now his face has turned serious. 'So has my mum.'

'Oh, and is that a problem?'

'Yes, a big one. Huge.' I blink at him.

'Yes, my sisters made me watch *Pretty Woman* sixty million times.'

'Why is it such a problem?'

'Starting with the fact that I hadn't told her I was going to New York. My sisters are livid, apparently they would have given me shopping lists.'

I smile at that; he looks resigned. I'm not sure what he wants me to say, though. It's nothing to do with me if his mum's mad at him because he didn't tell her he was leaving the country. He's a grown man. 'Unfortunately, what she's really mad about is that I didn't tell her I was romantically involved with anyone – her words, I hasten to add.'

I shrug my shoulders. 'I still don't see how this is my problem.'

Hudson slumps back in his chair and runs his hand through his hair. For once he looks serious and very sad. 'She's been ill, recovering from chemo and radiotherapy. Breast cancer. She's been given the all-clear but ... she's ... well ... she wants to meet you.'

'Me. Why?'

'I might have told her you were my girlfriend when she saw the video.'

'Why would you do that?'

He jerks back in his seat. 'Er, hello.' He taps the screen and the bloody video plays again. 'My mum, like every other woman on the planet, seems to think this is a tender moment, not that I was trying to get into your knickers.'

I laugh. Classic Hudson. 'Were you?'

'It worked, didn't it.' This is said with an accompanying devilish glint in his eye and with a sudden rush of heat, I remember the desperate desire and want of our last night together.

'Can't you just tell your mother we broke up?'

He gives me an uncharacteristically sarcastic fake grin. 'Wouldn't that be the easiest course of action? Unfortunately, I missed the window of opportunity.'

'What?' He's not making any sense.

'It would have been callous to dump you just after a trip to New York, especially as you paid the air fare – Mum knows I'm broke at the moment.'

He's got to be kidding me.

'I'd never have heard the end of it from my sisters, taking advantage of you, and Mum would have been disappointed. I thought I'd give it a month or two.'

'Good of you,' I comment.

He grins at me. 'I thought so.'

'I had no idea there were acceptable lengths of time for dumping someone. Is it written down anywhere? What is it? Three days after dinner? A week after sex? Two weeks after meeting the family?'

'Not sure but I didn't dump you in time. Mum had the *talk* with me this week. He sighs. 'She's worried about me –' he puts his fingers up in air quotes '– flitting from girl to girl. I got the lecture about growing up and then the emotional blackmail. So, I said I'd bring you home.'

'You lied to her, basically.'

He holds up a hand.

'She's been so ill this year, she's decided it might be her last Christmas and she wants it to be perfect. She's going to be fine, of course.' I'm not sure whether he's saying it because he believes it or because he needs to believe it. It's difficult to tell, his jaw line has hardened. 'I just want to … to give her what she wants. I figured, we'd pretended once, we could pretend again.'

I immediately shake my head. 'No, no way. That was a one-off business arrangement. I'm not interested.' I cannot spend more time with this man. For dozens and dozens of reasons.

His catches his lip with his teeth. 'Please, Becs.' There's real pleading in his voice and the puppy-dog eyes are back. I shake my head as he says, 'It's just a few days. For my mum. She's had such a shit year.'

'I can't.' I rise to my feet, even as guilt is tugging at me like the guy rope on a hot-air balloon. He loves his mother and he's prepared to lie to her to make her happy. But I can't spend any more time with him. It's too dangerous. 'This conversation is over.'

'I'll tell your sister,' he calls, laying down his trump card.

I stop and sit back down with a thump, staring at him disbelievingly. He wouldn't. I'd never live it down. Paying for a date. Shit, she would crow about that for evermore. I'd never be able to show my face at another family gathering again. I can hear her now, the triumphant, vindictive pitch in her voice, 'Do you remember that time Rebecca had to pay someone to come home with her?'

Then my brain clicks into action. This is Hudson Strong. He wouldn't. He's not that unkind. But he is desperate. I can see the stricken look in his eyes when he talks about his mum.

'You wouldn't. There was a non-disclosure clause in the contract.' I lift my chin, I'm still fighting. Perhaps there's a compromise somewhere. 'I'd sue.'

He lifts his beer and takes a leisurely sip. 'You'd sue?'

'Yes.'

'No, you wouldn't. Then everyone would know. Besides, I read that bit of the contract. The non-disclosure bit was for while we were there. Not afterwards.'

Is that true? My mouth drops open. No. That's not right. My contracts are duck's arse watertight. I have a reputation for it. No loopholes. I pull out my phone. I need to read that contract right now. I pull it up and scroll to the section.

'Becs.' Hudson puts his hand over my phone. 'What are you doing?'

'Checking the contract,' I snap.

'Do you realise how mad that sounds?' he says quietly. It's the quiet in his voice, almost pitying, that penetrates.

'What do you mean?'

'You're more worried about the contract being correct that anything else.'

'It's what I do,' I say coldly. It's who I am. I feel twisted up inside because I've messed up so badly. How could I not have made the non-disclosure period in perpetuity? It's the most basic error.

Hudson looks at me and his hand lifts to my face. 'You look tired, Becs.'

I swallow. I have no idea how to respond to this. Kindness. Concern. For a moment, it's tempting to admit to weakness. I am tired. Worried. Disconcerted. Out of sorts.

'It's been full on at work. My MD is going to retire and a couple of muppets will be taking over.' My lip curls at the thought of Dick and Dom.

'Apart from New York, do you ever take a break? Not that it was much of a break. You were on the phone all the time.'

There we go.

'I take plenty of breaks,' I say blithely which is a complete lie.

'What are you doing for Christmas?'

'Not sure yet.'

'I thought your folks were coming to London? Don't they have a place in Kensington?'

'You're well informed.'

'Jenny was telling me over dinner about how she likes going food shopping in Harrods.'

'Well *Jennifer* won't be shopping there this year, they've cancelled the trip to London. Too much going on with wedding plans.'

'That's rough. I'm sorry, Becs.'

'Don't be. It's fine.'

'But what will you do?'

I stare at him. 'Christmas is just another day. I'll have breakfast. Do a bit of work. Have lunch. Have dinner. Go to bed. I'm not going to die because I'm on my own and off work for two days.

He blinks and tilts his head to one side as if studying a rare specimen. I bristle.

'What?'

'Nothing.'

I don't want to talk about this anymore. 'I need to go.'

'What, to do some work before you have dinner and go to bed?'

'Who are you to judge?' I don't need to point out that he needed my money to get his career back on track. 'Are you back in your studio?'

Rather than being chastened, his bloody gorgeous face lights up, properly, like he's in the full beam of a spotlight in the theatre.

'Yeah. And I've sold a piece so I can pay you back.' He digs in his backpack and pulls out an envelope. 'Here you go.' Without pausing, he carries on talking. I want to laugh at his blasé attitude. The money which was once so important is forgotten even though he fulfilled his part of the bargain. And he hasn't used that fact as leverage for what he wants. 'I picked up a new piece of wood at the weekend, which I've been working on. Making a table.' His hands move with the light, sure touch of a ballet dancer, as he describes the design and talks about the grain of the wood and the curve of the piece. It changes the whole timbre of our conversation. His sheer enthusiasm and obvious pleasure calm me and stop all the scratchy thoughts in my head. I stare at him, mesmerised. He is happy. Hudson is Hudson. He's himself. He knows himself.

'Becs.' Hudson waves a hand across my face. 'You've drifted off again. Am I boring you?'

'No, just a lot on my mind. I really ought to be going.' I can feel myself weakening.

'Come for Christmas,' he says suddenly. 'It'll kill two birds with one stone. Give you something to do and you can meet my mum. I'll pick you up on Christmas Eve and take you home on Boxing Day. Two nights.'

'I can't,' I say, lifting my chin.

'Yes, you can and you owe me.'

I do. Especially now that he's paid me back, not that I'm about to admit that. 'No, I don't.'

A wicked smile crosses his face. 'Yes, you do. Remember Sydney.'

## Chapter Eighteen

I wake up the following morning, bright and early. It's one of those clear, crisp winter mornings with a coating of frost on the balcony rails outside my window. Seagulls are wheeling over the steely grey Thames, their raucous calls piercing the chilly air.

Even though it's seven-thirty on a Saturday, I check my phone. There's a WhatsApp message from Hudson.

I don't bloody believe it, the cheeky sod has sent me a contract.

As I left the bar last night, thoroughly pissed off that he'd won, his parting shot was 'I'll send a contract over.' I shot him the middle finger.

Easy to do when you're walking out the door but I'm going to have to be on my best behaviour because Hudson has made it quite clear that if I upset his mother in any way, he'll be straight on the phone to my sister.

If I have to go to meet Hudson's family, I want to make a

good impression at the very least. That's pride talking. Surely his mother is going to take one look at me and realise I am not Hudson's type and that I'm barking up the wrong tree, never mind being in the wrong flaming forest. And I bet his sisters – all three of them will be there – are going to see straight through our faux relationship. His family strike me as a lot more down to earth and having emotional intelligence, unlike mine, although my mother did surprise me on that last trip. She seemed to have softened – quite a lot, actually.

Fresh out of the shower, I grab the notes I once made about his family to refresh myself. Micky and Geoff are his parents. DD, PP and CC are his sisters. I pick up my phone and call him.

'Morning, Becs,' he chirps. I'd forgotten he's a lark.

'I need to know what your mother likes and your sisters and your father.'

'Why?'

'I need to get them gifts.'

'No, you don't. They won't mind.'

'If I'm coming for Christmas, I'm not coming empty-handed.' God, I sound so prissy. But I can't bear the thought of turning up, being out of place and adding insult to injury by being mean. It didn't matter when Hudson came home with me, our family is unemotional and not touchy-feely in the least. Hudson's family sound the absolute opposite.

'Mum likes scarves and brooches. PP is mad about snails, DD is into horse-racing and CC makes her own jewellery. Dad loves his garden.'

'Snails?'

'Yes, always an odd child. She collects them.'

'She collects snails?'

He sputters out a laugh. 'Not the real thing, like little ornaments or pictures or stuffed toys.'

I relax a little. I thought he was making it up, but there's enough added detail there to reassure me he's telling the truth. It gives me enough to go on. I like a challenge.

'What do you think of the contract?'

I want to deny I've read it. I close my eyes and shake my head even though he can see me.

'You call this a contract?'

'I thought I'd done quite a good job.'

'Hmm,' I say, perusing the sheet of paper that I've printed off.

According to the *contract* our agreement commences at eight-thirty on the twenty-fourth day of December two thousand and twenty-two and will terminate by four-thirty on December the twenty-sixth.

'You do know that if you were paying me that would be fifty-six billable hours.' I tell him.

'Good job I'm not paying. You owe me, remember.'

I huff out a sigh. 'We don't need a contract.'

'I seem to recall someone insisting that we did, to protect ourselves.'

'That was a proper contract. Not a back-of-a-fag-packet job.'

'This is a proper contract.' There's laughter in his voice. 'I got it off the internet. It cost me two pounds fifty.'

'You were robbed.'

I grin to myself at how much fun I'm going to have ripping this baby to shreds. It's not a lengthy document. One side of A4. I dig out a red pen especially for the job.

'*Becs will not bring her straightening irons,*' I read. 'You can forget that. That's non-negotiable.'

'Okay,' he agrees, far too easily. 'But don't blame me if it short-circuits the very ancient electrics in the house and we have to go without Christmas lunch.' I ignore him and cross the clause out.

*Neither party will reveal the details of this agreement in perpetuity.* I'm not even going to deign to comment on that one. Sneaky bastard. He's nailed my loophole.

'*Rebecca will enjoy herself.* Bit presumptuous of you, isn't it?'

'You will,' he says and I can hear the confidence in his voice.

I read on. 'No *resting bitch faces allowed.* Bloody cheek. I can't help how I look.'

'Yes, you can. Just because someone's an idiot, you don't have to show it.'

'And you can forget this one. *No laptops or mobile phones allowed – except for half an hour on Christmas Day to wish distant family a Merry Christmas.*' I can't not check my emails for a whole fifty hours. What if something came up?

'*Joining in family games is mandatory.* What sort of games?' Now I'm starting to get nervous. What sort of games do they play? I have a funny feeling we're not talking Bridge or Canasta.

'Nothing too challenging.'

'Hudson, that's not helpful.'

My eyes stray back to the final clause of his ridiculous contract. It turns my stomach inside out.

*Being unbuttoned is obligatory.*

## Chapter Nineteen

A week later, I slap the revised contract with red slashes all over it into Hudson's lap, narrowly missing his balls, as soon as I get into the car, a beaten up old VW Golf GTi.

I've resolved that we are *not* going to have sex again. We're a pretend couple. Which all sounds perfectly logical when I'm apart from him but now I'm next to him, my willpower is wavering. Sleeping with him again would be so easy, but it's the wrong thing to do for my own self-preservation. I like Hudson. I like him a lot. Too much. I am determined to put some emotional distance between us. I have to. I don't want to lose myself again.

'Whoa! Watch the boys,' he says. 'What's bitten you this morning?'

'It's half-past six and I've only had one coffee.' I smooth down my red wool dress, admiring the full skater skirt. I'm rocking the Christmas look this morning, not that I need to impress anyone but I like to be well dressed. It gives me that competitive edge.

Of course, I'd asked Hudson what the dress code was and there was a blank silence on the other end of the phone before he said, 'There isn't one.'

I sighed because sometimes he is such a boy. There's always a dress code.

His follow up of an airy 'it's all very casual' didn't reassure me in the least. Men always say that about their families and then you arrive to find that they dress for dinner every night, with obligatory family pearls.

Despite Spanish inquisitor style questioning, over the course of several phone calls in the last week, the canny bugger's given very little away. To my question 'Where will we be sleeping?' he responded, 'In a bed,' in his usual cheerful teasing tone. Is that a sofa bed in the lounge, his boyhood single bed or in the spare room? 'Don't worry so, Becs. You'll have a good time.'

'Mm,' I say darkly but I remember the last time he said I'd have a good time. I refuse to think about Ellen's Stardust Diner.

'What time are we expected?' I ask as he pulls out into the slow trickle of early morning traffic. It's still dark and London is just stirring. The roads are quiet – at the moment – they will be chaotic later as the diehards spill out of the office and head home for Christmas Eve.

'Around lunchtime but we'll stop for breakfast.'

We're heading to Kingham, a village north of Oxford, a place I've never been but every time I mentioned that I'd be going there for Christmas, colleagues said how pretty it is.

I've never heard of it before but then when I travel I tend to go abroad.

I did look up the journey and it's going to take us two hours.

'How are Jenny and Jon?' asks Hudson as we head out of London on the A40.

'Good,' I say, I don't even bother correcting him. My mother was rather taken with him calling her Jenny.

'So what do your parents do?' I ask, studying Hudson's hands on the steering wheel. His fingers are long and elegant and suddenly I have a flash of them stroking my body.

'My mum potters these days – literally, she makes things out of clay and she decorates them.' The vagueness of this description is both worrying and intriguing.

'What sort of things?'

He screws up his face. 'Fairy homes and unicorn stables. That sort of thing.'

She sounds barking. I can't begin to imagine how hideous they must be. Perhaps I can buy one as a wedding present for Laura and Andrew.

'And my dad runs a farm shop. He's really into organic farming and rewilding and all that stuff.'

I nod. They sound quite eccentric, not like my sort of people at all. Way out of my comfort zone. I've been brought up in a staid, sensible family and I know exactly where I am with them. Everything is straightforward and quite routine. There are no surprises. I always know what to expect. Just how I like it. 'DD works for a local racing trainer doing all their admin. He's her husband. CC makes jewellery and PP does something to do with soil conservation. She goes round the country collecting pots of mud. I think she counts worms as well.'

I smile politely. Oh my God, they sound as mad as a box of frogs. This is going to be the Christmas from hell.

'And how's the preparation for your big exhibition going?' I feel invested in his work even though I've never seen any of it in the flesh.

'Really great,' he says. 'I've just finished the final piece and I'm so pleased with it.' He starts telling me all about it, in that buzzy, enthusiastic way of his, taking both hands off the steering wheel at one point. I mean, I love my job but I couldn't ever get this passionate about it. I'm good at it and I like the praise I get, I like the mental challenge of making sure there are no loopholes that can be exploited, the very precise language required and the prestige of being exceptionally good at the work. Despite all this, there are some things I don't like. The partners love wheeling me out as an example of someone who's broken through and yes, I made partner, one of the youngest to do so, but I had to work a damn sight harder than some of the other partners just because they have an appendage between their legs.

After an hour and a half's driving, we stop for breakfast in a service station on the M40 and Hudson polishes off a full English while I have a croissant and black coffee. Where does he put it? I eye his biceps across the table. He's well built, with those beautifully defined muscles, especially on his very firm, flat stomach and just thinking about it and the line of hair dipping beneath his waistband sends my thoughts in a wayward direction. I guess making furniture must be quite physical.

I look up and realise Hudson is looking at me with a grin on his face. Oh God. He's turned into a bloody mind reader. I decide to brazen it out. 'What?'

'Nothing,' he says, all innocence, which doesn't fool me at all. I fold my arms and wait for whatever he's sure to say. His eyes dance with their perennial mischief. 'You should never play poker.'

'I've got a very good poker face,' I say. 'I'm known for it at work.'

'You were looking like you want to jump my bones again.'

'I was not,' I snap, annoyed that he's so close to the truth. 'Let's be clear. I am here because you are blackmailing me. Which, by the way, is a criminal offence. Section 21 of the 1968 Theft Act.'

He gives me a very direct look. 'I love it when you go all stern lawyer on me. It's really hot.' I ignore the quick flutter in my belly.

'I am not going to sleep with you again.' I'm not sure I even believe this.

He tilts his head, eyes crinkling with that teasing glint of his. 'You know you get this funny little dimple in your cheek when you tell fibs.'

And, of course, I fall for the line and lift my hand to my face.

He laughs delightedly. 'You're so easy to tease.'

I glare at him. I don't like being teased. It always makes me feel wrong-footed. Like I'm the only one who doesn't get the joke. I never quite know how to handle it. I shoot him my best ice-queen glare which has absolutely no bloody effect. He still looks all too pleased with himself.

'Is there anything else I need to know about your family? That they would expect me to know?'

He shakes his head. 'Don't think so, no. They'll grill you because you're the first girl I've brought home in a while.'

'How long is a while?'

'Few years?'

'Really? I'm surprised.'

'Don't get me wrong … I just never bring them home. I don't want anyone getting ideas, least of all my mum.'

'And you don't feel the slightest bit guilty about misleading her this time?' I drawl and to my surprise I think I can see a slight tinge of shame on his face.

His jaw tightens. 'What she doesn't know won't harm her. I'm not going to lie, just let her assume.'


The village of Kingham is very pretty and extremely rural. I ignore the knot of panic that ties itself around my intestines. We turn down a narrow country lane which we follow for what seems like several miles. The knot tightens. We really are in the middle of nowhere. I check my phone still has a signal. Only just. There's one bar on the display.

'You do have WiFi, don't you?' I ask, my voice thin and high.

He glances at me and I lift my chin, embarrassed by my weakness.

'Hmm, it's a bit spotty. But it's Christmas, Becs. What do

you need WiFi for? You're not going to do any work, surely. Everywhere must be closed.'

The thought of no WiFi triggers a swirl of nausea. I might be sick. I have to be available. What if something happens and no one can contact me?

I'm about to answer that I'm never out of touch with work, I'm always available – but available for what? I have a couple of contracts to go over while I'm here but both clients won't be back in the office until New Year. He's right, it is Christmas. I realise that I use work as an excuse to keep out of the family's way when I stay with them. I can only take so much of my sister and my mother, we're so different. They've both moved on since my dad died, and I feel left behind. Work has become my refuge. For the first time ever, this strikes me as being a bit sad.

We turn into a gravelled driveway. In front of us is a sprawling golden stone building, with a grand old creeper tracing its way across the façade around the stone-mullioned diamond-paned windows. It's not what I was expecting at all. I shoot a look at Hudson. There's a wistful smile on his face.

'Home sweet home.'

'It's lovely.' I stare up at the slate roof and the fancy barley-twist chimneys.

'Yeah.' His mouth twists. 'Another reason why I don't bring girls home. I'm not about to make anyone lady of the manor. They tend to fall for the house.'

I think Hudson is underestimating his charms but his ego doesn't need feeding so I don't say anything.

As I open the car door, a pack of dogs comes running

out to greet us. Actually there are three of them but they're so bouncy it feels like double that – a lively Cocker Spaniel who almost turns somersaults of delight at seeing Hudson, an enthusiastic Labrador whose tail wags like a manic windscreen wiper and a tiny Yorkshire Terrier with a pink bow tied around a little pineapple tuft of hair.

'Hello, hello, hello,' says Hudson squatting down and fussing over them before scooping up the Yorkshire terrier, who's dancing under the feet of the other two dogs. 'This is Trixie. She's small in size but big on attitude. That's Prudence, the Lab, and the completely mad dog is Eddie – he's barmy even by Cocker standards.'

I nod. I'm not scared of dogs, just not used to them. We've always been a strictly non-pet family even though I begged for years for a puppy. They're not clean, I was told. Prudence leans against me, her big brown eyes looking soulfully up at me. She leaves a cloud of blonde hair across my knees.

'That one will do anything for food, she's hoping that you've got a stray carrot on you. Come on.'

He gets our cases out of the boot of the car, both of us breathing plumes of steam in the cold morning air. The grass around us is still crisp with frost and I huddle into my long cashmere coat with a sudden shiver, pushing my hands deep into the pockets.

We walk through the unlocked front door – they obviously don't worry about burglars around here – and step onto the well-worn flagstones in the porch. They have that slight polished sheen of age. The house must be several hundred years old but it smells fresh with the scent of beeswax, lavender and pine. In front of us beside a big stone fireplace is a ceiling-height Christmas tree, covered with a hodge-podge of ornaments and decorations. It's nothing like the colour-co-ordinated designer trees that my mother commissions each year. This looks like a bit of a dog's dinner to be honest and the cross-eyed fairy at the top looks drunk. I stare up at her.

'Hideous, isn't she,' says Hudson, rolling his eyes. 'But my mother refuses to throw anything away that we made as children. PP made that when she was seven. It's had pride of place at the top of the tree ever since.'

I spot a few wooden animals dusted in glitter and a robin with an alarming traffic-light-red chest. 'Did you make those?' I ask, remembering him saying he started whittling when he was a child.

'Yes. I'm much better now but like I said, Mum never throws anything away.'

There is a real mix of decorations and the more I look, the more there is to look at. It's a bit of a visual adventure. Completely and utterly tasteless. My mother would be horrified.

'Huds, darling.' A small woman in what looks like a voluminous velvet tent comes darting out and throws her arms around him. She's wearing odd socks, one bright green covered in what looks like llamas and the other an orange football sock. She barely reaches his shoulder but she's clearly his mother, she has the same bright blue eyes and mop of curly hair, although hers is tied back with a piece of garden twine. Then she whirls around and holds out her arms. 'Rebecca, welcome. It's so lovely to meet you.

I've heard absolutely nothing about you. Why is that? This naughty boy has been keeping you to himself.'

As she wraps herself around me, the scents of apple, cinnamon and ginger embrace me. She smells of Christmas. She holds on tight and squeezes me even though we've never met before. I'm not used to such effusive welcomes. I stand stiffly with my arms clamped to my sides and give her a forced smile. She doesn't seem to notice.

'I've been making the gingerbread house today. Do you like gingerbread? We've got bloody tons of the stuff. Honestly, the children insist I make one each year and then they never eat it. You'll have to take some home with you.'

Before I can make any response, she's ushering us, like a border collie on a mission, through a door into a big airy kitchen full of light that streams in through a big lantern roof window. The wooden units are painted pale blue with blonde wood counter tops, and it looks straight out of *Country House Interiors*, except for the clutter. There's stuff everywhere. Pots of utensils, shallow trays of oils and vinegars, a plate full of chutneys, mustards and sauces, and piles of recipe books here, there and everywhere.

A woman jumps up from the island in the middle, which is dominated by a big bowl of fruit. 'Huddy, little bro.' She hurls herself at him, closely followed by a second woman who is sitting on a big squashy sofa beside a wood burner. A third woman folds her arms, leans against the wall and rolls her eyes. 'The prodigal son is back.' Despite her words, there's a ghost of a smile on her face.

'Put him down for God's sake,' booms a loud plummy

voice. 'Hello, son.' Hudson's father pumps his hand like he's trying to extract water.

I stand watching as they all crowd around him, talking and hugging. I might as well be invisible and envy tugs at me as I see how delighted they are to see him and how welcoming they are. Even the third sister has now muscled her way in and he's standing with his arm draped around her shoulders. They're all chattering away, it's like an aviary in here, and I notice they constantly touch each other. It's a world away from what I'm used to and I want to turn tail and run. What am I doing here? This was a terrible idea.

'Everyone, this is Becs.' Hudson shakes everyone loose and draws me into the circle. I'm immediately surrounded.

'Rebecca.' He introduces me to everyone and they're all ultra-friendly. 'You're blonde,' exclaims CC, the youngest, kissing me on either cheek. 'He normally goes for brunettes.'

'And gorgeous,' says DD, turning to Hudson. 'How did someone like you pull her? Punching, bro, punching.'

'Nice to meet you. Hudson says you're a lawyer. Know anything about property disputes?'

'Dad, don't start,' warns Hudson, as the others all chorus, 'Dad, no.'

'He's obsessed,' adds Hudson.

'So would you be if…'

'Hush, Geoffrey,' says Mrs Strong. 'Would you like a cup of tea or something stronger?'

'Champagne,' bellows Geoffrey. 'You look like a champagne kind of girl.'

CC is already removing flutes from one of the cabinets.

It's not even twelve o'clock. It's like being dropped into the circus ring.

I catch sight of something on the side and as they're all faffing with champagne and glasses, laughing and arguing, I take a closer look. It's clearly one of Hudson's mother's fairy castles and it's quite extraordinary. It's about thirty centimetres high, made of pottery covered in a pale blue shimmery glaze and so utterly bonkers that it's fascinating. The amount of delicate detail is astonishing. There are tiny pumpkin windows, growths of toadstools, hidden fairies with gossamer-fine wings. Little eyes peer from under sills and through the tiny doors. The intricacy is astonishing and in spite of myself I'm mesmerised by its whimsical crazy beauty. I decide that although it is completely beyond the bounds of taste, I actually quite like it.

'Do you like it?' asks Hudson's mother, pressing a champagne glass into my hand.

'Mmm, Mrs Strong.' I say a little stunned. 'How long does it take you to make one of these?'

There's a united groan from behind me and I turn to face them. She clasps my hand. 'It's Micky, darling. And I'm afraid I go missing in action when I'm working. This one took me three days. I had to have a lie down when I finished.'

'And she means three days,' says Hudson. 'Seventy-two hours straight. As children we learned to fend for ourselves very early on.'

'Just as well,' retorts Micky. 'Otherwise, you'd have starved.' She pats the ceramic castle with a fond hand.

'Hideous, isn't it, but they put food on the table.' I think she's being self-deprecating in that very British way.

Before I can say anything – thankfully – CC grabs my arm and leads me to the sofa, while Hudson sits at one of the bar stools, next to his other sisters and father. Micky darts around the kitchen, like quicksilver in constant motion. The only signs that she's been ill are the dark shadows beneath her eyes and the lines fanning from her eyes. I sip my champagne as the family catches up, asking about each other's work, friends and other family. They interrupt each other constantly, shout each other down and tease one another. I watch with fascination. It's loud and chaotic. They also seem so happy and relaxed. No one is trying to outdo anyone, they all seem interested in what each of them is doing.

Hudson catches my eye and winks. I smile back at him a little uncertainly as I watch the family dynamic unfold.

Geoffrey is all for opening another bottle of champagne when Hudson suggests that we go upstairs and unpack. As soon as we leave the kitchen, there's a silence.

'Don't start talking about us until we've gone,' calls Hudson.

'Wouldn't dream of it,' CC calls back. 'But she seems nice enough. Better than your usual floozies.'

I wince. I'm not sure that's much of an endorsement and it's a salutary reminder that I am just another one of Hudson's many women.

'Don't worry. You passed the test,' he says.

'What test?'

'The champagne test. You didn't even look at your watch. And you didn't say anything rude about Mum's art.'

'I've never seen anything like it.' I'm so going to buy one for Laura, she'll hate it.

'Bizarrely they go for a bomb. They really do keep the place afloat. When we were kids we had no money. This house is a money pit. I used to do all the repairs, that's how I got to be so handy. Dad is completely useless. Mum is the practical one.'

Upstairs he leads me to a room painted in dark racing green with pale cream wainscoting. It's tasteful and elegant but manages to be very homely too with a big double bed piled with an assortment of cushions, none of which seem to co-ordinate in any way. The throw tossed over the end is deep green silk with sprigs of yellow orchids embroidered on its surface. It's beautiful although rather worn – there are a couple of patches where the silk has shattered and quite an accumulation of dog hair. My mother would have had it replaced immediately. I lay a hand on the soft fabric and stroke its delicate surface.

'It was my grandmother's. She lived in Japan for a while and brought it back with her and gave it to Mum as a wedding present.'

I wonder if it's too precious to be thrown away.

'You okay?' Hudson asks. 'You seem a bit quiet.'

'Fine,' I say. My head is reeling a little after the noisy encounter with the Strong clan. It's difficult to figure out if they like one another or not.

I start to unpack.

'Do you want to toss for the bed again?' he asks levelling another one of those very direct looks at me and I know he's thinking, *Because it didn't really work last time, did it?*

'I'll take the right side.'

'To be on the safe side?' he asks with a sly smile. 'What if I forget which side of the bed I should be on?'

'You won't,' I retort.

'I'm used to sleeping on the right side.'

'You'll have to get unused to it for two nights. I'm sure you can manage that.'

'I'll do my best but don't blame me if I get … what was it, confused?'

'I had jetlag,' I snap, irritated beyond belief by the telling quirk of his lips.

'Mmm,' he says in an airy way as if he doesn't believe a word of it.

'Look, Hudson. Let's make this clear. Sleeping with you is not part of this arrangement. I am not going to sleep with you.' Even though I really want to.

To my surprise, he glares at me. 'I don't recall asking you. To be honest, I'm getting a bit pissed off with this assumption of yours that I've somehow forced you. You're the one that keeps coming on to me.' He holds up his hand, spreading his fingers out.

'That night in the bar,' he ticks off one finger, '"Unbutton me," you said. The first night in New York you made the first move when you got in my side of the bed,' he ticks off another finger, 'and the last night in New York, I seem to recall you dragged me into a cupboard.' His quick smile is

225

sour as he ticks off a third finger. 'Why not just be honest with yourself? We have great sex. Why not enjoy it? We're both consenting adults. Neither of us expects anything from the other. We could just enjoy each other.'

He steps forward, standing in my space, six foot of pissed-off male. My stomach does a loop the loop. Even angry he's gorgeous.

I stare at him. I know he's right. I swallow and snatch up my toilet bag, marching into the ensuite bathroom. I bloody hate being in the wrong.

I throw my toilet bag onto the shelf by the basin and sigh. There's no way I'm going to acknowledge I'm in the wrong. Denial is a sound defence. I'm not lying, just not admitting. Pleased with this decision, I unpack my toiletries, arranging them on the side.

It has one of those old-fashioned club-footed bathtubs and white painted wooden floorboards. It's very French provincial chic with lacy white curtains at sash windows, white towels and green accents of a glass vase, a toothbrush glass and a simple soap dish.

I've always preferred clean lines and contemporary styling but even I have to admit this room has a certain charm. There are bottles of Neom bath foam beside the bath and I stop to take a sniff. A fantasy of sitting breast deep in bubbles with Hudson behind me slides into my head.

I take my frustration out on my toiletries, arranging and rearranging them on the pretty wooden cabinet, trying to banish the image. Not going to happen. This room is far too romantic for my liking. I stalk back into the bedroom, head held high. Hudson is hanging up his clothes and shoots me an unreadable glance but doesn't say anything. I follow his lead and start unpacking the rest of my things. Unlike the room we shared in my mother's house, there is only one wardrobe and it feels odd putting my clothes in with his. Using different wardrobes made things feel more compartmentalised. Nice and separate. This feels as if we're being squeezed together and I really don't like it. Or is it because there's a worry that I might get used to it and it might become normalised? That's how things become norms. They slip under your guard and, before you know it, they're entrenched.

'Do you fancy a walk before lunch? We could take the dogs out,' suggests Hudson, his voice calm with no sign of that earlier flare of anger. I'm not going to say sorry but I nod and say equally, 'That sounds like a good idea,' before I've thought it through. It's a terrible idea. I don't have dog-walking clothes with me.

'You'll probably want to put some jeans on and some different shoes.'

I grimace. 'I didn't bring any jeans with me and please, do I look like a girl who owns walking shoes?'

He laughs, his usual good humour restored. 'No, Becs, you don't but we've got tons of wellies, there'll be a pair that fits and you can borrow a coat from someone.'

## Chapter Twenty

The cold has seeped into my bones, my feet are freezing and my nose is bright red but I'm not alone; Hudson is looking equally rosy-cheeked as we troop into the boot-room, the dogs charging ahead as we disrobe, removing our hats, scarves and gloves. We leave a rainbow puddle of wool behind.

'There you are,' cries Micky, peering through the door from the kitchen. 'Into the lounge with you. There's a nice fire. Hot toddies all round.'

I follow Hudson into a large sitting room dotted with various sofas. Logs are burning merrily in the large grate in the fireplace, giving off a lovely cosy warmth. Geoff is in there already, half hidden behind *The Times*. He acknowledges us with a brief nod and disappears behind the paper again. I feel I ought to sit next to Hudson but it's not like my mother's house where everyone perches politely on the edge of the sofa and makes small talk. PP is on one of the sofas sprawling full length, her shoes kicked off and abandoned on the floor beside her. DD has taken another sofa, having shoved off its cushions to make herself comfortable, while CC has arranged herself on the discarded cushions by the fire. There's one last two-seater sofa, a slightly shabby affair that I can see, in its heyday, would have been upholstered in a beautiful pale blue damask.

Hudson shakes his head. 'Dad, you were supposed to get rid of this. I fixed it as best I could last time I was here but there's only so much I can do.'

'You know your mother hates throwing things away,' replies Geoff from behind his newspaper. 'There's still some life in it.'

'This thing died before the start of the twenty-first century.'

He heads towards the sofa and puts one hand out to stop me sitting down straightaway. 'Careful.'

He grabs a throw from the back and puts it down over the threadbare fabric. There's a dull gleam of a spring at one end and he sticks a cushion over that.

He sits down and pats the space next to him. 'I think we'll be safe enough. Just don't make any sudden movements, the whole thing could collapse. If I don't take it to the tip, it will still be here next time I come home.'

I gingerly sit down. The sofa holds although there's an ominous creak from beneath me. Hudson swivels round, stretching out his legs onto my lap. I lean back into the lumpy cushions, feeling the weight and warmth of his limbs on mine. It feels oddly comforting and no one bats an eyelid at what I consider a very public display of affection.

Micky bustles in with a tray of whisky glasses and plonks it on the table. 'Help yourselves,' she says, before plucking the newspaper from her husband's fingers, handing him a drink and draping herself across his lap.

'Ma, the sofa?'

'Yes, dear, don't fuss. It's fine.'

He rolls his eyes and leans carefully out of the sofa to scoop up a drink and hand it to me, before snagging his own.

'Cheers,' he says. 'Merry Christmas.'

In a sudden flurry everyone grabs a drink and there's a chorus of 'Merry Christmas'. I wait for stilted conversation to begin but no one says anything. They all seem quite happy with their own thoughts. It's all so laid-back and easy. No one is standing on ceremony and they don't feel they have to act any differently because I'm a guest. I've never stayed anywhere like it before. I take a cautious sip of my drink and just about manage not to choke. It's a proper hot toddy: whisky, more whisky and a dash of lemon and honey. My second drink of the day and it's not even six o'clock yet. As the warming liquid slides down, I relax. It's rather nice not having to talk, to just be. There's an overriding sense of contentment in the room. They're all so comfortable with each other. No pressing need to make inconsequential conversation. It's refreshing. Hudson has closed his eyes, one hand limply resting on my arm. I study his face. Peppercorn pin-pricks of bristle dust his jaw, his lashes sweep the top of his cheek and his lips are slightly parted. I'm familiar with the little scar just above one eyebrow, the chicken pox scar on one cheek and the mole just below his lower lip. I feel proprietorial towards each feature, as if they are mine alone to touch, to stroke, to smooth across.

A movement across the room catches my eye and I turn to look. DD is studying me, her expression watchful and assessing. I give her a tentative smile. What's she thinking? Can she see that I'm infatuated with her brother? Has she seen it all before? I suspect the answer is yes. I close my eyes, partly to avoid looking at Hudson and partly because it's so lovely and snug in here. It's the most chilled I've been for a long time. I'm dopey and relaxed.

When I wake, I'm nestled against Hudson on the two-seater sofa. Fuck. How did that happen? I must have slipped down in my sleep and his legs are still across me but I've twisted so they're over my hip now and I'm between him and the sofa back, my head just beneath his chin. His arm is around me. Tucked up against him, it's warm and wonderful. I lie there relishing the thump of his heart. All my senses are like horses in a starting gate. I can hear his breathing, feel its rise and fall and its heat brushing the top of my head. I don't want to move, even though I really should. I inhale the smell of him, so familiar, so Hudson. It's that slight touch of lemon, along with the woody scent that he always carries. His hand is lightly stroking my back. I want to unfurl against him, stretching out, length to length. Being this close is torture. I move very slightly, getting the kink out of my neck, and his hand slips under my jumper, his fingers gently skimming over my skin, almost absently. He's so tactile I'm not sure he can help himself.

Everyone else in the room is dozing, while CC is absorbed in a book. No one is paying us any attention but even so I feel I ought to move. I really ought to move but it's so nice just lying. Oh God, is this cuddling? I freeze. I'm not a cuddler.

'Shh,' murmurs Hudson, 'Relax. You're on holiday. Let yourself chill.' His fingers have slipped to the small of my back and are lightly massaging the muscles there. I force myself to sit up, moving away from him. This is getting too cosy. Too normal. Too familiar.

Outside the light is fading and Micky springs to her feet and starts switching on the lamps around the room. Like animals emerging from hibernation, everyone uncurls and straightens and we all blink blearily at each other. I smile, more at myself than anyone else, trying to imagine my mother in this situation. She and my sister would be so uncomfortable. As a family, have we ever been this comfortable together? Or allowed ourselves to be this natural? I can't recall a time like this ever. When we were children, Laura would have been jockeying for position, wanting to be centre of attention. She was a restless, needy child.

A flash of understanding blossoms, with white-hot clarity. No. I want to deny it because it shatters too many deeply held convictions. My mother had been trying to tell me something at Thanksgiving. I glance over at Geoff – he seems to be equally casually affectionate to all of his offspring. There's no sense that any one of them is better or more important than the others. I feel slightly sick in hindsight. Poor Laura. It was my dad's attention she was desperate for.

Suddenly I could see it so clearly. Nothing she'd done had been good enough for our father. He was a hard taskmaster. He wouldn't have approved of Hudson – he's not a professional. Father expected me to marry well, a banker, a lawyer, someone well connected in the city. But I'm sure he would have wanted me to be happy.

I stiffen.

'What's the matter?' asks Hudson.

Hudson makes me happy even though I fight against it all the time. Why shouldn't I be happy – just for the holidays?

'Right, I must go and perform in the kitchen,' says Geoff, standing up. 'I need my favourite child to assist and be sous chef.'

All three sisters roll their eyes and Hudson laughs.

'No takers?' Geoff pulls a mournful face.

'Dad, you don't need any help,' says CC. 'We only get in the way.'

'You just want someone to pour your wine.' Micky winks at me across the room.

'Of course, my darling.'

'I hope you aren't expecting anything too fancy this evening,' says Micky, her face suddenly anxious. 'You did warn her, didn't you, Hudson?'

'Mmm,' he says, airily and I look at him. Warn me about what?

'Thank goodness. I must go and lay the table for tomorrow. DD, you can help me. PP, go and help your dad. CC, can you switch on the tree and sort out wine glasses?'

'What about Hudson?' asks CC immediately looking sulky.

'I'm looking after my guest,' he says with a smug expression.

'Is there anything I can do to help?' I ask.

'No, dear,' says Geoff, and cuffs CC's ear as he walks past. 'C'mon you, child. Come get your poor old pa a drink.'

Within seconds the room is empty and I ought to disentangle myself from Hudson but fuck it, I'm fed up with fighting it. I deserve to have some happiness. He's right, we do have great sex. He makes me feel great. I seem to have spent most of my life living within self-enforced parameters. Being the perfect daughter, the perfect employee. Being Rebecca Madison. For the next two days I could just be Becs.

He stands and stretches. His perennial Henley T-shirt rises to reveal his flat stomach. My breath hitches. I want him. The sharp stab of desire dries my mouth. I stare at him.

He looks down and his voice is husky as he says, 'Rebecca,' and holds out his hands. I'm so relaxed, I put mine in his and he pulls me up. Chest to chest we face each other and he lowers his mouth. I return the kiss as soon as his lips skim mine. Magnets north and south. I can't stay away from him. Can't resist him, especially not when he says my name like that.

I pull him closer to me, a touch of desperation. I don't

want this kiss to finish. Every time I've convinced myself this would be the last time I haven't been able to stop myself. His hands are delving in my hair, loosening my ponytail, his fingers trailing over my ears. My breasts are pressed up against the hard muscles of his chest, his thighs against me, and I want to press closer still.

'Get a room, will you.' We pull apart, a little breathless. CC is grinning from ear to ear, holding out two glasses of prosecco. 'I brought you a drink. Want me to chuck it over you? Cool you down.'

'No,' growls Hudson, frustration vibrating in his voice. I know how he feels. I blush bright scarlet as if I were fifteen again. I do not make out on other people's sofas in other people's homes. Why is it, around Hudson, I lose my composure and all sense of sophistication?

'I'll just go to the loo,' I mutter and scoot out of the room, grateful that CC seems amused rather than anything else. As I pass the kitchen I can hear the radio and Geoff and PP are singing away to 'Last Christmas'. Peeping through the door, I see him with his arm around his daughter, hamming it up. Both of them are laughing. This house is so openly full of honest emotion. I feel like a girl looking in through a window into a world I don't know.

I stare at my flushed cheeks in the mirror. My make-up has worn off, I've got faint smudges of mascara under my eyes, which look smoky rather than tarty, and my eyes are bright. I actually look okay. Happy.

Taking my time I wash my hands, a little entranced by my own reflection. Is this what Hudson sees when he looks at me? It's an enticing thought. There's definite chemistry between us. I can't deny that. But does he feel anything for me? I want him to like me. I want him to more than like me. I catch my lip in my teeth as the realisation strikes, like a icicle stabbing into my heart. Like all the other women, he's completely charmed me. I've only gone and fallen for Hudson.

## Chapter Twenty-One

We congregate in the kitchen; apparently the dining table is now reserved for Christmas lunch. Micky is sitting down directing her daughters as to how the table should be laid and I notice she looks a little pale.

Everyone is talking in bright voices, obviously trying to ignore the fact that she's flagging. She's been so bright and effervescent all day it's easy to forget that she's been so ill.

I feel the pain of their unspoken fear. When Dad was ill I tried so hard to put on a brave face in front of him even though it must have been obvious that's what I was doing.

As if sensing my unease, Hudson slips his hand into mine, reassuring me. I squeeze it back. His leg is pressed up against mine – or is it mine against his? Both of us wanting to get closer to the other. I wonder if anyone else in the room is aware of the soupy sexual tension between us. It's almost as if we need to reaffirm life. I'm clenching my fists to stop myself running a hand along his lean, muscular thigh. The urge to touch him is so strong it's almost frightening. I can feel him watching me and I look up; his eyes have darkened and his gaze drops to my mouth. My breath hitches and, more by instinct than anything else, I lick my lips. His thumb insinuates its way under my palm to graze the soft skin in the centre. The soft, insistent stroke ignites a low, persistent ache between my thighs. I can feel the tight spiral of want coiling inside me. I swallow hard and have an insane desire to laugh. Despite the formality of my mother's party, no one had noticed me dragging Hudson off to a cupboard. There's no chance of that here. Although everyone is busy chatting, I'm aware of the careful, wary scrutiny of Micky and the three girls, even if they seem oblivious to the low simmer between us.

Micky seems to have a second wind and opens another bottle of champagne and Geoff places a large plate on the table.

'Dinner is served,' he announces rather grandly.

The plate is full of thick-cut white-bread sandwiches and everyone leans forward to grab one.

'Dad,' groans CC. 'You've forgotten the tartare sauce.'

'No, I haven't. I didn't want any.'

Immediately good-natured bickering breaks out over the benefits of tomato sauce over tartare sauce. Warily I pick up a sandwich and lift the bread.

'What do you say, Rebecca?' asks DD and everyone goes quiet and looks intently at me. 'Tartare or tomato sauce.'

The way they're all staring at me, you'd think it was a life or death issue.

'Neither,' I say.

'What?' Geoff looks horror-struck.

I grin because I've got this. When I was at university fish finger sandwiches were my staple diet. 'Malt vinegar every time.'

There's a collective 'Ah.'

'Never thought of that,' says CC. She sounds impressed.

Hudson nudges me in the ribs and I realise I've just passed another test as well as dodged a bullet. 'Nice work, Becs,' he murmurs, in such a sultry tone I swear my knicker elastic has just started to smoulder.

We munch through the mound of sandwiches and it's the most stress-free Christmas Eve I've ever enjoyed. No one is fretting about food tomorrow or timings until CC jumps up.

'Has anyone got any wrapping paper I can borrow?'

'CC, you do this every year.'

'There's some in the bottom drawer of the bureau in the dining room, dear,' says Micky. 'There are spare tags in there too.'

'See you later, losers.' CC departs with a vague wave of her hand.

'Are you coming to Midnight Mass?' asks PP.

'Not bloody likely,' says CC. 'I'm off down the pub.'

'It will be rammed,' says DD, pulling a face.

'Excellent, lots of people to scrounge free drinks from.'

'I might come with you,' says Geoff, rising to his feet.

'Is no one going to the church?' asks Micky in a plaintive voice. 'What about you, Rebecca?'

I've been trained to be a good guest, to submit to the hostess's requests, but Hudson's hand tightens over mine.

'Becs has had a busy week. And we had an early start,' he says.

'You just want a guilt-free Christmas shag,' says PP, absolutely nailing it. 'Going to mass'll put the kibosh on that. Standing in a chilly church for an hour and a half isn't conducive to a festive shagathon. Your balls will shrivel up.'

Geoff shudders and his wife pokes him in the ribs with an elbow. 'Catherine Strong. Don't be so vulgar,' says Micky.

PP and DD just grin at her and I feel a blush rising up my cheeks.

Hudson turns to me, shaking his head. 'Every year Mum suggests going to Midnight Mass. She thinks it's the proper thing to do at Christmas.'

'It is,' protests Micky. 'But you're all Philistines.'

'I think they probably did go to church, didn't they?' says Geoff.

'Whatever.' Micky shakes her head as the rest of the family laugh.

'How about we go to the carol concert on the green?' suggests DD, putting a consoling arm around her mother, who immediately perks up.

'Now that's an excellent idea.'

It sounds hideous to me. Voluntarily standing outside in the middle of winter for a couple of hours. No thank you.

'We'd better get a move on, then,' says Hudson looking at his chunky watch.

Somehow, the decision is made and we're scattering to all four corners of the house to get ready to leave in five minutes. My head is spinning. This is spontaneity pushed to the limit.

'You going to be warm enough?' asks Hudson, eying my red coat. I hadn't planned for protracted outdoor periods.

'I haven't brought anything else.' I pride myself on my capsule wardrobe packing and I hate admitting that I'm not prepared. This is not Rebecca Madison territory. I'm like a boy scout – I'm always prepared. I didn't envision any of this. I thought it would be a civilised Christmas spent indoors eating and drinking like most normal families.

Hudson disappears and comes back with a large quilted down anorak which has seen better days. 'This'll keep you warm.'

He seriously expects me to wear that.

'Becs.' He raises an eyebrow at my not-as-well-hidden-as-I-thought disdain. 'You would look gorgeous in a paper bag.' The compliment floors me and I have no comeback. There's a warm glow in my chest that seeps up my throat. All I can do is stare at him. People, men, don't say that sort of thing to me. I suppose I've been working so hard to fit into the masculine world. I dress to look female, but there's a distinct look-but-don't-touch veneer. Buttoned up, I guess you'd say.

He steps forward and touches my face. 'You do know that, right.' With his other hand, he pulls a strand of my hair which, okay, I admit, I left curly today, and wraps it around one finger. I swallow and look up at the strange intensity on his face and the half smile on his lips. Awareness buzzes through me but also more. For some bizarre reason I want to cry. It's as if he's the first person that's ever really looked at me or seen me. The me that I keep tucked away. I've never been gorgeous to anyone before.

There's a loud rap on the bedroom door and CC pokes her head around the door. 'Come on you two, there's time for hot, sweaty sex later.'

Hudson shakes his head. 'Sorry about her. We've tried to lose her several times, but she always finds her way back.'

'I heard that,' calls CC from outside the door.

He does the zip of the coat up for me and kisses me on the nose. I sigh and look up at him.

'Don't look at me like that,' he says cupping my cheek. 'The sooner we get out of here, the sooner we can get back.'

We both give the bed one last look as we hear Geoff bellowing downstairs that everyone needs to get a move on.

## Chapter Twenty-Two

The carol concert is actually a lot of fun, although I'm separated from Hudson from the off, but I don't mind. His sisters and mothers treat me like one of their own and never miss the opportunity to take the piss out of Hudson. I enjoy their irreverence; it's as if I've been in a corset for a long time and someone has loosened the stays and I'm allowed to breathe again, to press my lungs out to my ribs. The extra breath brings a sense of light-headedness and silliness as if I've been breathing in helium.

'When are you going to Hudson's exhibition?' asks DD. 'We could meet up for cocktails afterwards. I haven't been out on the lash in London in ages.'

'I'm not sure yet,' I say, surprised by the sharp dig of disappointment that in all likelihood I won't ever meet her for cocktails or get lashed with them. I have no plans to go to Hudson's exhibition. Although I'm starting to wonder why not. I could go and take a look, see what all the fuss is about. He's not going to be there all the time, is he?

'We need to fix a date, then,' says PP.

'Where do you live?' demands CC. 'I bet it's nicer than Huddy's place. We could crash at yours.'

I imagine the chaos she'd bring with her to my pristine flat. 'You're more than welcome,' I say and I mean it. I'm proud of my beautiful apartment with its wonderful views across the Thames. It would be nice to show it off to someone for a change.

'Excellent. We should make a weekend of it,' says CC. 'I haven't been shopping. There isn't a Primark round here for miles.'

'You can't shop at Primark,' says PP and delivers a brief lecture on throwaway fashion to which CC responds by sticking her fingers in her ears and singing 'Good King Wenceslas'.

'You're such a child. I bet Becca wouldn't be seen dead in Primark. I love your red coat, where did you get it from?'

'Watch out, she'll be asking if she can borrow it,' warns DD and then prods her sister. 'I'm first in line.'

'Do you know,' says Micky, linking her arm through mine, 'I often think I should have stopped at one.'

'Ma,' complains CC. 'Then you wouldn't have had me. The others were just practice, to reach perfection.'

I smile as I listen to their banter. Despite their words, it's obvious they all absolutely adore one another.

There's quite a crowd gathered on the green around a Christmas tree decorated with plain white lights. On one side there's a lorry trailer and a brass band on the truck bed and on the other the church, its stained-glass windows lit from within. Volunteers in hi-vis vests are handing out song sheets and rattling buckets of coins for donations as they pass through.

Hudson comes to stand next to me. A headtorch has appeared on his forehead. And I laugh at him. 'You look a right dork.'

'You won't be saying that when you,' he lowers his voice, 'want to read my song sheet.'

I spit out another laugh. How does he manage to make *read my song sheet* sound like an innuendo?

'I think your song sheet's quite safe.'

'Shame,' he murmurs against my cheek. I start to giggle. Me, giggling. I am so not a giggler but tonight I feel light-hearted, free and happy. There's no expectation on me to behave in a certain way or be anyone or anything but myself.

'Are you ticklish?' he asks suddenly.

I raise an imperious eyebrow although I'm smiling. 'Like I'd tell you.'

'Hmm, I shall have to find out then, won't I?' His smile is positively wolfish and my heart does a funny ping in my chest.

'I'll look forward to it.'

We're halfway through the first carol when I look up and find him watching me.

His eyes gleam in the dark and we share another one of those long looks that turn my insides soft and dampen my knickers. From nowhere a desire to push his hand down my trousers to alleviate the almost painful throb of need rears up with frightening intensity. I want him with an urgency that takes my breath away.

CASSIE CONNOR

He grabs my hand and tugs me backwards out of the sight line of his family. Tugging harder, he leads me back across the green and pulls me into the porch of the church.

He kisses me. A hungry, needy kiss. I feel as if he wants to devour me – or is that because I want to devour him? His hot mouth glides over mine and my knees threaten to go. I want more of this. So much more. He pulls away, resting a tight hand on my shoulder as if he's trying to regain his balance.

'Fuck, it's been too long, Becs,' he says. 'I haven't been able to stop thinking about New York. I want you so badly.'

The words light me up inside like the Eiffel Tower. Having that power over him, him wanting me so badly.

'Why don't you then?' I ask because how can I not. He is so fucking hot and I want him inside me right now.

He grabs my hand, saying quickly, 'Look pale and sad. Sick,' and marches over to where Micky and Geoff are standing. 'Becs has got a migraine, I'm going to take her home.'

'Oh sweetheart,' says Micky. 'I'm sorry. They are such horrid things. Yes, you get yourself to bed and hopefully you'll be right for the morning.'

Behind her the three sisters pull faces of strident disbelief, they know exactly what he's up to. What we're up to.

'Feel better soon,' says CC with a quick snigger. 'Yes, get yourself to *bed*,' adds DD.

'I'm sure Hudson will make you feel better.' PP's grin stretches her face from ear to ear.

Hudson pays no attention as we walk away, our pace so

fast that by the time we've left the lights, we've fallen into a half run, half stumble.

'They all know.'

'So,' replies Hudson. 'Do you care? If it weren't so bloody cold, I'd have you on the floor right here and now.' The rasp in his voice does absolutely fuck all for my control.

It's a relief when the lights of the house loom up. Hudson jams his key into the lock and yanks me through the door. From the other side of the house, a chorus of joyful they're-home barking breaks out. He stops in the doorway and kisses me as I fight to unzip his coat. I need to feel his skin. We begin to undress each other, breathless and impatient, grabbing kisses where we can. It's as if we can't bear to break contact but at the same time we can't co-ordinate. I'm trying to unwind that bloody scarf, while he's tugging at the zip of my jacket. It's an unruly mess and neither of us cares as, entwined, he backs me up towards the stairs.

'If I don't get you upstairs, I'm going to take you right here and I'd hate for my family to get an eyeful of my arse when they come home.' His voice is low and hoarse with need.

I give him a slow smile. I have all the power and I love it.

'Better come upstairs with me, then,' I say, taking his hand and leading him upstairs.

As soon as we're through the bedroom door, we're both peeling our clothes off. There's no finesse, no seduction – we just want rid of the barriers. I want to feel his warm body pressed up against mine. I pull my sweater over my head as he takes off his top. He's bare-chested and my mouth dries as I look at his smooth, muscular torso. He's bloody gorgeous. Our eyes meet and he leans forward and pushes a hand into my bra, freeing one breast. Without a word he drops his head and his mouth closes over my nipple. It's exquisite – that intense burn of desire as his tongue swirls around my sensitive skin. 'Hudson,' I say as I pant out an agitated breath. His hands are in my waistband and in seconds he's pushing both my trousers and pants down while I'm unzipping his jeans. We're in danger of falling over in one of those romcom sex moments. With feverish fingers, which, to be honest, are hopelessly amateur, I'm trying to push his jeans down. Our seesawing movements end as I topple backwards onto the bed and he lands on me, his hands immediately fisting into my hair, kissing me with open-mouthed kisses. The feel of his warm skin on mine is heaven and I squirm beneath him. Somehow we manage to get our trousers off.

'Stop,' I say, panting.

'What?' He has a bleary, lost look on his face, the disappointment so sharp I can almost taste it. Disappointed Hudson is so cute.

I laugh, a breathless hoarse sound. 'Socks,' I say and scramble to a sitting position to remove mine. With a disgruntled pout he throws himself back on the bed. 'Jesus, woman.'

'I can't have sex when we're wearing socks,' I say. 'It's unsexy.'

He bends one leg, lying back his arms above his head,

his cock standing to attention, eager and urgent. 'You think this is unsexy.'

I swallow. Fuck no. I want him inside me. I straddle him. Socks forgotten, I rise above him. His hands reach up to my breasts and I watch his eyes as I lower myself onto him. I'm already anticipating the feeling of fullness and it turns me on even more. I'm wet and slick as I take him inside me, allowing myself just an inch. I stop and I look down at him. My eyes meeting his.

'Yes, Becs,' he pleads. His eyes are almost glassy as they beg me to carry on. I slide another inch, just holding gently squeezing my muscles around him. He's panting slightly and it's such a turn on. Half of me wants to sink down, down and clench him tight into me while a new me feels confident enough to want to tease and torture, myself as much as him. I'm taking control back. I slide up out of reach and he slides his hands from my waist to my arms. 'Ah, ah!' I give him a sinful smile and push his hands over his head. 'No touching.'

His eyes widen. It's the first time I've taken charge in the bedroom with him and it thrills me. I slide down again and he lifts his hips. I stop and shake my head, my hair tumbling down across my breasts. 'You have to stay still.'

His eyebrows quirk with amusement but he gives me a tiny nod. I lower myself again, watching his face. I can see the tension and the pleasure in his eyes, hear the tiny hoarse gasps as I slide slowly, slowly down.

His jawline is tight as I move, taking my time and eking out my own pleasure.

'You're killing me, Becs.'

'That's the plan.' I lean forward and gently roll one of his nipples between my fingers, rocking his cock inside me. It feels so good. Soo good. Too good. I stop. It's too intense, the build-up. I think I'm going to explode. Hudson groans my name and moves his hips again. Pleasure is building, for both of us. I hold on, savouring the spiralling heat but it's no good, I need more. I begin to ride him, setting the pace. He grips my hips. 'Becs. Fuck. Yes. Yes. Oh God, yes.' It's a delicious chorus that drives me on, faster. I grind down hard on him, the fullness of him filling me to the core. And then there it is, I fly. I cry out, lost in the pleasure that consumes me. Hudson is watching me through half-lidded eyes as the orgasm rolls up and through me. Then Hudson closes his eyes, his face half agony, half ecstasy. I feel him pulsing as his hips drive upwards. 'Becs.' He comes with a groan which is both guttural and heart-felt and it throbs through me.

I collapse on top of him, aftershocks of pleasure exploding through me. We're both breathing heavily.

'Jeez.' Hudson strokes the hair from my shoulder, an arm loosely wrapped around my waist. His body beneath mine is warm, hard muscle and I revel in the skin-to-skin touch. 'You should come with a health warning. I think you might have killed me.'

I nip his shoulder. 'Stop being such a wuss.'

He laughs, his arm tightening to give me a squeeze before he pulls the duvet up and tucks it around me and then he places a kiss on my temple. For some weird reason, the gentle touch makes me well up and there's a strange blooming sensation in my chest, like there's a balloon expanding inside my ribcage.

Gradually my body settles, the fireworks dimming to a low contented buzz, our contours accommodating and aligning to each other. Contentment. Happiness. Security. I feel safe here as peace steals over me, softening the usual tension that's caught in the tendons of my neck, the knotted muscles in my shoulder and the stiffness I carry in my back.

We're lying in the dark, the moon shining through the open curtains at the window. The flakes of snow have thickened and they dance and swirl outside in the night sky. Hudson is absently playing with my hair.

'Christmas Eve,' he murmurs. 'Didn't expect to be doing this. My family like you, though.'

'Is that a surprise?'

'I was worried you'd be all Rebecca Madison with them.'

'I am Rebecca Madison.' Even as I say it, I'm half-hearted because I'm not that woman at all.

'Snooty you.' He strokes the side of my mouth as if to lessen the insult. 'You know what I mean.'

And I do – somehow, I've become Becs. 'They're…' They're not what I was expecting at all, but instead I say, 'They're great.' I don't want to be too fulsome in my praise. 'I like that they don't let you get away with anything.'

Actually, it's a whole lot more than that. It's kind of rocked my foundations a little. These women like each other. Genuinely like and support each other. And what's more they've gathered me into their circle, just because I'm Hudson's friend. No other reason. They've included me, accepted me without reservation. My mother and sister would be primed, like beady-eyed hawks, ready to swoop and make judgements on anything from someone's clothes, manners, looks, values, job or background. They're not picky in their prejudices.

'I really like them,' I add a little belatedly.

'Of course you do.' There's a touch of long suffering in his voice. 'They give me such a hard time.'

I laugh at the pout on his lips and lean up to kiss it away. 'You're so hard done by.' I'm teasing him. Me teasing Hudson Strong. There's a little flip of happiness low in my belly.

His hands slide down my back, smoothing over my butt cheeks. 'You'll have to make it up to me.'

'How do you suggest I do that?' My voice is flirty and throaty as I gaze at him. He shifts beneath me and I can feel him growing hard again.

'I'm sure you'll think of something,' he says.

## Chapter Twenty-Three

'Someone saw Christmas in with a bang, then,' says CC, as Hudson and I walk into the kitchen the next morning.

'Merry Christmas to you, too,' says Hudson. 'You're just jealous.'

'Tell me about it,' she says, with a mournful sigh from her perch on top of one of the kitchen counters, where she's sitting swinging her legs. She's wearing a pink unicorn onesie which is completely at odds with her next statement: 'I think my little vag might have dried up.'

'Too much information,' says Micky, holding her hands up above her head, waving a very sharp knife. This morning she looks a lot brighter.

With the exception of me and Hudson, everyone else is still in their dressing gowns and pyjamas.

'Happy Christmas, darling.' She kisses Hudson on the cheek before turning to me, her bright eyes studying my face. 'Happy Christmas, Becca. How's your head this morning?'

'It's fine,' I say before realising she's not talking hangovers. I'd completely forgotten about my convenient migraine the previous evening. Several pairs of eyes give me knowing looks as Micky says, 'That's such good news, there's nothing more miserable than a migraine, especially on Christmas Day.'

Over in the corner of the kitchen, Geoff, wearing a silk paisley robe from which a pair of very skinny hairy legs protrude, is peeling a mountain of potatoes, while PP is scrubbing parsnips. Micky goes back to expertly slicing smoked salmon with the lethal-looking knife, while issuing orders. 'Hudson, would you take the cream cheese out of the fridge and put it on the table? DD, could you chop some lemons? Becca, would you mind getting knives out of there.' She nods over to the row of kitchen units and drawers. I like that I'm expected to pitch in – none of that stiff sitting and standing around like a spare part of my mother's. It occurs to me that I always feel like a guest at my mother's home, rather than part of the family.

We sit at the scrubbed pine table and tuck into a breakfast buffet. There's smoked salmon, cream cheese and bagels, bacon butties with wholegrain mustard, sausage baps oozing with tomato sauce, a pile of hash browns surrounded by onion rings, waffles and maple syrup as well as a very small plate of black pudding. I'm perplexed by the eclectic collection of breakfast. Micky, seeing my quick frown, pats the back of my hand and leaves her warm fingers resting across mine. 'Everyone is allowed to have their favourite breakfast on Christmas Day. Hudson said your favourite is cream cheese and smoked salmon with bagels.'

I raise an eyebrow. Hudson made that up.

'It's one of my favourites, too.' She continues, smiling happily as if this fact alone makes us kindred spirits, and gives my hand a quick squeeze. She's really rather lovely. I want to hug her, even if my favourite breakfast is smashed avocado on sourdough with a squeeze of lemon.

A man appears at the back door and DD leaps up from the table and launches herself at him. It turns out that this is her husband, who stayed at home last night because he had the horses to feed this morning and then had to ride out with the lads. (As in stable lads, I realise after a few seconds of wondering why you'd go out with your drinking buddies on Christmas morning.)

'Missed you,' he grumbles into her hair as they melt into each other's arms. I watch as her arms tighten around him and she burrows into his chest. I turn away, unused to this honest, open affection, and ignore the quick stab of envy.

'Come and have a seat, Jonty,' calls Micky and shuffles along the bench to make room for him. 'I made extra onion rings—'

'Made. You got them out of the freezer,' pipes up CC, snatching one up. 'But they're pretty good for frozen.'

'Save one for Jonty, CC. Oh, this is Hudson's girlfriend, Becca.'

'Hi,' he says and lifts a large hand. He's really tall and

lanky and I wonder how he sits on the back of a racehorse. Aren't jockeys tiny?

I smile at him. He's not especially good looking but he has a kind face and there's a soft warmth in his spaniel-brown eyes but when he smiles back, his whole face lights up and I watch DD's face soften as she looks up at him. Love shines from every feature. He sits down next to her and although neither of them speaks to the other – there isn't the space within the conversation as everyone around them begins to talk – you can tell that they're a couple. There's a togetherness about them, a comfortable ease, and when they turn their heads slightly to look at each other, it's obvious there's a silent conversation going on there. Their interaction is so brief and yet, somehow, I can tell they are completely in sync.

'Sickening, isn't it?' Hudson whispers in my ear.

I roll my eyes at him. 'I think it's a grown-up relationship. Not something you'd know anything about.' It's supposed to come out teasing but it comes out slightly snarky and I instantly feel ashamed. I know Hudson's had lots of girlfriends, he's never claimed otherwise, but it's wrong of me to make an issue of it. After all, that's why I offered him the original contract – he's a safe bet. Or rather he was supposed to be.

After breakfast we move through to the lounge where overnight a pile of gifts has appeared. I've added my little collection which stand out jewel-bright in their perfection. Some of the presents are wrapped in newspaper, stamped with very rudimentary Rudolphs and tied up with green garden twine. Others are wrapped in birthday wrapping paper and others in battered gift bags which have clearly been used a time or two.

'Bagsy be Christmas Elf,' crows CC and pulls a green hat with large ears on either side onto her head and immediately dives under the tree to retrieve a large gift bag. 'This is for Mum and Dad, from me. Open it now.' She's jiggling with excitement as together they open the large bag. They take out two large pieces of metal and she jumps up to put them together. 'It's a sculpture for the garden.'

It's one of those finely balanced pieces of garden art that will move in the wind. It's clever and beautiful.

'Do you like it?' asks CC, her hands clasped in front of her. Her excitement is palpable as is her desire to please.

'Oh darling.' Micky sniffs and throws her arms around her daughter. 'It's beautiful. You're so talented.'

CC sits back on her heels. 'I was rather pleased with it, especially as it's a prototype. I might have to borrow it to show the garden centre, I want to sell them to them.'

I stare. 'You made it.'

'CC is broke. She always makes her presents,' teases Hudson.

'The materials cost me,' protests CC.

'Or me,' mutters Geoff but he's smiling. He genuinely doesn't seem to mind that his daughter is still struggling to make a living.

'It's just a loan, Daddy. You know I'll pay you back.'

'He's just teasing, darling,' says Micky.

Micky hands out the newspaper-wrapped presents. 'I'm

saving the planet,' she says as DD examines one of the reindeers.

'I'm just trying to figure out if this is a six-legged dog with a red ball on its head or a mythical beast with an angry bollock,' DD says with a laugh and everyone joins in. All of Micky's presents are handmade pottery and they're all beautiful including my very own fairy castle. It's glazed in soft pale colours, pinks, blues and greens, and dotted with delicate dragonflies and hidden fairies visible only from tiny eyes peeking out of windows. I've never owned anything so whimsical and impractical and I love it.

I'm spoiled by these lovely people I barely know. PP has given me a hardback notebook, across which is written the words, 'My lists of things I was right about.' It's so me. Geoff has given me a string of carved wooden robins to go on my Christmas tree. DD and her husband have given me a set of personalised Post-it notes in varying sizes which read, 'Rebecca's Word is Law!'

The pile of presents has diminished and I'm nervous now. Hudson picks up the package I've wrapped for him. What seemed like a jokey idea now seems a bit presumptuous. I didn't want to get anything too impersonal – that's my pride – but then again I didn't want to get him anything too personal – so I went for an in-joke which now seems ridiculous.

Before he opens mine, he hands me a small parcel and I'm relieved to see that it is small and slightly squidgy. There's nothing more embarrassing than someone going to town on a present when you haven't. Sometimes the-thought-that-counts is just bollocks.

We open them at the same time; thankfully no one else is watching us, they're all involved in their own unwrapping. From the birthday paper – yes, it was Hudson who hadn't got around to buying any Christmas paper – I pull a red beanie hat. It's made from the softest cashmere and it's exactly the same shade as my coat.

He gives me that lopsided smile, which I know means he's slightly uncertain. 'Thought it was about time you had your own hat.' I nod. Oh God, this is embarrassing. I think I'm going to cry. It's so thoughtful and so understated but so perfect.

When he finally pulls the little book from my carefully wrapped froth of ribbon, he bursts into laughter.

'What?' asks CC, snatching it from him. *'The Care and Feeding of Hamsters.'* Her frown is confused. 'Are you two getting a hamster?'

Hudson is still laughing, holding his stomach. 'It's … it's a private joke.'

She gives the pair of us a suspicious look and shakes her head. 'I'll never understand couples. Remind me never to get a boyfriend. It's bad enough having a brother.'

# Chapter Twenty-Four

I t's probably the nicest Christmas Day I've had in years. It's wonderfully informal and relaxed. We don't eat Christmas lunch until nearly four o'clock and it's a wonder that Micky is still standing, let alone managing a roast dinner, after the amount of champagne she's consumed. It's a Strong family ladies' tradition that they only drink champagne before lunch and by my reckoning by then we're on the fifth or sixth bottle. Hudson's on the Brewdog, his father alternates between fizz and whisky, while poor old Jonty is stone-cold sober because he's got to drive back to the stables later. We're still at the table at seven o'clock and the red wine is flowing as is the conversation. There's much laughter and teasing. I'm even wearing a paper crown – which is unheard of – while CC is trying to foretell my future with a Magic Fish, a sliver of blue cellophane. Apparently, depending on the way it curls in the palm of my hand, it predicts whether I'm passionate, resentful, fickle, false or dead. You'd think we'd all know if I'm dead.

Everyone is arguing over whether the fish is moving its head or its tail, when it suddenly flips off my hand and lands in the gravy boat.

'Oh my God, it's swimming,' screeches CC, as the fish writhes for a few seconds before sinking out of sight in the gravy. My mother would have been horrified but Micky simply grabs a spoon and fishes it out.

'I'm not wasting good gravy,' she says. 'I was planning to heat it up to have on cold Yorkshire pud for breakfast.'

I can't help smiling; having tasted the gravy and the big, puffy Yorkshires, it doesn't sound such a bad idea. I think I might have fallen down a rabbit hole.

It's all hands on deck to clear up and then we slump in front of the television to watch *Skyfall*. I'm not going to admit to anyone in the room that I've never seen it before. The television never goes on at home on Christmas Day. In fact, it strikes me that the festive season at my mother's home is deadly dull. There's plenty of food and numerous drinks parties, at which the same people gather, but it's like being on duty the whole time. No wonder I've never been a big fan. Christmas present has been a hell of a lot more fun than Christmas past. I feel like I've had a bit of a Scrooge-like epiphany as I look around the room at the Strong family. Forget about worrying about falling in love with Hudson, I think I've fallen in love with the whole family.

I don't want to leave tomorrow. The thought of going back to my barren London existence makes me feel cold inside and out. I shiver. Hudson, whose arm is draped across my shoulder, pulls me in for a hug.

'You okay?' he asks.

I nod and swallow. I can't look at him. There's a twist in my stomach as I think about tomorrow and saying goodbye to him. I feel hollow at the thought; it's literally like someone has scooped out my chest cavity. It frightens me.

Next to me, Hudson is warm and he smells good. I've not even seen the furniture he's been making.

The fire is making me drowsy, that and all the booze I've drunk over the course of the day. I close my eyes, leaning against Hudson and before I know it, he's gently shaking me. 'Come on, hamster chops, it's time for bed.'

I smile sleepily at him. He's so gorgeous and he's just so bloody kissable. As if he's read my mind, his mouth finds mine. In his eyes, there's definite promise despite the soft brush of his lips over mine.

When we go upstairs, it's as if he can read my mood. He puts one of the bedside table lamps on before he turns to me and takes me in his arms. We stand there together, our arms around each other, his forehead resting against mine. His chest is solid, so broad, and I could stay here for ever, absorbing his quiet strength. I reach up to kiss him on the jaw, tracing the slightly stubbled skin with my lips, feeling the texture of him as if I'm trying to imprint him on my mind for ever.

He peels my clothes off gently; there's none of that blind rush to get naked. Just a slow seductive peeling of layer after layer and then he lays me down on the bed, after folding back the duvet. We don't say a word. He kneels above me, his eyes on mine as his hands skim across my body, fingers trailing down the valley of my breasts, brushing across my hips, smoothing down my thighs. Does he feel it too? The last time.

With his eyes he checks back, after each move, each kiss. I hold his gaze and watch him as he cradles my hips bones in his hands and kisses his way across my stomach. For a moment he lays his head on my stomach, as if he's listening to the blood singing in my veins. Our breaths are quiet, deep and even. I push my hands into his hair, massaging his scalp. I can see the profile of his face in the dim light. We're saying goodbye with our bodies. He stands up and takes his clothes off and I'm holding tight to each breath as I watch him. The light creates shadows on the planes of his torso and I reach out to touch his warm skin. He captures my hand and lowers himself on to the bed, lying on his side beside me and pulls the duvet up around us. I turn to face him and we look at each other in the dim light, our eyes searching each other's faces.

Something is different but I don't think either of us is prepared to acknowledge it. We're in a dark cocoon outside of time and real life. We lie in silence, facing each other, just holding hands, no other touch.

'You okay?' he asks in a whisper.

I nod. 'You?'

'I think so. Thanks for coming. It meant a lot. I've not seen Mum so full of beans for ages.'

'I had a good time.'

'I knew you would.'

He leans into me and I meet him halfway to kiss him. It's a slow, languid kiss. Soft and warm. A gentle dance as our tongues lead and follow. I sink into it, enjoying the sensation, my arm around his broad back. I feel anchored and safe. Ripples of awareness start to build as parts of me are awakened. There's no frantic foreplay or teasing. Our kiss deepens. We know where we're going and there's no hurry to get there. It's safe, steady and all the more electric because we're taking the time and savouring the moment. It's like eating a chocolate bar tiny piece by tiny piece and letting each one melt in our mouths. The silence contains our breathing, slow deep intakes of breath to sustain us through the intensity of the moment. His cock is nudging me; it's wet but so am I, and I spread my legs to accommodate him and he teases me for a moment. Then he stops. 'I've had a good time too, Becs. A really good time.'

I want to look away but I can't. I see the sincerity in his eyes and know that he's telling me more. I can't do this but I can't say no either. I look up at him and I want him as much as ever, if not more. I close my eyes because I don't want him to see that wanting is not enough though. He slides in, his weight heavy on me. He moves again, slow, slow thrusts. It's the double-edged sword of the pain of intense pleasure. I can't help the cry that escapes. It's worse still because I know this is the very last time. Tomorrow I will say goodbye and I'll mean it.

'Oh God, yes, Becs. You feel so good.'

'Hudson.' I breathe his name. He's still moving tantalisingly slowly but the need is building. I lift my hips to take more of him as he groans my name again.

'I want you so bad,' he says, his thrust this time harder, followed quickly by another and then another. The pace has changed but we're in tandem. I'm so ready for him, I lift my hips to cradle him as he slides into me again and again. I grip his forearms, my legs rising to link behind his hips, locking him onto me. I tense as the swell builds and I'm straining towards the end, desperate and needy for the release, and tears start to run down my face because this is the end. It has to be. My cries are incoherent as the spasms of pleasure short-circuit my brain. I'm all sensation and feeling. Unbuttoned. With a low-pitched groan, he comes, bringing my own shuddering orgasm.

He collapses on top of me panting, his head in the crook of my neck and shoulder, his breaths dragon-hot on my skin, our chests heaving against the frantic beat of our hearts. I welcome the weight of him, his body sprawled over mine, as the aftershocks, rolling through me, subside enough to make me aware of our surroundings. Our ragged breathing punctuates the silence of the night. The chill air touches my shoulders but the rest of me is warm beneath the blanket of Hudson. The very fabric of him warms me inside and out. I'm home. Beyond the doors of this room, the rest of the world is a million miles away, a million breaths away. It's just us.

Neither of us say a word – I'm not sure either of us can manage it but I know that we're both very aware of each other. We've crossed a line. I've crossed a line. After that nothing can ever be the same again. It's not just the amazing sex, though.

It's more. I've fallen in love with Hudson. Fathoms deep. I might drown if I don't pull myself out, but it's too late. I'm in love with Hudson Strong and it's the worst thing that could have happened.

'Well, that was ... something,' says Hudson at last, raising his head to look at me, his eyes are searching mine. I know what he's looking for and I can't give it to him.

'It was,' I reply and then I say in true Rebecca Madison style, 'Amazing sex. I'll definitely miss it when I get back to real life.' I hate myself even as I'm saying it, but I need to make it clear, it was just sex. This has been a nice interlude and I've upheld my side of the deal. Tomorrow life returns to normal.

He lifts himself from me and rolls onto his back, his arm above his head, his hand on his forehead. His hip is still touching mine and we're thigh to thigh, so he hasn't completely withdrawn but there's definite distance there as if we're recalibrating. It would seem that neither of us wants to talk about what just happened. So why do I feel disappointed when I should be relieved?

We both lie in the dark not saying anything. This is how it's supposed to be. A civilised end, where two grown-ups go their separate ways as per the contract.

'What time do you want to leave in the morning?' I ask, suddenly desperate to go back to real life.

'After breakfast,' he says.

'Great.' I say with a coolness that hides the rollercoaster drop in my belly.

I turn over, turning my back on him. Tomorrow we'll say goodbye and that will be it.

## Chapter Twenty-Five

Only another couple of miles to Chelsea, thank fuck. I glance at Hudson. We've exchanged the grand total of fifty-one words in the car since we left Kingham. (OK, I'm not completely exact on the numbers, it's not like I counted them, but it's remarkably few words for a two-hour journey.)

My phone has buzzed with several messages from CC, who set up a WhatsApp group before we'd even reached Chipping Norton.

*Missing you already.*

*You're the best girlfriend Hudson has ever had, and he's had a ton.*

I'm not sure why she thinks this would reassure me.

*What's your address?*

*Where's the nearest tube station?'*

*What's your favourite cocktail?*

*Is Hudson still grumpy?*

'*Yes,*' I type back. '*Grumpy as fuck.*'

'*Normal operating procedure. He's a grumpy bastard.*'

Really? I don't have Hudson down as grumpy, well, not until today. I feel as guilty as fuck because I'm pretty sure it's my fault, but I never made promises. This was always going to be temporary. I didn't lead him on, did I? We're twenty minutes from Chelsea. I take in a breath, about to speak. Home is getting closer and I want to get this sorted so that when I step out of the car, the line is drawn and we never have to see each other again.

'Are you going to spit it out or just keep sighing?' asks Hudson, a touch snippily. His hands on the beleaguered steering wheel have tightened.

His tone pulls my guilt strings even tauter. It's not Hudson, he's normally Mr Sunshine and Roses.

'What are you trying to say?' he asks.

'I was trying to decide what day we should break up. Or whether we should have a huge row in the car and decide we're incompatible?'

'God, you realise I'm really going to get it in the neck from my family. Why did you have to be nice to my sisters? Can we hold fire for a week or so? I can already imagine the grief.'

'Makes no difference to me,' I say. Once he's dropped me off, I'm never going to see him again and that suits me just fine. It hardly matters what the date is. I'm sure in a day or so, CC will soon find some other novelty to interest her. 'When does your exhibition start? Would that have any bearing?'

He frowns and shrugs his shoulders. 'It starts on the seventh. So any time after that works.'

It hits me with the strength of a punch to the sternum. I'm not going to see him again. This really is the last time. There's no reason for us to see each other again. Not unless we were both inclined to have mind-blowing sex, which I have to say is tempting but also terrifying. Oh my God, will anyone else ever measure up to Hudson? And that right there is another reason to move on. He's ruined me for anyone else. I have to move on.

'Not sooner, why not now?'

'Hmm,' he says tilting his head to one side, flicking the indicator as we take a final right turn into the car park of my apartment block. 'I don't think my sisters will believe that we broke up on the way home and they'll be really pissed off with me if I break up with you.' He lapses into thought for a minute. 'I know. You go back to work. Sleep with a colleague and I dump you.'

'Er, excuse me. There's no way I would do that.'

'They don't know that.'

'But I do. I don't want them thinking the worst of me.'

'That's a bit unfair,' he says with a growl and glares at me. He actually looks a bit cross. 'So you're happy that they think the worst of me. My own family.'

'I liked them, I don't want them to hate me,' I say, which is ridiculous – I'm never going to see them again but despite that I want them to think well of me. I think I'm a little infatuated with Hudson's family.

He pulls into a parking space.

'But it's all right if my own family hate me?' he snaps

'Oh for God's sake, Hudson.' I'm irritated beyond belief because yes, I'm in the wrong and it shouldn't matter what his family think of me. I'm never going to see any of them again. 'You'll get the chance to redeem yourself. They'll forgive you.'

He huffs. 'You're a corporate shark, Becs. How about January the eighth?' he suggests.


I get out of the car and he gets out of the other side, moving around to the boot to retrieve my suitcase. My hands feel clammy despite the cold December chill and the grey damp mist around us. This really is it. Goodbye.

Do I kiss him? Shake his hand? Give him an arm's-length clap on the arm?

He lifts my case out of the boot and we stand facing each other, our eyes locked on each other's faces. I can't look away. My stomach ties itself in knots on top of knots.

'Well, this is goodbye,' he says and hands over my case. I'm just about to point out he's inadvertently dropped his Dr Who scarf when his faces creases into a naughty grin. 'Unless you want one last, mind-blowing, farewell orgasm? I'm happy to oblige.' It's so Hudson. He's so fucking irresistible. He's so forgiving.

Honestly, I swear to God, my vagina has just lit up in neon lights shouting, *Wahay, yes.* I can't. I really can't. I absolutely must not go there again.

I hesitate, almost swaying on the spot. My body wants

in, but my head is slamming on the brakes. There's a down and dirty battle going on. I try to shape the word 'yes' but self-preservation kicks in. Not sense. If he comes up to my flat, his presence will be forever embedded in the place; a Hudson-shaped outline will be imprinted in my bed and the memory of him being there in my space will be branded into my brain.

I open my mouth. The word 'no' comes out with an almost but not quite inaudible sigh. I shake my head to emphasise it, in case he didn't hear me or heard the obvious reluctance in my voice. My heart cracks a little. This is the end of the road. It's the right decision.

'Thanks for this weekend, Becs. Look after yourself.'

'You too. Good luck with the exhibition. I hope it goes well.'

'Thanks, it wouldn't be happening without you.'

I shrug, with careless nonchalance, even though that was his cue to invite me. 'Glad I was able to help. Besides you helped me.'

'Yeah and then you helped me.'

'That wasn't by choice.' Dry humour fills my words. 'Blackmail was involved.'

'But you had a good time, didn't you?'

My mouth twitches. I owe it to him to be honest. 'I did. Your family is great.'

'As long as you don't have to live with them.'

'You don't mean that.'

'No, I don't,' he acknowledges.

We're rapidly running out of things to say.

'They liked you, though,' he says. 'Especially CC. You're honoured. She never likes anyone.'

'She likes the location of my flat,' I joke.

'Well, there is that.'

I swallow. I like the idea of the sisters coming to stay. They're fun and they don't know me. I can be a different version of me when I'm with them.

'Well, thanks for driving me home. I ought to…' I turn and nod up towards my balcony as if any second I'm going to fly up there like Superwoman.

'Yes,' he says.

Neither of us move.

'Well, thanks again,' he says.

'Thanks, Hudson,' I say, my tongue savouring his name.

'No problem.'

For fuck's sake, this is getting painful.

I grab him, slap a kiss on his lips and turn to go. If I can get this over and done with it will be easier. One of us has to get on with it. He spins me round, pulls me into his arms. 'What sort of kiss was that?' he asks. 'We can do a lot better than that.'

That's what I was afraid of.

'Hudson, no,' I say, pulling back. If *he* kisses *me* I'll be a goner.

'If you ever change your mind, Becs, you've got my number.'

'For a booty call?' I say with a jokey, flippant smile. Inside I metaphorically hold my breath. Shit, I want so much more than that. I want to see him again. I really don't want this to end.

His smile slips. 'Not your style.'

'No, it isn't.' I'd always want more. I've fallen in love with Hudson Strong. I want it all with him but I know I can't have it, so I have to add, 'I'm not sure I'm built for anything else but if I were...' He looks directly in my eyes and smiles sadly.

# Chapter Twenty-Six

The lift doors are just sliding closed when a hand grabs them to halt their progress.

Marcus Carter-Wheeler shoulders his way through. 'Morning, Rebecca. Not in New York this year?'

'Evidently not,' I say looking down at myself to labour the point.

He laughs. 'That's what I like about you, you don't suffer fools. What brings you in this morning?'

I stare at him. What the fuck does he think I'm doing here? What would he say if I turned round and said, 'I'm such a sad bitch, I've got fuck all else to do the day after Boxing Day'?

'I just wanted a bit of peace and quiet to go over the Lawson contract one last time.'

He laughs. 'Me too, it's a mad house at home.'

I nod politely but rather than think of my own silent, sterile apartment, I'm thinking of the happy chaos at Hudson's family home. 'I can imagine,' I say.

'Have a good Christmas, did you?' he asks. Oh God, he's in chatty mode again, but an involuntary smile breaks out over my face and I can answer with honesty. 'Yes. I did.'

'Jolly good. It gave me a view of retirement. I'm actually looking forward to it.'

And yet here he is in the office on Wednesday, two days after Christmas.

When I leave the lift at the fourth floor and bid him goodbye, I'm still thinking about Hudson's sisters.

The office is deserted. Of course it is. Everyone has better things to do. God, since when did I start feeling sorry for myself? This is what I signed up for. I've always been the keen one. An eager beaver – shit, that's so not the right phrase – I've definitely got an eager beaver. I miss Hudson. I woke up this morning in an empty bed and the regret almost flattened me. There's this fierce ache of longing and it frightens me. It's almost physical, a hole in my life. I hate it. This feeling of loss, yearning and despair. For fuck's sake, my life is brilliant. So why am I sitting here at my desk gazing into space remembering Hudson's voice when he calls me Becs, when he tells me he wants me, when he said, 'I'm not built for anything else but if I were…'

I pull his Dr Who scarf out of my bag. I brought it into the office to send back to him. And then I do that stupid thing. I sniff it. Of course it smells of him. Wood shavings, lemon and just him. That indefinable Hudson smell. My stomach turns over, contracting with sudden pain.

I drop the scarf back into my bag and open the file on my desk, ignoring the sick feeling roiling through my gut.

I bury myself in my work or at least I try to. I find

myself staring out of the window at the slivers of leaden winter sky that glower through the city skyscrapers. Even my head feels heavy as I try to work.

My phone rings at 11.30 and I reach for it, grateful for a distraction.

'It's Marcus. Do you want to come up for a coffee and a chat? Although you'll have to bring your own coffee. No idea how the coffee machine works up here and the barista isn't in today.'

'Sure, give me five minutes,' I say as pleasantly as I can. What the hell does he want? Another chat? The approaching retirement is obviously making him demob happy. Bully for him, but I'm really not up for a convivial chat with the boss today. And I'm certainly not bloody making him coffee.

At the last minute I relent and take the lift downstairs. I nip to the Costa just across the road and order two flat whites. It's not because I'm feeling generous, I'm in need of caffeine and it would be tactless drinking one in front of him. He is still the boss.

'One coffee – don't get used to it,' I say, sliding the cup across his desk.

His eyebrows lift in surprise. 'Thank you. I wouldn't expect someone your level to make me coffee.'

'Marcus, if that's supposed to be some kind of compliment, just don't. You're a grown man – you should be able to make coffee and not rely on your PA.'

He laughs. 'Thank you.' He lifts the coffee to his lips. 'Ah, that's better.'

I wait. What has brought me up here for only the third time? Did he just want coffee? Or did he have something else to say.

'I wanted to follow up on our last conversation about my succession plans.'

He pauses deliberately, waiting for me to jump in and fill the convenient silence, but I don't bother. I already gave him my opinion.

'If I don't appoint Richard or Dominic, who should I appoint?' A deep crease appears in his forehead, his bushy eyebrows curving like caterpillars about to face off. I stare at him.

He's still looking at me, clearly waiting for an answer.

'I thought it was a foregone conclusion,' I say.

His mouth twists and he takes a sip of coffee, glaring unhappily down at the liquid. 'You have excellent judgement. You're right. Neither of them has what it takes but they both expect the post. I need to appoint a far better candidate. I value your opinion. Who would you suggest?'

I mentally flick through the other board members.

'Would you consider an external hire?' I ask.

There's a pained look on his face. 'What does that say about our board?'

They're all incompetent patriarchal fuckers. Of course, I don't say this because a beacon has just lit up in my head.

'You could appoint me,' I say. Fuck! I said it out loud.

He stares at me and reaches for his papers on his desk, shuffling them and clearing his throat. What the hell possessed me? But at least he's not laughed out loud. Probably too damned shocked.

Actually it's a fucking brilliant suggestion. I'd rock it.

Of course, he'd never go for it, maybe that's why I said it. But just imagine if there was a woman at the top. I'd change things. I remember Hudson's sisters all being so supportive. There's room for collaboration. I've been one of the worst, treating other women as competition. We could boost each other, support each other. Maybe I should leave and set up my own legal firm. Run things my way.

*If I'm the boss, I could have my cake and eat it.* The thought flashes into my head so briefly it's like a lightbulb filament burning out before I can grasp it and then my brain explodes, busy speeding off considering new premises, hiring employees, poaching Mitzie . . . and I miss what he's saying.

'Sorry, could you say that again?'

His eyes twinkle in what some might say is an avuncular manner. It freaks me out.

'I said, I think that's an excellent idea.'

'What?'

'I really don't know why I didn't think of it before,' he says with a delighted chuckle.

Seriously? He didn't think of it in the first place. And he's seriously telling me that he hadn't considered me? Could it be because I'm a woman? What fucking century are we in?

'But it's the perfect solution. You would make an excellent MD. You've got more talent in your little finger than that pair of fuckwits.'

I goggle at him. I've never heard him use language like that before and definitely not about his nephews.

He leans over and holds out his hand. I shake it. He beams at me. 'That might just be one of the best decisions I've ever made.'

'And the rest of the board?' I ask because I can't believe he has the sole decision making power on this.

The ruthless glint that I know better appears in his eye. 'They'll do what I tell them.' He softens momentarily. 'They'd be mad not to. You're the obvious candidate.'

I raise a sarcastic eyebrow at him. So obvious it only occurred to him five minutes ago after a month of speculation. Funny that.

'Quite right, m'dear. I'm a dinosaur but it doesn't mean I can't accept when I'm wrong. We need to move with the times. You'll ensure that happens.'

He looks at his watch. 'I think we should go out to celebrate. Would you like some lunch?'

I can hardly say no and besides it beats a turkey and cranberry sandwich from Pret. There's no food in my fridge – nothing new there then – and who else am I going to celebrate with?

# Chapter Twenty-Seven

It's Friday night and I've just got in from work. I can't be arsed to cook anything and I'm perusing one of an extensive selection of take-away menus. I throw it down on the table. I don't know what I fancy tonight. I don't even bother to question what's wrong with me, I know exactly what the problem is. I huff out an exasperated sigh, yank open the fridge and grab a bottle of champagne. It's been there a while but what the hell, I can celebrate on my own. Managing Director at thirty-three isn't too shabby. Why not?

There's a very good reason why not, which I realise the minute the fizz of bubbles crowd on to my tongue. It reminds me of Hudson's family and Christmas day.

Kicking off my heels, I wander over to the window and stand there looking out. I seem to be doing that a lot of late. Yet again I'm gazing out thoughtfully at the lights, wondering what other people out there are doing. I knock back the champagne with a quick angry thrust of the glass. I've got it bad. I've got an itch and it needs scratching. I put the glass down and lie on the sofa. I touch myself through the fabric of my trousers, the seam rubbing against me. There's a fierce ache of desire between my legs but a few urgent strokes show me it's not enough, it's never going to be enough. I moan in frustration and roll over, putting my arm across my face. It's Hudson I want. I consider the vibrator in my bedside table but I know it won't be the same. Nothing will ever be as good as him.

I pick up my phone and then put it down again. Don't even go there. Instead, I stomp into the kitchen and pour myself a second glass of champagne. I stick on the TV and flick through the programmes. I'm still channel-hopping ten minutes later. My glass is empty. I refill it. It's just a booty call. It doesn't mean anything.

I pick up my phone. I close my eyes. I'm mad. How would Hudson respond if I typed in, *I miss you*? I swallow. This neediness is alien. I call up his name on my text messages and stare at it for a few seconds. I put my phone down. I'm going to have a hot bath, more champagne, do some work. Anything to distract me.

I eye the phone. I could just say hello. He's probably out in some bar having fun, not even looking at his phone. He'll see my message later and think I'm some sad sack. And then I have the most magnificent brainwave of my entire life.

*I have your Dr Who scarf.*

I press send. Completely innocuous. Innocent. Nothing to see here. It's done.

I swallow down regret and then joy of joy, I see three wavery dots appear. I hold my breath.

*Would you like me to come and collect it?*

I close my eyes. Fuck, yes. Yes. Yes. Yes. It's just good sex. That's all.

*'Yes. Now?'*

Shit, I've pressed send. No going back now.

My heart is racing.

The dots are back. Then they stop. Then they're back. I watch, catching my lip between my teeth. Then nothing. No response. I've just made a complete tit of myself. I throw the phone down on the sofa and duck my head in my hands. I am twat of twatsville. I wait for a full ten minutes, or at least it feels that long, before I check my phone again. Still no response. I close my eyes and throw myself back into the sofa wishing the cushions would swallow me and my shame.

After another glass of champagne and a search of Google to find out if you can recall a text – you can't, not after it's been read – I decide to run myself a bath. I fill it with my Neom bubbles, which will hopefully help me to sleep and calm down the ants-crawling-through-my-system feelings.

I've just stripped and pulled on a silk kimono-style robe when my front doorbell rings. My heart lurches. It can't be Hudson, surely. To get up here, visitors have to be buzzed up.

I look through the little spyhole and my heart sky dives in my chest. I yank open the door.

Hudson grins at me.

287

'I've come to collect –' he pauses, his voice dropping to that level that pings straight to my clit '– my scarf.'

Of course he has. Relief rushes through me so intense that I feel my face go pink.

I can't help the broad smile that stretches across my face as I drink the sight of him in. Everything inside me melts and softens.

The next second we're kissing and I've no idea who made the first move but I know it's the right one. My breath hitches as his delicious mouth is on mine.

'God, I've missed you,' he mutters as his lips nibble at the corner of my mouth.

I thrust my hands into his hair and pull his lips back to mine.

Things are heating up at a rate of knots but my heart is singing. He's here. He's here and I never want to let him go. His hands are smoothing over the silk fabric down my back to grip my bottom, hauling me up against his rock-hard erection.

'Were you going to bed?' he asks.

I shake my head. 'I was just about to have a bath.'

His eyes light up. 'I love a bath.' His hands are already untying my robe and slipping inside to grasp my hips. He's pushing me inside the flat. 'Which way?' he whispers.

Walking backwards, I take him down the hall to the main bathroom. I've always liked this room but I have a feeling after tonight I'm going to like it a whole lot more.

The room is scented with jasmine and neroli and the bubbled water is waiting.

Hudson stops and gives me that wicked grin and then

surprising me, he reaches forward and snags one of the hair scrunchies from the shelf below the mirror. 'Turn around,' he says. He eases down my robe and then scoops up my hair, pressing a kiss to the nape of my neck before smoothing my hair into a ponytail and doubling the scrunchie around it to make a floppy bun.

I turn my head and look at him over my shoulder, catching his naked appreciation of the view. 'Like what you see?' I ask.

'You are so fucking gorgeous, Becs.' He stands back as if he wants to absorb every bit of the view.

'Why don't you get in?' he asks. The invitation in his words sends a tingle through my body.

'Are you going to join me?'

'Eventually.'

Oh God. My eyes widen at the soft promise in his voice.

As I take one step into the bath, he grasps me by the waist. I'm straddling the floor and the bath, my legs wide and he sits down on the edge and grins wickedly up at me. He traces a finger up my inner thigh and I close my eyes as it hovers at the apex of my legs.

'So soft,' he murmurs as he leans forward and places a kiss where his finger has left off. My knees soften. His fingers brush my labia and he leans forward and blows a soft breath over my clit. I have to hold on to his shoulder, my knees are wobbling. The anticipation heart-stopping. I close my eyes, willing him to move.

'Do you know, Becs, I love the smell of you. Do you taste as good?' He looks up at me. 'Do you?'

The dirty words bring a blush to my cheeks but I love it. It ratchets up the aching need another notch.

'I don't know,' I manage. My nipples have peaked and I'm shaky with desire. I want him to touch me.

'I think you do. Do you want me to taste you?' He looks at me. Oh God, he wants an answer. I nod but his eyes are wicked. 'Not good enough, Becs. Tell me what you want.'

I stare back at him. It feels like he can see into my soul. He knows what I want but he's going to make me say it. He wants me to admit that I'm desperate for his touch.

I swallow and hold his gaze. 'I want you to taste me.' I pause because I know he wants more from me and he knows that saying the words will turn me on even more. 'I want to feel your tongue.'

He's still looking at me, holding my hips. I feel so wet. I clench my internal muscles, trying to give myself some relief from the burning ache.

'Where?' he asks, his voice low and throaty.

I swallow. He wants it all and I'm powerless. 'My clit,' I whisper, 'I want you to lick my clit.'

'Just lick?'

'Suck.' I breathe out the word. Every nerve ending in my vagina is throbbing with desperation and then before my knees give way, he breaks my gaze and he kisses my inner thigh again. I swallow as his lips trace their way up, up. I'm trembling with heat, need, want.

At the first rasp of his tongue, I jerk and let out a sigh. It's so good. I pant out a breath, trying to gain some control but it's … it's sublime. The lap and stroke of his tongue, teasing the sensitive bundle of nerves. I hardly dare breathe, I don't want him to stop. I hear myself moaning softly. His hands are stroking my bottom, one finger slides down my seam and hovers over the firm ring of flesh there, pushing gently. The intense sear of pleasure makes me whimper his name in panic. 'Hudson.' My senses are overwhelmed. I feel sensuous, wicked and dirty, so dirty, and I want him.

'Do you want this?' he asks, reading my mind.

'Mmm,' I manage.

His tongue toys with me, while his finger presses gently. No one has ever touched me there.

He pushes one finger gently inside me. I groan at the illicit thrill that immediately shudders through my body. There's a moment to adjust to this new sensation and then his other hand moves up my thigh and he sucks on my clit. A burst of pleasure explodes before I can catch my breath and stop the cry. He moves up and kisses my stomach as he slides two fingers into me, taking me prisoner to every feeling. My knees are going to buckle. My orgasm floods through me. Hudson is all that is holding me up now as my panting fills the quiet room. I collapse forward, my head on his chest as he strokes my back. 'Jesus, you're incredible, you know that.'

It takes me a while to return to reality. I finally lift my head and look at him.

'The scarf's in the other room,' I say.

He bursts out laughing and hugs me to him. 'Becs, I love you. You're hilarious.'

Those three little words. My heart expands. But I know they're the jokey kind of 'I love you', the 'I love your sense of humour', 'I love the way you think', 'I love that you said that.'

To hide the stupid jiggle of hope, I drawl, 'So are you planning on taking any clothes off, anytime soon?' I sink into the bath, glad to rest my legs, which are still having trouble holding me up.

He immediately pulls his T-shirt over his head. I lie back and watch him, making no effort to conceal my admiration as my gaze moves over his chest and down to the hair around his belly button.

'Like what you see?' he asks teasingly as he yanks off his trainers and socks.

'Not bad,' I reply.

Without any self-consciousness, he undoes his jeans and pushes them down along with his boxers. His erection jumps free.

'Move up,' he says and he gets into the bath behind me and lowers himself so that his legs are straddling my hips and the firm hard length of him is pressed against my back. He lies back against the end of the bath pulling me against his chest, his lips nuzzling my neck as his hands drift down to my breasts. He cups them but leaves his hands there.

'This is nice,' he says and sighs into my hair.

'Mmm.' I relax back against him and close my eyes, still not quite able to believe that he's really here. For the first time since I came home, the restless, irritated, scratchy feelings leave me. Peace settles on me. I'm content just to be, I don't feel the need to say anything or try to make conversation. I idly stroke Hudson's forearm, luxuriating in the feel of his arms around me, his solid presence at my back.

The bubbles start to disappear and the temperature of the water is no longer quite so soothing.

'Time to get out,' says Hudson and he sits up and pushes me down the bath so that he can stand.

He climbs out of the bath and takes the bath sheet from the back of the door. Holding out his hand, I get out and he folds it around me and hugs me to him. No one has ever cosseted me like this. I lift my eyes to his and he smiles and kisses me lightly on the lips. I catch sight of his naked form, his skin darker against the white of my towel. His back is strong and the muscles ripple as he moves. His erection is pressed up against me.

I free my arms and wrap the towel around my bust. My hand slides along his waist and down his belly until I can grasp the end of his cock. Hudson sucks in a breath and once again those blue eyes are locked on mine. It's a powerful aphrodisiac watching him as I stroke him. His eyes are half lidded as he watches. His mouth falls open and I hear his inward suck of breath. I increase the pace very slightly and grip a little tighter on the down movement. I'm rewarded with a low, guttural groan as his hips push forward slightly.

'Fuck. Yes.'

My hand moves firmer and faster and I take his mouth in a kiss, our lips gorging on each other, our frantic rhythm matching my strokes.

With a shudder, he pulls back. 'You have to stop,' he gasps, breathing heavily. 'I need to be inside you. Now.'

I don't stop, I slow right down and watch his tortured face with a feline smile.

'Becs, you're killing ... fuck's sake, stop.' He gapes and clamps a hand over mine, his mouth capturing my lips, his tongue thrusting greedily into my mouth. I stop, distracted by the kiss.

'Condoms,' growls Hudson, his eyes a little wild. 'If I don't get inside you in the next ten seconds...' The threat dies away as I rip open a square packet from the bathroom cabinet and slide it over his dick.

He pushes me up against the wall and slides in, looking at me intently as his arms rest against the tiles above my head. 'Come for me, Becs. Now.' He pulls back and glides in again in a hard, firm thrust, and again and again, all the time watching me. He takes one of my nipples into my mouth and sucks hard, pain and pleasure fight it out, and then he lifts his head, a gleam in his eyes as he thrusts harder and deeper. The orgasm slams into me and I cry out, my muscles clamping onto him, and a second later he shudders and I feel him come inside me as he calls out my name.

## Chapter Twenty-Eight

Overnight I've burrowed into Hudson's chest, and I wake up with my nose pressed up against his skin, my knees against his hip. The weight of his arm rests across my waist, anchoring me into place. I smile sleepily to myself, remembering last night.

'You're twitching. It's like sleeping with a hamster.' Amusement quivers in his voice.

I move my head and look up at Hudson's face. His eyes are still closed but his mouth has quirked in a smile. I sigh and settle back in as he seems quite content and I'm in no hurry to go anywhere. I doze for a while listening to the steady beat of his heart beneath my ear. That solid rhythm is so Hudson, the steadiness of him. It's funny, when I first met him I thought he was unreliable and a bit flaky but he's anything but, although he does his best to hide it. I sigh and his arm tightens around me and he drops a kiss on my head. I could get used to this.

No! No, I couldn't. I mustn't. This is just blissed-out

post-coital euphoria. It's not real. We had a great time but I know from past experience things would change, especially now I've got this amazing promotion. I'm going to have to put the hours in. My job will take even more of centre stage. It will spoil everything between us when I refuse to compromise. It's not the right time for me to put someone else first.

He yawns and I feel I ought to be a good hostess, although I'd rather stay put.

'Do you want a coffee?' I straighten up beside him.

'In a while,' he murmurs, rolling onto his side and reaching forward to trace my collar bone. It's oddly tender and I can't help myself, I lean forward and press a soft kiss on his cheek.

'What are you doing today?' he asks, his eyes not meeting mine; they're focused on his hand, smoothing over my skin.

'Shopping,' I say firmly. I need to go, although part of me is willing him to suggest we do something different, together.

'For anything specific?' He smiles into my eyes. 'I bet you're a very good shopper.'

'Of course I am. Efficient. Organised. Methodical.'

'You make it sound like filing. Shopping should be fun.'

I give him the look. 'I'm buying a new suit for work.' It won't be fun, it will be serious business. 'I've been promoted at work and they're announcing it at the board meeting on Monday. I want to look the part.'

He sits up and pulls the duvet up over his chest. 'Promoted. That's awesome, Becs.' He hugs me and smacks a friend kiss on my lips. 'Well done, you. What are you now?' His eyes light up with enthusiasm, 'Contracts Empress of the Universe?'

I push at him, touched by his genuine pleasure for me, and laugh. 'Not yet.'

'So what are you?'

I feel suddenly shy. Although I'm proud of my achievements, I don't like boasting about them. I've worked hard for everything but I don't feel the need to tell everyone. 'Managing Director,' I say in a quiet voice.

'Becs!' He swoops me into his arms for a hard squeeze. 'That's amazing. I bet your family are so proud of you.'

Actually my mother and sister were. They sounded thrilled for me when I told them on a FaceTime call. Okay, maybe it was a bit of oneupmanship. See, Laura, I don't need to get married.

'Oh my God, we should totally celebrate. I know this great place for lunch. We can go shopping, find your suit and then go eat.'

'You do not want to come shopping with me,' I say.

'I do ... I'd like to see you in your underwear in the changing room.'

Ah, that's more like the Hudson I know.

He gives me a devastating smile. 'I bet you were planning to buy a black suit and while I think you're as cute as hell in one, I know you can do better. I'm thinking red.'

'Over my dead body,' I say.

'Not this very lovely body,' he replies, his hand sliding down to my breasts, his thumb swirling around my nipple.

He's doing it again, sneaking under my skin, making me want more.

'I have to get in the shower,' I say, forcing myself to get out of bed. Without looking at him, I take clean clothes with me and firmly lock the door of the bathroom. I know what will happen if he comes in with me. I turn down the water to cold, almost as a punishment for enjoying myself too much with Hudson.

I take a deep breath and step out of the bathroom, fully dressed. Hudson is wearing my dressing gown, which doesn't meet across the chest and only just covers his bum – God, he looks cute in it. What's more he's made me a cup of coffee.

'You're dressed,' he says with a mock pout.

'I told you I'm going shopping.' My tone is terse.

'You don't want me to come.'

'No, Hudson, I don't want you to come.' I'm firmer now but he's still not getting the message.

'If I don't come, I know you'll buy something really boring,' he says with that familiar twinkle in his eye.

My heart sinks. Please don't charm me.

'It's a suit for work. It makes a statement about who I am and sends a message to the people I work with.'

'But you're not boring,' he says.

'Hudson, I have to go. Just close the door behind you when you leave.'

For a second it takes the words to sink in and then he gives me a sad smile. 'Seriously, Becs.'

'Seriously, Hudson.'

He stares at me so hard as if he's trying to look inside my soul.

'You don't mean it.' Again that smile touches his lips.

'I do. You have to go.'

He sighs and takes a sip of his coffee. 'So, last night. Just a booty call?'

A lump the size of a golfball fills my throat. 'What did you think it was?'

'Really, Becs, you're going to do this?'

'Do what?' I snap. I don't need this.

'Turn your back on us.'

'There is no us. What are you talking about?' My heart contracts in terror. He's not supposed to be talking like this. He's supposed to be free and easy. That's what I signed up for. He supposed to find it easy to walk away. He's not supposed to make this hard.

'Becs,' he says, still looking at me.

'We had a deal, remember. We both got what we wanted from it. And we agreed an official end date.'

'Is that what you really want?' he asks softly.

I grit my teeth before saying, 'Yes.'

'Don't do this, Becs.' There's an expression in his eyes that almost takes my breath away.

'Do what?' I'm being deliberately obtuse.

'What if I said I'd fallen in love with you.'

My laugh is slightly hyaena-like. 'Hudson, you're the love 'em and leave 'em type.'

He raises an eyebrow. 'I never said that. You did. Because it suited you to believe that.'

'What about your business partner?'

'I told you. That was a misunderstanding on her part. I never made any commitment to her but it doesn't mean I'm not capable of making one.'

'Good for you.' I'm being deliberately cruel now.

'What are you so scared of?'

'Scared? Don't be ridiculous. I have a career that I've worked incredibly hard at. I'm about to be made MD. I've got nothing to be scared of. And I've had enough relationships to know that men can't handle coming second to my ambition.'

'Why should they?'

'Exactly! You're like the rest of them. Five minutes in, why aren't you home for dinner? Why are working on a Sunday?'

'But surely questions like that show that they care about you.'

I give him a pitying smile. 'No, they show that they can't hack my job being more important than they are.'

'But it shouldn't be if you love someone. They should be as important and you can work together, both of you making compromises. If you're in a relationship, you can work these things out.' Then he makes the fatal mistake of saying. 'A job isn't everything.'

'It is to me,' I say. If it wasn't, my dad would be so disappointed. No one is going to derail me.

'You're wrong, Becs. There's more to life. A lot more. I thought you wanted to be unbuttoned.'

'That was just sex. We had great sex.'

'Yeah, Becs, we had fucking marvellous sex.' With that he storms out of the bedroom and slams the bathroom door.

I've hurt him. I've been so focused on what I want, I hadn't thought about his feelings. But it's for the best. I snatch up my handbag and rush out of the flat before he can come out of the shower. It's the second time I've run out on him but this time it's definitely the last.

## Chapter Twenty-Nine

I t's officially the worst New Year's Eve ever. I've been invited to two black tie parties and neither of them holds much appeal. I'd rather stay home and watch *Grease* for the second time this week, except I know I'll sob over the final scene again.

But I've got to do something, I can't stay in and both parties are potential networking events. I opt for the event at the Grosvenor Hotel, figuring it will be easy to get a cab home from there.

It takes me ages to get ready, mainly because I inexplicably can't make up my mind what to do with my hair. When it's finally straightened to within an inch of its life and secured at the nape with a barrette, I'm ready to go. I'm wearing a black silk dress but it's more daring than I'd normally wear although from the front it's very severe with a high neck. When I turn around it's completely backless and my hair falls in a column straight down the middle. It's the sort of dress that leaves men wondering what's holding my tits up.

Walking into a party on my own doesn't faze me and I snag a glass of champagne from the waiter near the doors. As I turn to walk away she says, 'That's one cool dress.' When I turn back to acknowledge the compliment, she gives me a sunny, guileless smile. It reminds me of Hudson, the way he's so friendly to everyone, no matter who they are or what they do. 'Thank you,' I reply and smile back. 'I hope you're getting double time tonight.'

'Only reason I'm doing it.' She beams. 'My boyfriend and friends will be waiting up for me when I get home. We'll have our own celebration then.'

'That's nice.'

'Yeah. I think New Year's Eve is overrated. I'd rather be with friends and family.' She spreads her hand to indicate the corporate crowd and then realises she's inadvertently said the wrong thing.

I laugh. 'I know what you mean.' I'm thinking of Christmas with Hudson and his family.

'Rebecca! Good to see you.' Oh shit, it's Dominic Wright. He pumps my hand. 'Good Christmas?'

'Yes.' I nod and dredge up a smile. He introduces me to his wife. 'Alison, this is Rebecca Madison, one of our high-flyers.'

'Hello.' She looks around with a slightly puzzled frown. 'Are you here on your own?'

Dominic bays out a laugh. 'Married to the job is our Miss Madison. She's the original ice queen.'

Alison looks slightly horrified. Dominic has obviously

been on the pre-drinks. He's an even bigger tosser drunk than sober if that's possible. Thank fuck he'll not be running the company.

I give a tight smile, wondering if I can fire his sorry arse once I'm MD.

Through the crowd I see a dark head of curls and my heart lifts. Hudson. Then a group of people move into my eye-line and I've lost him.

'Excuse me, I've just seen someone I need to talk to.'

Dominic elbows his wife in the ribs. 'There, what did I tell you. Always on the job.'

Alison rolls her eyes; clearly she thinks he's a knob too.

I swan through the crowd, nodding at people I know, other lawyers – previous work colleagues who have moved on, current colleagues and a few clients. What am I doing here? I've done this for the last five years. I move forward and there he is, his back to me, an arm draped around a woman wearing a stunning bright fuchsia pink dress. Of course she is, someone Hudson chose wouldn't wear black. His fingers are stroking her skin, his head bent towards her. They're the picture of togetherness. My heart drops like a lead weight to the very bottom of the sea. Hudson is with someone else. Regret pinches hard, mean-fingered, with a sharp stab like a stitch in my side. Something inside me crumples and suddenly I'm close to tears. Me, Rebecca Madison. I straighten up and lift my chin. I will go up and say hello and move on. I was the one that pushed him away. It was *my* choice. His words come back to me. *What if I said I'd fallen in love with you?* I was right though; he is the love 'em and leave 'em type. He's moved on already. I paste a smile on my face and move towards them. She looks up first and then he turns.

'Hi,' I say, suddenly finding myself grinning at them. The pair exchange slightly startled glances, as well they might. It's not Hudson. Now I'm looking at him, he doesn't even look remotely like him. My heart doubles in size in my chest. Relief, happiness, triumph? I'm not sure which. It's a wonderful feeling whatever it is, even if my brain appears to have been playing some trick on me. Shit, if this is what love does to you, you can keep it.

My phone rings. It's two minutes past five in the morning. Groggily, I reach out to answer it without checking who it is.

'Happy New Year!'

'Hello, Rebecca Madison speaking.'

Oh,' a voice says followed by a nervous giggle. 'Rebecca, I didn't think you'd answer. I was going to leave a message.'

I blink as understanding dawns. 'Laura?'

'Yes, it's meee.'

'Are you pissed?' I ask.

'Not precisely,' she enunciates extremely carefully, because she clearly is, 'but I might be a bit ... wobbly.' Before I can say anything, she suddenly bursts out with, 'Iwantyoutobeabridesmaid.'

It takes me a moment to extricate the words and I'm shocked into silence. Am I dreaming or has an alien taken up residence in Laura's body. I'm definitely dreaming.

'Rebecca! Are you there? Mum, I think she dropped the phone.'

'So, Mother pressganged you into this then,' I ask, surprised by the disappointment I'm feeling.

'No.' Laura giggles. 'She's been feeding me champagne to give me courage.'

My sister is clearly smashed. 'Why don't you call me tomorrow, when you've sobered up?'

'No! Wait. Don't hang up. I won't be brave enough.'

'What are you talking about?'

'Rebecca, I've always been so jealous of you but I've had an epi... an epidural.'

'You're having a baby, what now?'

'No, silly. Oh, Mum says it's an epifunny, epifanny ... one of those things when you realise you've been wrong about something for a very long time.'

'An epiphany,' I say wondering what on earth she's talking about and whether I can get my mother on the line to get some sense out of her.

'Hear me out. I was always jealous of you.'

I refrain from saying, 'Tell me something I didn't know,' because the sooner she finishes, the sooner I can go back to sleep.

'But then I realised that it wasn't your fault that you were smarter than me. And of course you had it far harder than me.'

It is far too early in the morning for this crappy psychobabble. I throw myself against the pillow and ask wearily, 'And how do you figure that?'

'Nothing you ever did was going to be good enough for

Dad. You got straight As, you had to go to Cambridge, you got a first, you had to go work for the best law firm. You had to make partner. There was always going to be something else. It would never have stopped.'

'You mean if he hadn't died,' I whisper, my stomach turning over at the memory of his death.

'Yes. I never knew that until I met Andrew. He loves me, you know.'

Where is she going with this?

'He really loves me. For what I am. Not for what he wants me to be. Ditzy, stupid Laura.'

'You're not stupid,' I say because if nothing else, I'm honest.

'But I'm not smart, not like you, but it doesn't matter anymore. I love Andrew and I'm happy – really happy.'

She must have drunk a whole bottle of champagne on her own. She always was a lightweight when it came to alcohol. 'I don't need to be jealous anymore. And I'm really happy that you've found someone like Hudson and that you can be happy.'

I can't help myself and I just want to be difficult because that's how it's always been with us. 'Hudson and I have broken up.' Hopefully that will shut her up.

'No!' Laura's wail is heartfelt. 'Mum, they broke up. I'm putting you on speakerphone.'

'It's fine,' I say. Oh shit, I don't want to speak to my mother as well. 'It's for the best.'

'Why did you break up?' asks Laura.

'Because . . .' I lift my shoulders in a shrug that neither of them can see. 'You know. We weren't that compatible.'

'Is it because of your fucking job?' asks Laura.

'Laura! Language,' says my mother.

'You're the fucking MD now, Rebecca. You can do what you like. You have people to delegate to. Tell her. Mum. Tell her what you said to me.'

My mother's voice breaks through Laura's inexplicable anger. 'Rebecca, you've more than proved yourself. You are allowed to live as well as work.'

'I do live,' I retort. They don't know anything. But a little voice inside me adds, 'Do they?'

There's silence on the other end of the phone.

'Will you be my bridesmaid?' asks Laura.

'Have you got a date yet?'

'I'm not asking if you'll be available. I'm asking you to be my bridesmaid, no matter what the date is. Do you mean you'd cancel if something came up at work?

I'm appalled to realise that that's exactly what I'm thinking.

'It's the most important day of my life … and you still think your job is more important. I told you, Mum, I told you.' Laura's voice is rising. 'My big sister's job is more important than me just like it's always been. She was too busy studying to play, to go shopping, to swim when we were on holiday, to do anything – even when I begged her.'

I hear my mother make soothing noises in the background.

'You know something, Rebecca, I hero-worshipped you when I was younger. It wasn't just Dad who I wanted to notice me, it was you as well. And you can't even commit to being my bridesmaid. Well, fuck off.'

'Laura!' My mother's outraged tone is the last thing I hear before the line goes dead.

I'm wide awake now and pacing the balcony clutching a large mug of decaf coffee. My breath comes out in plumes of steam in the cold January night but with a sloppy cashmere sweater over my PJs and Ugg sheepskin slippers the chill in the air doesn't bother me. I still can't believe that Laura wants me to bridesmaid or that she got upset with me because I didn't commit. I didn't think she cared that much.

I spend the next half hour unpicking the past, sifting through my memories with fresh eyes. In my head Laura had been a whiny, attention-seeking brat, but now I see that I was the brat, too self-absorbed, too wrapped up in my own self-importance. I was the clever one, I had important things to do. All fuelled by my dad who wanted great things for me.

For himself? I remember Maude's comments at the party and my mother's. 'He wasn't an easy man to love. His affection had to be earned.'

Am I still trying to earn my father's affection? Am I still trying to live his dreams?

## Chapter Thirty

It's Monday, 4 January, announcement day. In my new suit, I'd like to say I feel like a million dollars as I grab a coffee from Barista Boy and stride across the lobby to the lift. I bloody should. I did blow a fuckload of money to look like this and the bright scarlet certainly makes a statement. My Mac lipstick matches the jacket perfectly. But the truth is I'm feeling like a ten-watt lightbulb. The light is on but that's about all.

I'm just antsy because I want this meeting done. That's all. In my head I draw a neat line under everything that happened last year. This is a new start. I have to forget Hudson and the great sex. Forget that he made me feel different. Forget that he made me look at things differently. This is the future. It's more than I dreamed of. My dad *would* have been proud of me. But I can't help wondering, would it have been enough? Laura has sown a seed which is in danger of growing into a triffid.

I ride up to the top floor in the lift, looking out over the city through the glass walls. There's a kick of pride in my chest but it doesn't quite balance that dull shitty little tug in my stomach.

What if it isn't enough for me? What if I want more? What if I want it all?

The thought strikes like an arrow slicing through every value and aspiration I've taken for granted throughout my entire life.

My vision blurs for a moment and I have to grab the handrail as a wave of dizziness hits me, almost spilling my coffee. Is this a panic attack? I grip the cold metal harder, my knuckles almost bursting out of my skin. I'm being ridiculous. This is just nerves. The announcement will be a bombshell. There's no doubt about that. Emails have been flying about, asking if anyone knows what the meeting is about. Marcus likes to be theatrical sometimes. On this occasion, I wish it wasn't at my expense. What the fuck is wrong with me? I straighten up. Since when have I given a shit about what anyone thinks about me? Get a grip, Rebecca. I take in a deep breath and tug at my jacket sleeves. The lift slows. I take another breath. I've got this.

I've deliberately timed it so that I arrive at the very last minute. I slide into my seat and take a good slug of coffee. An air of anticipation gently fizzes around the room, slightly suppressed because hey, when are lawyers ever giddy? But all the same everyone suspects they know why they're here. Dick and Dom are at opposite ends of the table and I get a kick of nerves as I see them at pains to be eyeing each other and remaining imperturbable. Neither of them knows the other hasn't got the job but they both know they haven't. There's a complex reverse pissing strategy going on with neither of them acknowledging the other has won.

At last Marcus walks in and takes his place at the head of the long table. It's positively Victorian. I'm going to have a round table. None of this top-seat, top-dog, testosterone-fuelled bollocks. He surveys the room, face by face, and frankly I want to cringe. He's playing the kingmaker or in this case the queenmaker. It's not fucking *Game of Thrones*. It's a mid-sized city law firm with lots of large-sized egos.

When I get back to my desk, a mere twenty minutes later, my phone starts pinging with congratulatory texts. The news has spread like proverbial wildfire. Most are politic rather than effusive. The exception to this is Mitzie. (It's noticeable that neither Dick nor Dom said a word to me but if looks could kill I'd be six feet under with a couple of pitchforks driven through my heart.) Despite this, I feel a touch deflated and I've no idea why.

*OMG. Go you. Awesome news. Please, please, please can we have a creche.*

This is followed by a couple of baby emojis. WTF? Mitzie. No!

*Are you pregnant?!!!*

*Yup. Completely up the duff. Shit timing. Guess who did all the driving over Christmas.*

Oh my god, poor Mitzie. I call her immediately. 'Shit, are you okay? What are you going to do?'

She laughs in my ear. Shit, she's hysterical. I don't blame her.

'Rebecca, I wanted to get pregnant.'

It takes me a full thirty seconds to get rid of the ringing in my ears before I say – with a distinct note of incredulity because, hey, this is Mitzie – 'You did?' The sky might as well have fallen in. 'You never said.'

There's a silence before she says in a small voice. 'I knew you wouldn't approve.'

It's a gut-wrenching punch to the stomach. I almost double over. Am I that bad a friend? I trace a line across my desk with one glossy fingernail (red to match the suit) and catch my lower lip between my teeth. Part of me is hurt that she needs my approval – she's a strong, independent woman – the other part feels guilty because it's the truth. She's worked so hard to get where she is, why would she throw it all away?

'Besides,' she adds, I suspect to make me feel better. 'It's not something I'm going to advertise when I work at Misogynists R Us. To be honest I was fully expecting to go on maternity leave and be made redundant. That's what usually happens.'

'Does it?'

'Madison! Don't tell me you've never noticed? Trudy Winters, Alessandra Keighley, Joanne Dickens, Ellie McGreggor, Sue Peters, Ivana Nugent, to name but a few. They were all managed out.'

Shit, they were all smart operators. I assumed they'd got baby brain or something and didn't want to work anymore. 'But isn't that illegal?'

'Technically it's very illegal, but there are always convenient loopholes. I've fought it as much as I could but they always manage to find a way. Difficult performance management targets, refusal to offer flexible working practices, or just made to feel very unwelcome until they resigned. I'm amazed no one sued for unfair dismissal.'

They probably knew it wouldn't get them anywhere. They'd never work in the City again.

'So what are you going to do?' I ask again.

'What lots of other women do. Go on mat leave, have a baby and come back to work. And if my new boss has any nous, she'll implement flexible working and an onsite creche. There's all that unused space on the second floor. You could probably make a profit from it. Open it up to other companies in the area. There's F all available at the moment.'

'I've got a few other things to think about first,' I say.

'You've got six and half months.' There's a hint of challenge in her voice.


The congratulatory messages continue to pour in, which is amazing as I've never considered myself that popular. It seems being the first woman MD in the 120- year history of Carter-Wright is really striking a chord, even among male colleagues. It's been decided that I will take over on 1 February, which strikes me as quite soon. Now he's made his decision, Marcus is keen to move on. He's already got his first golf tournament booked for the 2nd.

Things die down by lunch time and I take five to go to the loo.

Someone has just flushed next door and the door creaks in tandem with the outer door opening.

'OMG, have you heard?' a voice bursts out as someone else comes in.

'Yes. Can't believe it. Female MD. That's a first. Think she's going to shake things up?'

'You're having a laugh.' This is followed by a derisive snort before a voice, which I don't recognise, dripping with scorn, adds, 'Rebecca Madison is one of the old boy brigade. How do you think she's got so far? She's got iced water in her veins. She might as well be a bloke.'

'Ooh, savage.'

'C'mon, she's a bitch. You think she's going to change a thing. She's no sister. Where she's concerned, it's fuck the sisterhood. Remember when Mel split with her boyfriend and had to move back in with her parents, a two-hour rancid commute away. Her frigging boss couldn't be arsed to see how she was doing, all Frigid Knickers wanted to know was why she was late.'

They say eavesdroppers don't hear good of themselves. I've had enough and I'm ready to embarrass the shit out of this pair but my hand stills on the lock when first voice adds, 'Do you think she ever has fun? I mean, she's so buttoned up.'

My hand drops away from the door. Of all the things they've said – that draws blood. It scores a direct hit. That might be their perception of me, but Hudson has shown me that I can be unbuttoned. Thinking about him makes me feel a little sick. How can I miss him so much? My prized ability to compartmentalise anything I don't want to think about has been blown out of the water. Thoughts of Hudson are never far from my mind.

'God, can you imagine her letting go when she's having a shag. Or do you think she lies there thinking of England, giving the poor bastard commands. You will touch my clit. Squeeze my tit.'

Both of them burst into laughter.

The laughter adds humiliation to the twist of hurt I'm already feeling. Smoothing back my hair and buttoning my jacket as if I'm just about to go into court, I push my shoulders back and open the door.

The look on their faces when they see me is priceless. It fuels my snark perfectly. My smile is full on shark-going-in-for-the-kill, all teeth with lips drawn back and no warmth. I incline my head with regal grace and say, 'I'll bear in mind your comments about sisterhood.'

Without haste, I turn my back on them, refusing to look at them in the mirrors as I calmly wash my hands and use the hand dryer, giving them another polite goodbye smile as I saunter out of the toilets. Despite my froideur, inside I'm crying. I've been unbuttoned, shown another view of life, and I want to keep it. Perhaps I can.

## Chapter Thirty-One

B*ummer. You and Hudson, broken up! No! I'm soooo sad,* reads CC's text at six-thirty the next morning. This is followed by a second text filled with a dozen sad-faced emojis.

I don't fucking believe it. Hudson has dumped me, two days early. How dare he?

I'm late into the office, well late for me. It's eight-thirty instead of my usual seven-thirty and the gloom of a murky, drizzly January morning suits my mood. I've just fought my way off the underground, my nose rammed into wall-to-wall wet-dog-smelling wool coats and I'm Pissed off. Yes with a capital P. But I've no idea why – well, apart from Hudson not sticking to our agreement. It was supposed to be the eighth, not the sixth.

I have to shove my hands deep in the pockets of my coat. I could quite happily stab three-quarters of the human race this morning. I catch my reflection in the glass-fronted reception as I swing into the lobby. I snatch off the cashmere red beanie hat, releasing the torrent of curls. Okay, so I've decided I quite like my hair curly these days – no one needs to make a thing of it. But they all are, and if one more person tells me it really suits me I might actually kill them with the nearest pair of scissors. Mitzie even went as far as saying it made me look more approachable. I'll be putting salt in her coffee the next chance I get.

People give me a wide berth as I storm through the open-plan desks to my office.

'Love really doesn't agree with you, does it, babe?' drawls Mitzie, who's sitting in my office waiting for me. On the plus side she has two cups of coffee in front of her. One of them had better be for me. 'Cute hat.' She nods towards the hat in my hand. 'Is it new?'

'No,' I snap and toss it onto the spare chair in the corner. 'And I've no idea what you're talking about.'

'Oooh! Who pissed on your bonfire this morning?'

I round on her and then droop, realising that I, Rebecca Madison, am behaving like a complete tool. What is wrong with me?

But I know what's wrong with me. If this is love, it can shove it. I hate this hollowed-out, wrong feeling. I hate the neediness of wanting to feel Hudson's arms around me. I hate … I hate fucking everything this morning.

'I thought I'd pop in and run something by you. Here, have some coffee, you look like you could use it.'

'Thanks.' I take it from her. 'Do you think I'm one of the boys?'

'Pardon me?' She gapes at me and stares at my chest. 'Not from where I'm sitting.'

'You know what I mean. Do you think that I'm just like the rest of the stuffed shirts on the board? Be honest.'

It's worrying that she catches her lip between her teeth before she says anything. 'How honest is honest?'

'Shit, Mitz, don't pull any punches.'

'You asked me to be honest.'

I sigh. 'That bad?'

She shrugs.

'So why have you never left?'

'For one thing, I wouldn't have got a job anywhere else at the moment – I was too much of a maternity risk. Hey presto.' She waves a hand down at her barely there bulge. 'And secondly, I quite like the work and I don't have as much to do with the he-men as you do. A lot of women here respect you and look up to you. They'd like to have your balls.'

'I don't want to have my balls,' I say and there's an uncharacteristic whine in my voice.

She pats my hand with a patronising smile. 'Just say the word. You're the one that has the power to change things. Change the culture.'

'Change the culture?'

'Rebecca, you're still in the same century as all the dickheads on the board. You've proved yourself a thousand times over. There's more to life than work.'

'So everyone keeps telling me.'

'Perhaps because it's true.'

I shake my head. That's not what my dad told me.

• • •

After Mitzie leaves, I get my head down and manage to do some work, which is great until I check my phone. My WhatsApp seems to have blown up and I've been added to a brand-new group. *Staging An Intervention.*

*Becca, are you okay? You didn't reply to my text. We're here for you. What are you doing this evening?* This is from CC. It never occurred to me to respond.

Patience is not her strong suit, in fact it doesn't appear to be her suit at all.

Within thirty seconds of that one, she'd sent another.

CC: *Where are you? You okay?*

PP: *He's a dick, even if he is our brother.*

CC: *I'm disowning the stupid prick.* She's added a row of aubergine emojis.

Five minutes later CC sent this message:

*It's a code red, ladies. We're all going to Becca's tonight. The situation calls for Margaritas.*

DD has joined. *Will be there.*

PP adds her answer. *KK. Who's bringing the tequila?*

DD: *I will because I'm the only one with any dosh. Becca send your address with post code for SatNav. I'm driving up this afternoon.*

PP. *Me and CC are getting the train. Gets into Paddington Bear at four-fifty. Leaves at ten past two.*

I double check my watch, just in case there's time to stop them. Fruitless because it's now two o'clock.

They're on their way.

CC. *See you soon Becca. Don't forget the address.*

. . .

Shit, it's really official. Hudson has formally broken up with me. My stupid heart cracks a little. Which is really, really stupid because why am I upset over the break-up of a fake relationship?

How did Hudson break the news to the family? Did he mention it in passing? I play the conversation in my head.

*How's Becca?*

*Her? Oh, we broke up, I'm seeing …* Portia, Jocasta, Camilla, Beatrice… delete as appropriate.

I plan to hold out on my family for as long as I possibly can. They don't need to know any time soon. Oh shit! Except for the wedding. Hopefully it's a good year away. I'll have to hire myself another date. Maybe I could contact Hudson again for the event. My heart flickers with false hope like the wick of a dying candle. Maybe not.

I stare down at my phone not sure whether to giggle or cry. Whether I like it or not, I've got three houseguests arriving in about three hours and I'm a little overwhelmed by their unconditional support. Despite Hudson being their brother, they seem to be on my side.

CC: *Seriously he's a twat sometimes.*

PP: *He can't help himself – he has a penis.*

I laugh out loud at that one.

DD: *Give him a chance, knowing him he's running scared because he knows you're perfect for him.*

I can't help feeling a little guilty that they've assumed that Hudson is the one at fault. Our contract had always said that we'd have a no-fault break-up.

## Chapter Thirty-Two

'There you are. We had to start the party without you.'

CC and PP are sprawled in the corridor outside my flat, their legs splayed out in front them. There are several empty gin and tonic cans beside them.

'Sorry, we drank yours. It's way after six.'

'How did you get in?'

'We blagged our way.' CC winks at me. 'Buzzed the fella in number thirty-two and offered him a blow job if he let me in.'

My mouth drops open. I'm horrified.

'It's okay, he's gay.'

Oh my Christ, that's even worse. The poor man might be scarred for life.

She shrieks with laughter. 'Chill, Becca, I'm joking.'

PP shakes her head. 'Sorry about her. We waited for someone to go in and did the old slip-in-behind-them.' She shimmies her shoulders as if to demonstrate their adept manoeuvre.

'Sorry, I got caught up in something.' I'm only ten minutes late.

CC shoots me a disapproving look as she rises to her feet. 'Hudson said you were a workaholic. Although Pot. Kettle. Black. How are you feeling, honey?' She steps forward and wraps her arms around me and PP follows suit a second later. They both smell of the same fabric conditioner, the one Hudson uses. It brings a flood of memories. Their bodies are soft against mine and I give into the weakness and hug them back and despite feeling a bit of a fraud, tears prick at my eyes. I'm never going to hold him again like this.

'Hey, it's okay,' says PP. 'We're here for you.' She gives me another squeeze which is the worst thing she could have done because I actually start to cry, full on sobbing.

'Oh, honey. He's not worth it,' says PP.

She gets a glare from CC. 'He is our brother.'

'I'm trying to be nice.'

And I choke out the standard break-up words that I've despised all my life, 'But I l-love him.'

'Come on,' says CC. 'Let's get shitfaced.'

I wipe away the tears with the back of my hand and try to summon up a smile. Now that they're here, despite the inconvenient flood of tears, I'm really happy to see them.

When I open the front door, CC scoots past me into the open-plan lounge-diner-kitchen which takes up the corner of the building and stands at the picture window putting her hands on the glass to peer at the night sky. 'Shut the front door, Becca. This is fab-U-lous.' She spins around and grins at me. 'What a hole.'

With that she switches on the nearest table lamp and throws herself onto the sofa, bouncing up and down on the midnight blue velvet cushions. 'Lush. Where are we sleeping?' She jumps up nearly tripping over the bags she's dumped in the middle of the floor. Funny, the place immediately looks more lived in.

She's already darting ahead of me before I can show her and PP to the guest room.

PP scoops up her overnight bag with a sigh. 'She's like a dog, makes herself at home everywhere and assumes people will love her.' It's such a good description I let out a small laugh.

CC, with the same unerring ability as a Labrador sniffing out food, has already found one of the guest rooms.

'Wow, I love this,' she says, poking her head into the ensuite bathroom. 'Great shower. I could so live here.'

I raise an eyebrow. I'm not in the market for a flatmate.

She gives me a twinkly-eyed smile that reminds me of Hudson. 'Don't worry.' She winks. 'I'll invite myself to stay once you're married.'

My laugh is snorted through my nose. If I'd been drinking anything I'd have spray-painted the walls. 'We've split up, remember.'

'Yes,' says PP, threading her arm through mine. 'A temporary setback, that's all. Mum and Dad loved you, they never like Hudson's girlfriends.'

'Great to know,' I murmur. 'Always good to get the parents onside.' I think my brain is going to go into meltdown. This is getting out of hand. I don't know what to say to them. Married, for fuck's sake. That was never going to happen. Our break-up is fake, our whole relationship is fake. I'm a fake. I'm normally pretty ruthless, I do what I have to do to get a job done, but there's this weird guilt plaguing me at deceiving these lovely people. I had no idea I was going to fall in love with his bloody family as well as him. God, if I tell them the truth, they'll hate me and for once, I actually do give a … what people think of me.

'You do know, you're perfect for him,' persisted CC. 'You don't take any crap. Least of all mine.' Despite her guileless grin I sense shark-infested water. CC is a conniving minx. She beams at me. 'That Prosecco isn't opening itself.'

An hour later, DD has arrived with more supplies and we've managed to down two bottles of Prosecco with a third on the go. There are a couple of Marks and Spencer lasagnes in the oven, which I think we're going to need to mop up some of the alcohol. I have a feeling the evening is going to get messy.

'Right,' says CC. 'Time to talk mastodons.' Everyone goes quiet. 'You know, the mastodon in the room, they're bigger than elephants.'

PP frowns. 'You know I'm not sure they actually were.'

CC throws one of my Graham and Green cushions at her sister. 'What went wrong with you and Huddy?' All three pairs of eyes are trained on me. They'll be getting the thumbscrews out at any minute. I swallow and shrug, my usual articulate self, shrinking into a stammering mess.

'Well. You know. We just decided, I mean, realised, that we weren't, well, it wasn't what we… And so we split up.'

This incoherence is as befuddling to them as to me. Why can't I just spit it out? Irreconcilable differences. That's what we agreed. It seemed so simple then.

'Did you have a row?'

'What did you argue about?'

'Did he cheat on you?'

I shake my head.

'Did you cheat on him?'

'No!' I say, outraged that they'd think that of me.

'Do you love him?' This last question is from DD, who is by far the most sensible sister. She fixes an unblinking gaze upon me. It's hard for me to lie at the best of times, even harder under the scrutiny of a Strong sister. My throat closes up. God, yes, I love him. So much so that it hurts and he has no bloody idea. He would laugh his socks off. Wasn't he the one that had suggested putting the 'no falling in love' clause into the contract? I seriously underestimated him.

'Of course she does,' crows CC, 'she's gone all pink.'

DD looks triumphant. 'Told you.'

'You have to fight for what you want,' says CC, 'You have to fight for Hudson. But without being stalkery about it.'

I have a lot more pride than that. 'I'd never reduce myself to being stalkery,' I say.

'But you need to see him. Talk to him. Tell him why he's wrong.'

'Or why you were wrong.' PP rounds on me. 'Who did the breaking up? Was it him or you?'

'I told you, it was mutual. We just agreed it wasn't going anywhere.'

'But you wanted it to go somewhere,' prompts CC. 'Bloody Hudson, he doesn't know when he's got a good thing going. I told him that this morning and he hung up.'

I keep quiet. Going somewhere was never part of the agreement. It was always temporary.

I liked temporary though. It suited me.

'You've got to fight for him,' repeats CC.

I nod and take a strategic sip of Prosecco so I don't have to say anything. The guilt is burning a hole in my gut.

'Yes, because you're perfect together,' says DD. 'I've never seen him so relaxed and happy with anyone before. But the best thing is that you keep him on his toes.'

Do I? I'm not even sure we're perfect together but I do know that I want him in my life, as much as I want anyone in my life. Perhaps we could carry on, on a temporary basis. I could draw up another contract which lays out the parameters. Weddings. Family parties. No long-term commitment. Keep it casual. Enough with the contracts. What is wrong with me? I'm so confused, I don't know what I want. It's all so complicated. How can I have Hudson and my career? It will end in heartbreak – mine.

We drink more, the girls formulating wilder and wilder plans. By the end of the night, CC and PP stagger to their room, singing Jess Glynne's 'Hold My Hand' at the tops of their voices. DD, who is slightly more sober, gives me a hug.

'You've got this, Becca. Just talk some sense into him.' I hug her back, the lies sitting on my shoulder like black shadows.

. . .

Just as I tumble into bed, the world swimming a little, there's a WhatsApp from Hudson. My heart does that funny wobble thing just at the sight of the little red dot next to his name.

*I'm the most unpopular man on the planet. Why didn't you tell them it was mutual?*

My mouth twists in an amused smile at the aggrieved words. I can imagine him saying them. Imagine the expression on his face. I miss him.

It's difficult to focus on the keyboard but I manage to tap out quite a coherent message. *I did try but this is your family we're dealing with, you know what they're like.* I take my phone to the bathroom for one last wee.

*What did you do to them? They've never liked any of my other girlfriends.*

I'm sitting on the loo smiling to myself as I type, *Maybe that should tell you something…*

The messages stop after that and I wonder if I've said too much.

As I'm about to switch out the light I get another message, and this is the one that breaks my heart. I've really blown it this time.

*You've still got my Dr Who scarf. Will you give it to one of my sisters?*

## Chapter Thirty-Three

I haven't been able to eat breakfast this morning, or lunch, and the solitary espresso I did chug down is sloshing around an empty stomach as the tube on the Northern Line goes round a bend. Even if it wasn't Saturday, I would have thrown a sickie. There's some football match on because the train is packed. I can't ever remember being this nervous. I pat my enormous tote bag. It contains Hudson's Dr Who scarf and also a contract. A new contract that I've scribbled down in five minutes flat. It's probably so full of loopholes it will collapse in on itself like a giant black hole.

The only thing that has kept me going this morning is the constant support of CC. She's sent me a message every hour, *Have you spoken to him yet?*

She and the others left early because they all had places to be, having dropped everything to rush to my side. Their last words as they left were still encouraging me to call him and fight for what I want.

Rather than message or phone him I'm going balls deep – I'm going to see him. I'm going to offer him a new contract. A temporary arrangement to keep both our families off our backs. It makes perfect sense.

I've kept the contract practical, spelling out the logical reasons why it makes sense for us to continue our fake relationship. I'm going to need a wedding date at some point and he can redeem himself with his family. CC and PP are both refusing to talk to him at the moment. And it suits me to have a temporary relationship with no long-term commitment and no real expectation of one another. With the new job, work will be my focus and the last thing I need is a boyfriend complaining he's not coming first. Hopefully Hudson's exhibition will be a success and he'll need to have the same dedication. In my head it all makes sense but now I'm headed to his exhibition, at the Design Centre, I'm starting to have doubts. I open my bag and take out the contract, skimming it one last time.

*This is a temporary contract between Rebecca Jane Madison and Hudson Strong and can be terminated by either party at any time with one week's notice.*

*The Client and the contractor agree to undertake a temporary relationship of convenience which suits either party for as long as it is beneficial to said parties.*

I read through the familiar legalese about each party's rights and responsibilities, all of which I've written thousands and thousands of times over the years. It's all quite straightforward. Less straightforward is the additional clauses section:

*The following activities will be permitted:*

*Unlimited kissing*

*Sexual relations*

God, I rewrote that particular clause over and over. Sexual activities sounds a bit kinky, sexual intercourse sounds a bit blunt and matter of fact and I'm still not sure about sexual relations – it's a bit Clintonesque.

*Hand holding*

Is that too prescriptive?

*Dates*

Is that too demanding? Is it extending the parameters of the contract too far?

*A minimum of two accompanied official visits to parents per annum.*

That would be normal in a real relationship, wouldn't it? Although I wouldn't mind hanging out with his family more often.

The train pulls into the station and I get off at The Angel absorbed into the flow of people all heading to the exit.


The uniformed security guard at the entrance hands me a guide to the venue. It takes a while to work out where Hudson's stand is within the huge glass-ceilinged hall. Once I've got my bearings, I take a deep breath and set off along one of the wide aisles. I'm too focused to really take in any of the displays on either side of me. I'm like a Hudson-seeking missile, locked on target and ready to go. My hand is in my handbag nestled into the soft wool of his scarf. I hope he's pleased to see me. If he isn't I can always pretend I was passing and thought I'd drop it in.

Emboldened by this plan of action, my pace picks up and I'm counting my way along the stand numbers: 112, 113, 114 and, there it is, 115. Hudson's furniture is stunning – it's more than stunning. It creates deep avarice; I'd love to own one of these pieces. His designs maximise the sinuous lines of the wood grain to create beautiful shapes which are both practical as well as aesthetic. They're simply gorgeous and judging by the number of sold signs I can see, I'm not the only one that thinks so. I smile, pleased for him. Although where is he? I look around but I can't see him anywhere. Maybe he's gone for coffee. I take the scarf out of my bag and drape it over the small desk in the corner, which has obviously been made by him but also looks as if it's being used during the show for admin. If I go off looking for him, he'll know I've been here. God, I'm sad. I want him to know that I've been here. It's my own *Sleepless in Seattle* Empire State Building moment. I'm leaving the choice to him but he'll know I was here.

Across the way I can see a sign for refreshments, so head towards it. I'll come back in ten minutes. As I'm walking away something catches my eye and I turn. Hudson has just arrived back on the stand. I stop and drink in the sight of him, my heart skipping a few beats. It's only when I take the first step towards him, I see the blonde girl beside him. She wraps her arms around his neck and kisses him on the mouth. His hands go to her waist. A tight knot grips my stomach. I am so dumb. He doesn't need me, someone who can't commit. Someone who threw his love back in his face. Because I know now that Hudson was telling me he loved me. God, I really have messed things up. I should never have come.

And I've left that bloody scarf.

As I'm staring at them through suddenly blurry eyes, Hudson pulls away and looks over her shoulder. He sees me and something flits across his face – guilt or regret, I'm not sure which, but I don't need him to see my humiliation up close and personal. I turn and hurry away, before I make an even bigger fool of myself, dropping the contract into the nearest bin.

Done. Over and done with it. I take out my phone and see the latest message from CC. *Go see him!* My mouth twists in a moue of disgust. It's so tempting to reply and tell her I've crashed and burned but she doesn't know the truth – I don't deserve her sympathy or support, much as I want it. To stop myself indulging, I turn my phone off.

I can't bear to go home but I hop back on the Northern Line. God, how did Hudson fill my life so quickly? There are so many memories. The train pulls into Leicester Square and on impulse I get out. I wander through Covent Garden down to the Strand, through Somerset House, until I find myself on the river bank. I decide to walk home. It's one of those bright winter days that holds the promise of spring but there's a lot of winter to get through still. The future spreads out in front of me like a vast landscape I'm never going to get across. How can I feel so lonely when in fact I had so little time with Hudson? I suppose it's because it gave me a glimpse of another life. Without meaning to he's given me so much, the friendship of his sisters, a greater understanding of other women, and the ability to start being true to myself. I've spent so much of my life moulding myself to what others expect and hiding the real me behind severe suits and straightened hair. I should be grateful to him; after all, he's stuck to the terms of our original contract. It was never supposed to be more than that one weekend. Things between us always had a finite end.

It takes me an hour and a half to walk home and as I near Chelsea Harbour, the light is fading. My footsteps drag. I really don't want to go home, to be on my own, but it's getting cold as the sun goes down. There's a bite of frost in the air.

I hurry into the building, glad of the warmth in the lobby even if it's deserted. I rarely see anyone here, apart from my neighbours who are too disorganised to buy milk on a regular basis. The lift takes for ever and finally arrives to take me up to my floor.

I'm taking my keys out of my bag as I walk down the corridor when I'm aware that someone is there.

Hudson is sitting outside my door. He gets to his feet. I'm really going to have to make a complaint about the building's security.

'Don't you ever answer your phone?' he asks and then holds up the contract. 'And what the fuck is this?'

I open my mouth and nothing comes out.

In one quick move he tears it in two and then he stands there looking as shocked as I am.

'It took me hours to write that,' I say hotly, blatantly lying, suddenly furious with him.

'Well, you wasted your time,' he snarls. 'Is it really what you want?' He sounds cross but at the same time there's puzzlement on his face as if he doesn't know why he's cross.

I find my voice. 'No.' I lift my chin. Time to fight for what I really want. I've been doing it all my working life, but now I realise what's really important. 'I want a proper relationship … with you.'

He swallows and I brace myself.

'Okay.'

'Okay?' I ask. My voice is slightly plaintive or is it aggrieved? After all the turmoil my heart has been through since New Year's Day, this calm acceptance is a bit of an anti-climax. I stare at him and he stares back.

'You're going to make me say it, aren't you?' he snaps. It really is not very romantic.

'Say what?' Honestly it's like bloody stand-off at the OK Corral or something.

He releases a heavy sigh. 'You don't ever give me an inch, do you?' His face slowly creases into one of his smiles, the ones that send tiny darts of happiness into me when our eyes meet. I've never felt like this with anyone else.

I walk up to him. We study each other and then he brushes my hair back from my face.

'The first time I saw you, I wondered what was

underneath that cocky, confident exterior. You were a challenge because you didn't need me.'

And now I do.

I hold my breath. Is this contingent on me still not needing him?

'You're so easy to be with. You don't expect me to look after you but when I do –' he smiles '– you turn soft and sweet, like a hamster.'

'I've heard hamsters can be quite vicious.'

'What I like about them is that they're self-contained. Their happiness is not dependent on someone else. They make their own way.'

I can see what he's doing. Trying to justify his fears. Thing is, I've realised we just have to step off the cliff and find out if *we* work.

'Hudson,' I say and stop his mouth with a quick kiss. 'You're talking bollocks. I've fallen in love with you. I do need you but my life won't stop if you're not around. It just won't be as good.'

He laughs. 'And that, right there, is why I love you back.'

I grin at him. 'I knew that.'

'No, you didn't.'

'Yes, I did.'

He puts his arms around me. He cups my chin.

My heart melts just a little.

'I love you, Becs.' He pauses, 'Just a little more than my fucking family, who, I might add, have not stopped giving me grief since I said we'd split up.'

'That's why you're here. You want to get back in their good books.'

'That and a booty call.' He grins at me.

'I love you too, Hudson Strong.'

'Now we've got that slushy stuff over with, can we go inside, have mind-blowing sex, then dinner? During which time I can tell you what a fucking star I am and how you, Ms Managing Director, are looking at Heal's' latest supplier and the *Evening Standard*'s "hottest new designer".'

I let us into the flat but instead of heading to the bedroom, Hudson leads me out to the balcony.

'It's not quite the Empire State Building –' he cups my face with both hands '– but that's when I fell for you.'

'Funny, I fell for you when you put that hideous hat on me.'

'Hideous hat…'

Our teasing ends in a scorching kiss which we have to take inside before we shock the hell out of the neighbours.

# Epilogue

'We're going to be late,' says Hudson, following me out of the shower, giving my nipple what's supposed to be a quick farewell kiss, except he lingers a moment before handing me a towel.

'And whose fault is that?' I grin back at him, my heart warming at the very sight of him, as he wraps a white towel around his hips. Honestly, after six months you'd have thought the honeymoon would be over but Hudson is as irresistible as ever. Being with him gives me a sense that I fit, that there's a Rebecca Madison-shaped space in the world for me that isn't just about work.

He gives me his naughty grin. 'Yours for being so hot.' He pulls me in for another kiss. There are drops of water running down his chest and I track one, running my palm down his warm skin. He captures my hand with one of his and deepens the kiss.

I have to wrench myself away. 'We'll be even later,' I say regretfully. I could quite happily stay in the hotel suite all afternoon. We're at Murcott Manor, which is only a few miles away from Hudson's family home and not entirely dissimilar with its golden Cotswold stone buildings.

'Mmm,' he says, pulling me back against him. 'I could make it worth your while.'

I laugh. 'Nothing, not even you, is worth upsetting Laura today.'

I walk back into the bedroom, casting a quick glance at the rumpled bedsheets and pick up my watch from the dressing table. I'm going to have to get my skates on to look presentable.

'You're gorgeous, you don't need to worry about how you look,' says Hudson, reading my mind as usual.

'I look post-shagged,' I retort and glance at my watch again. I'm due in my sister's suite precisely five minutes ago and I haven't even got my bridesmaid's dress on yet.

'I could dry your hair.'

'No, go put some clothes on and stop distracting me.'

'Me!' He puts a hand to his bare chest in mock aggrievement.

For a moment we smile at each other.

Once I've done my hair and make-up, I'm only half an hour late.

I take the silk dress from the padded hanger. It's a soft pale blue bias-cut dress with spaghetti straps and as I pull it over my head, the skirt flows around my legs with a soft whisper. It's a far cry from the peach puffball I'd imagined my sister would take great delight in putting me in.

Hudson comes over and strokes my bare shoulder, dropping a quick kiss on it.

'Gorgeous,' he says again, his voice husky this time.

I swallow down a quick lump of emotion. 'Thank you,' I whisper. I'm so in love with this man, he turns me inside out with the smallest gesture.

'Good luck,' he says.

I smile at him and look around, patting my dress. I wish it had pockets.

He holds up my clutch. 'Don't worry, I won't forget it. And, yes, your phone is on silent and I will let you check it once an hour in case there's a crisis that only you can handle.' He's teasing me but he's also reminding me how well he knows me. I've changed a lot in the last six months but not that much. Being the boss means you can delegate ... if you want to.

I leave him and head down to my sister's bridal suite at the other end of the corridor.

At my knock the door is thrown open and Laura stands there in an ice-white silk bustier. Her make-up is flawless and her hair is arranged in an elaborate up-do, through which tiny white orchid flowers are threaded. I hold up my hands in instant apology. 'I'm sorry I'm late.'

I follow her into the suite. 'Where is everyone?' The bridesmaids and mothers are supposed to be gathering for pre-ceremony champagne and the reveal of the dress.

Laura gives me a triumphant smirk. 'I lied about the time. You're actually five minutes early.'

I think of my hasty shower with Hudson. 'What! Why would you do that?'

Oh no, does she want some sisterly heart-to-heart?

Please God no. Like I said, I've changed in the last few months but, again, really not that much.

'Er hello!' She taps her watch.

'I'm always very punctual.'

She snorts. 'Unless Hudson is in the room.' She sends me a knowing look.

'I don't know what you mean,' I say, but I can feel the pinkness in my cheeks.

She steps forward and taps one of them. 'You have that post-coital glow ....' I lift my chin and then I grin at her because I can't deny it.

'He's good for you.'

'Thank you. Now are you going to get this party started?' I might have softened, a little, but I'm not prepared to discuss my feelings with my sister, even if she is getting married today. Being a bridesmaid is a baby step towards us having a better relationship but I don't like to rush things.

As the champagne cork is popped, my mother arrives, along with the other bridesmaids, all seven of them friends of Laura's from high school and college, a few of whom I know slightly. After a glass of fizz, we help Laura into her ecru duchesse satin dress. My mother discreetly wipes tears from her face and I hand her a tissue. Laura does look beautiful and I find my eyes watering. I think the pollen from the lilies in her bouquet is setting me off.

The service goes off well and once the photographer has taken a trillion and one pictures, I slip away to find Hudson. Not an easy task among a guest list of three hundred people but when I survey the crowd on the lawns, like a heat-seeking missile my gaze lands on him. Even as it does, he looks up and we exchange that secret smile of acknowledgement. I'm always aware of him; it's as if my heart hums when he's in the vicinity.

He excuses himself from the two women he was chatting with, who I recognise as friends of Laura's. As he saunters across the grass, tucking the cream leather bag, which matches my LK Bennett shoes, under his arm, they both watch him with speculative expressions. I wonder if it's because he's carrying my clutch with such casual aplomb.

'It's a good look on you,' I say, nodding to the bag.

'You look beautiful,' he says, cupping my face and kissing my cheek as if I'm something infinitely precious and delicate.

'You're supposed to say that about the bride.'

He shrugs and kisses me again, murmuring against my lips, 'I'm not crazy in love with the bride.'

Our eyes meet, holding another of those unspoken conversations. Sometimes I can't get enough of him and others, like now, I'm just happy to be, enjoying a moment of sweet serenity.

Arm in arm we wander to the lower level of the garden near the lake and tuck ourselves into the dappled shade of a drooping willow tree.

'This is nice,' he says, pushing the strap of my dress off my shoulder and trailing kisses across my collar bone.

It tickles slightly and I giggle. 'Behave.'

'Do I have to?' He pouts but there's that ever-present twinkle in his eye.

'Today, you do.'

'You're no fun,' he teases and puts an arm around me. We stand in the shady spot for a few minutes. It's nice to take a breather from the bustle of the day. Since we arrived this morning – apart from that quick half hour to ourselves – we've been on family duty, setting out wedding favours, delivering flowers, buttonholes and posies to the six groomsmen and seven other bridesmaids and basically being on call for the extensive wedding party.

I hear heels crunching on the gravel path nearby and Hudson and I glance at each other, wondering if the guests will spot us, half hidden among the slender leafy branches.

From the conversation, they clearly don't.

'Laura and Andrew make a gorgeous couple, don't they?'

'They do. You know he used to go out with Rebecca.'

'Yeah.' There's an unkind laugh. 'Have you seen her plus one?'

'Yes!' This is said with considerable enthusiasm. 'He is smoking hot. I thought my knickers would go up in flames.'

I waggle my eyebrows at Hudson, grinning at him.

'Mine too.' There's a tinkling laugh. 'Do you think she hired him for today?'

Hudson and I exchange a glance, our lips twitching in unison.

'What?'

'You know, like in that film. I can't remember what it's called but it's the one where she pays someone to be her date at the wedding. He's so good looking he could be a model or something.'

I raise my eyebrows at Hudson and smirk at him. He lifts his chin and winks at me, striking a pose with his hands on his hips. I clutch my diaphragm to stop the giggle leaking out.

'You mean like some kind of escort?'

'Yes, you're going to want some sort of back-up when your sister is marrying your ex.'

'Wonder how much she had to pay him?'

Hudson pinches his lips together, his eyes sparkling with mirth, and I can tell he's dying to laugh. I've had to slap a hand over my mouth and I'm shaking with amusement; it's actually painful trying to keep it all in. Any minute now both of us are going to burst into giggles.

I straighten up and take a deep breath, trying to plaster a dignified look on my face. I tuck my hand through his arm and give him a tug forward to step out of the shadows.

'Afternoon,' I say as both women's eyes widen. They're the two that Hudson was talking to earlier.

'The film you're thinking of is *The Wedding Date*. Don't tell anyone,' I say, putting a finger up to my lips, 'but you should try hiring a date, it's worth every penny.' I wink at them.

Open-mouthed, the two women simply stare at us. I give them an insouciant smile and we're about to walk off when Hudson adds, 'It helps to draw up a good contract. I can recommend an extremely good lawyer.'

Together we saunter off, hand in hand, almost choking on the laughter we're trying to hold back.

## Acknowledgments

The biggest thanks go to you, yes you, the reader. Thank you for picking this book up and if you've got this far, for investing in Rebecca and Hudson's story. I hope you've enjoyed it as much as I enjoyed writing it.

YOUR NUMBER ONE STOP

# ONE MORE CHAPTER

FOR PAGETURNING BOOKS

**One More Chapter is an
award-winning global
division of HarperCollins.**

**Sign up to our newsletter to get our
latest eBook deals and stay up to date
with our weekly Book Club!
<u>Subscribe here.</u>**

**Meet the team at
<u>www.onemorechapter.com</u>**

**Follow us!**

 **<u>@OneMoreChapter_</u>**

**<u>@OneMoreChapter</u>**

**<u>@onemorechapterhc</u>**

**Do you write unputdownable fiction?
We love to hear from new voices.
Find out how to submit your novel at
<u>www.onemorechapter.com/submissions</u>**